Canyon of Death

Faith in the Parks, Book 2

J. Carol Nemeth

"Rock of Ages" is a Public Domain Hymn published by Augustus M. Toplady who died in 1778.
https://www.umcdiscipleship.org/resources/hymns-public-domain-and-copyright https://www.umcdiscipleship.org/resources/history-of-hymns-rock-of-ages-cleft-for-me
http://www.pdhymns.com/index.htm

ISBN-13: 978-1-946939-89-0
ISBN-10: 1-946939-89-7

Dedication

I would like to dedicate this book to the memory of my father, the Rev. James W. Pruitt and to my mother, Mary Sue Amick Pruitt. My parents instilled in my siblings and me the love of camping and the outdoors at an early age. I still remember our first camping trip in an old canvas army tent that closed by tying long strings at the door, and it had no floor. We slept on old army cots. I must have been three or four years old. We soon graduated to one with a floor and a zippered door where creepy crawlies were encouraged to stay out. My parents introduced us to the national parks and monuments as well as state parks, and we traveled from the mountains to the coast as often as we could. We climbed lighthouses, descended into caves, swam in the ocean, visited presidents (homes), and saw where man took flight to name only a few places. Thank you, Mama and Daddy, for spreading our wings and giving us the love of travel!

Acknowledgements

My appreciation goes to Loretta Yerian, my son-in-law's sister and the editor of the Williams-Grand Canyon News and the Navajo-Hopi Observer for her willingness to share her wealth of knowledge with me. Not only did she sit with me one evening, giving me the opportunity to bombard her with questions but she dug into her treasure trove of newspaper articles and shared those with me as well. Thank you, Loretta! What a blessing you and the time I was able to spend with you were to me.

I would also like to thank my son, Matthew Nemeth, who allowed me to pick his military brain on wounds, dessert survival, setting traps, etc. He's active duty Army Special Forces, and I'm very proud of him. He made certain suggestions concerning the things near the end of the book (no spoilers here). Thanks, Matt. I love you so much, and I appreciate all your help! I enjoyed our discussions and look forward to picking your brain in the future!

Thank you to my daughter, Jennifer, who is the model for the cover of this book. She's wearing my old park service uniform. She looks beautiful and like the real deal!

Thank you, Diana Corbiser, for your photographic skills. We had a blast that day at the photo shoot, and the pictures turned out beautiful.

To Cynthia Hickey, my publisher, thank you for all you do for me. You never fail to produce a beautiful cover, and this one is no exception. I can't wait to see what you do with the rest of the series.

As always, I'm thankful for a husband who loves me and supports me. He sent me cross country on a research journey, allowing me to take my time and enjoy myself, stopping whenever and wherever I wanted. I visited the Grand Canyon and researched for this book, enjoying every minute. Thank you, Sweetheart! I love you! The only way it could have been better was if you had been able to share it with me! Next time!

Jeremiah 29: 11 "For I know the thoughts that I think toward you, saith the Lord, thoughts of peace, and not evil." (KJV)

Prologue

W ow, this trail is treacherous." The tall hiker planted his foot against a large rock to steady himself and surveyed the canyon wall along his left side. "Did you see which way the mountain goat went? I lost sight of him just over there."

"Yeah. He slipped behind that huge boulder." His shorter hiking partner pointed to a large, craggy formation, nearly twice the height of an average man, just below their position. He scratched his goatee-covered chin before yanking off his ball cap and wiping his arm across his forehead. "I wanted to snap his picture but he disappeared. Want to check it out and see if we can catch him back there?"

"Why not? We've gotten some amazing pictures out here. Let's go for it."

Both men edged carefully down to the "boulder" that turned out to be part of the canyon wall. The trail led to the right and away from the wall just before this point creating a divide between the wall and the trail. Scrub vegetation covered the side of the formation.

"Hey, long legs. You jump first then you can catch me," chuckled the shorter of the two hikers.

The taller hiker rolled his eyes and easily jumped across the divide, grabbing hold of the side of the rock formation. Pushing the vegetation aside, he pulled out a flashlight and glanced around the opening before turning back to his hiking partner.

"I don't see any snakes. Go ahead and jump. You'll make it. I'll give you a hand."

When the second hiker was safely inside the opening of the formation with his partner, they turned to take stock of the situation.

"Are you sure he went this way? Looks like a dead end to me."

"I'm positive he came back here. It has to go somewhere." The short man slid his hands further behind the vegetation, feeling for a fissure in the cliff face.

"Are you sure you want to be doing that? I mean, there still might be snakes and stuff out here, man. Don't get yourself bit. I can't carry your sorry carcass back up that trail." He nodded in the direction they had descended.

His hiking partner turned with a victorious smile as he tugged a clump of vegetation away. Behind it an opening in the rock was large enough for a man to walk through without ducking his head or having to enter sideways.

"Looks almost like it was put there. Intentionally."

"Yeah. Like it was chiseled out. Let's see where it goes." The taller man slipped through as his partner held the vegetation back.

As the hikers slipped into the opening, they realized they were in a small tunnel that ran approximately twenty feet before curving inward along the canyon wall. Light streamed from around the bend lighting the tunnel without the use of their flashlights.

The tunnel walls were dry and smooth, and the floor was scattered with fine rocks and sand. Around the bend, the tunnel opened into an enormous room that hugged the side of the Grand Canyon.

"Oh, my...are you seeing this, man?" The tall hiker gaped at the sight before him.

"I'm seeing it, but I'm not sure what I'm seeing. Do you think the park service knows about this?" His partner's chin dropped in awe. "There's no signs or postings on the rim or anything."

"Or on the trail map."

The mountain goat long forgotten, the hikers carefully explored the brightly lit cavernous room. Cliff dwellings built into the back wall extended several hundred feet in length. Various sized round holes in the floor indicated rooms were likely positioned beneath as well. A large overhang in front of the massive room allowed light in but would hide it from the outside.

Lower views of the canyon could be seen but nothing above the overhang. Whoever had lived here hadn't intended to be seen by the outside world.

"I think we better tell someone about this, man. If they already know about it, that's one thing, but if not…"

"Let's snap some pictures. Stand over there by that low wall. That's it."

With pose after pose on their digital camera, the hikers decided to get back and report their find. Who knows? One day they just might be famous.

Chapter One

"Rock of Ages, cleft for me,
Let me hide myself in Thee"

The faint melodic words floated on the morning breeze as Kate Fleming made her way toward Mather Point. She was about to catch her first glimpse of the Grand Canyon and her heart ticked an upbeat in anticipation. She'd waited a long time for this moment.

"Let the water and the blood,
From Thy wounded side which
flowed,"

The closer Kate got to the south rim of the canyon, the stronger the words grew. Definitely feminine in tone, there was a slight crackle as though she was elderly. It held a quality that indicated the a cappella soloist sang straight from her heart.

People dressed in heavy winter clothing meandered about as they snapped pictures and took selfies with the canyon behind them.

"Be of sin the double cure,
Save from wrath and make me
pure."

As the Grand Canyon came into view, Kate sucked in the cold morning air in awe, chilling her throat and lungs. Placing her gloved hands over her nose and mouth, she warmed them up again.

The Grand Canyon was the most amazing thing she'd ever seen. Gorgeous earth tones blended with blues, pinks and shadowy purples. With the morning sun still in the eastern sky, long shadows were cast on the western side of ridges and peaks. As a strong, cold breeze blew up from the canyon, Kate zipped up her olive-drab uniform parka and jammed her "Smokey-Bear" hat further down on her head.

> "Could my tears forever
> flow...."

"Shut up, old woman! I don't want to hear you singing."

The angry voice came from Kate's left, drawing her attention from the spectacular view. An elderly woman stood by the chain-link fence which protects visitors from going over the edge of the canyon at the overlook. Her rheumy eyes were focused on the horizon between earth and sky, her thin, arthritic hands raised toward heaven as tears streamed down her wrinkled cheeks. Two young men stood beside her, anger marring their faces.

"Shut up, old woman," one of them yelled. "Stop your screeching!"

Kate quickly approached them to see what the commotion was about. The woman certainly didn't seem to be bothering anyone.

"Excuse me." Kate put as much authority in her voice as she could muster. "What are you two doing here? This lady isn't bothering anyone."

The guys spotted her uniform, belligerence oozing from their expressions. "Well, she's bothering us. I don't want to hear her singing about...God." The last word was spat out with disgust. "She's gotta stop."

Kate laid a kind hand on the woman's arm. "Ma'am, I hate to interrupt you but can I hear your side of this situation?"

The woman's faded blue eyes turned to Kate, tears still wet on her cheeks. "Of course, my dear. I'm eighty-six years old. All my life I've seen pictures of the Grand Canyon, but I've never been here before. Well, now that I'm here, I can't help but be in awe at the wonder of God's creation. He did this." She waved a hand in the direction of the natural wonder spread before them. "It didn't just happen. All I wanted was to praise Him for how marvelous and mighty He is. One look at that view and anyone with half a brain knows God made it."

The two young men sputtered in anger at the pointed remark.

Kate held up her hand. "Fellows, this is a really big canyon. I mean, really big. There's plenty of room for you to see it and for this lady to sing as she desires. Why don't you just move along to another location and enjoy the view. Leave her in peace to enjoy it in her own way."

They cast angry glares in the woman's direction as they shifted their daypacks higher on their backs and left the canyon rim, hopefully to find a spot elsewhere.

"Thank you, miss." The old woman settled a gnarled, arthritic hand on Kate's arm. Gloveless, it felt cold even through Kate's parka sleeve. "I just don't understand how folks can look at that view and not give credit where credit is due. God made it, and He made it for us to enjoy. I just don't think some people want to believe He exists. It's sad really."

"Yes, I think you're right, ma'am." Kate patted the woman's thin shoulder. "And thank you for the reminder. You might want to go inside and warm up though. It's pretty chilly out here. Are you here alone?"

The woman smiled. "No, my son and daughter-in-law are here with me. They went to get coffee, so they'll be back shortly with a cup for me. I just didn't want to leave this view. I want to drink in as much as I can as long as I can."

"I understand," Kate nodded with a smile. "You have a wonderful day, ma'am."

Before Kate realize what she was doing, the woman reached out thin arms and wrapped them around her. Then she stepped back and smiled, contentment written across her wrinkled face.

"Thank you, my dear. These weary eyes have seen a lot of things during my lifetime, but this was the last thing I truly wanted to see before the Lord calls me home. I don't know if that'll be tomorrow or next year or the next, but I'm happy that I got to see this marvel of His handiwork."

Kate started to walked away, then stripping the gloves from her hands, pressed them into the woman's hands and hurried away before she could protest.

As Kate strolled along the canyon rim, she could hear the

woman's voice once again lift in praise. She reflected on her words. Kate hadn't given God much credit lately. She believed in Him, had even put her trust in Him, but He'd let her down. Pain sliced through her heart as memories flooded her mind. Nope. She wasn't going to think about all that right now. Whether God put this view here for her to enjoy or not, she could still appreciate the beauty before her. And she wanted to forget. Oh, how she wanted to forget.

Pushing the memories from her mind, she glanced at her watch. She needed to get to the visitor center to meet with Tasha Johnson. Kate had arrived yesterday afternoon. Just long enough to be assigned living quarters and to begin to learn her way around Grand Canyon Village and some of the government offices, but she hadn't yet met Tasha.

With a last long appreciative glance at the canyon, she left it behind and made her way to the visitor center near Mather Point. In spite of the cold wind that swept across the south rim, bundled-up visitors scurried from one overlook to the next, searching for that subtle difference in the scenery. Kate could appreciate that. She was sure she wouldn't get tired of the view any time soon.

Kate slipped inside the visitor center where it was much warmer. Straight ahead was a long information desk with a few park staff members answering questions and passing out park maps. To the right was the entrance to a theater where a video played every few minutes telling about the Grand Canyon National Park and its natural splendor. Exhibits of small wildlife and historical information were arranged to the left. Park visitors meandered about looking at these exhibits and taking in the video in the theater. So, where would she find Tasha Johnson?

"Kate Fleming?"

Kate turned at the soft feminine voice that spoke her name. A young African-American woman met her questioning gaze with a smile. Her flawless ebony skin, black eyes surrounded by long lashes and beautiful white teeth between full lips was striking. Her short, curly black hair set off her beautiful features.

"Yes, I'm Kate Fleming."

The young woman held out her hand. "It's nice to meet you at last, Kate. I'm Tasha Johnson. We've been expecting you."

Kate shook her hand. "It's a pleasure to meet you, Tasha."

"Have you been out to see the canyon yet? That's usually where everyone makes a bee-line to as soon as they arrive." Tasha chuckled. "And no wonder. I've been here three years and still can't get over the view."

"Yes. I just came from Mather Point. It's amazing. I'll be spending a lot of time soaking in the sights." Kate had wanted to work at the Grand Canyon for a long time, and she'd finally made it. But she hadn't planned to come alone. Shoving those painful memories away, she concentrated on Tasha's words.

"Well, I hate to rush you into your job, but I'm going to take you out to the sight and introduce you to the archeologists." Tugging on her parka and her uniform ball cap, Tasha eyed Kate's "Smokey-Bear" hat critically. "If you've got your ball cap, I think you'd better wear it. Much better suited to where we're heading. Good. You're wearing hiking boots. You'll need them."

With a quick trip to Kate's car to exchange hats, the women climbed into Tasha's park SUV.

"As my assistant, your help will be invaluable in keeping an eye on the archaeological team," Tasha explained.

"You're the park liaison, right?" Kate wanted to make sure she had her supervisor's title correct.

"That's right." Tasha flashed a smile. "I have a few projects I'm overseeing, so I need you to keep me informed. You'll be my liaison to the archeological team. My eyes and ears, so to speak. If they have questions you can't answer, bring them to me and we'll get them answered. There are regulations they must follow. I need you to ensure they follow them. If they don't, tell me and I'll deal with it."

"So, what is the team looking for? Anything in particular or just digging until they find something?"

"Oh, no. It's something in particular. A couple of hikers stumbled on a lost Anasazi city a month ago. The park invited the archeological team to investigate."

"What about the hikers? How did they find the site?"

"They were hiking on the Hermit's Trail and followed a mountain goat. It disappeared behind a rock formation and when they went to investigate, they found the city. They snapped a lot of pictures, too, but we confiscated them. No way could we let that out to the public."

"Won't they talk?"

"Probably, although they signed an agreement not to." Tasha stopped the SUV next to a gate with an electronic keypad. She entered a four-digit code and the gate swung upward, allowing them to proceed. "This is Hermit's Road and it's closed to the public except during the winter months. They just closed it last week, so we don't have to worry about competing with tourists anymore. Only park personnel and shuttle buses as well as the Hermit's Rest Gift Shop employees drive out here now. And of course, the archeologists. I'll give you the combination so you'll have access. You'll be driving out here all the time."

They followed the road along the south rim of the canyon to the Hermit's Rest Gift Shop and overlook. Tasha drove a half mile further down a dirt road behind the gift shop and parked beside a building comprised of two mobile construction trailers placed side by side.

"This is the archeologists' office." Tasha climbed out of the SUV. "You might find one or more of the archeologists here but usually they're on-site so it's harder to find them."

"Ok. Good to know." Kate exited the SUV and followed Tasha toward the trailhead. "So, they're not here now?"

Tasha glanced at the dark windows. "Probably not."

Kate's eyes were glued to the view before her. A completely different and amazingly colorful configuration of ridges, peaks and plateaus met her gaze. Tasha's chuckle beside her drew her attention back to her companion.

"Sorry. I'm just in awe of…well…this." Her hand moved in an all-encompassing arc. "It's… gorgeous."

"Yes, it is," Tasha sighed. "I just love it here. But," she pointed at the trailhead, "this is a very treacherous trail to descend. It's not maintained by the park as much as the other trails. So take your time and watch your step. It's going to take some getting used to."

Kate and Craig had hiked a lot of trails in the three years since they'd started dating, and she was confident she was in shape and could tackle it. This did look daunting. What would Craig have said to this bit of adventure? A pang sliced through her heart as it always did when she thought of Craig.

She swallowed hard. Don't go there. It hurt too much.

Tasha eyed Kate closely and laid a hand on her jacketed arm. "Are you ok, girlfriend? Your face is mighty pale. Want to take a minute before we head down? It's not that bad, really."

Kate met Tasha's concerned dark gaze and was touched. The young woman hardly knew her but had read Kate's expression like she'd known her a long time.

Kate flashed a smile in spite of the tears that threatened to spill from her eyes. "No, I'm fine. Really, I am. I just…remembered something…someone. It's okay. I'm ready when you are." She pulled her sunglasses from her jacket pocket and tugged her ball cap lower over her eyes. It probably wouldn't help hide the pain at the memories of Craig, but it was worth a try.

Tasha considered her a moment longer before nodding. "Okay. If you say so. But if you have a problem, just tell me."

Kate understood that she wasn't just talking about the difficulty of the trail. Did she mean she could talk to her about other things too? Would Tasha be a friend she could trust? Time would tell. But some things were just off limits. Totally.

The path down the Hermit's Trail was indeed difficult. In some areas they had to crawl over rocks and boulders while in other places the trail smoothed out for a few feet. Kate concentrated on following Tasha and pushed personal thoughts from her mind.

At a particularly steep and precarious spot on the trail, Tasha stopped and pointed at a large formation on the left of the trail.

"That's the huge boulder the notorious mountain goat disappeared behind. Funny how that goat lost his one claim to fame. We'll never really know what happened to him. But he led the hikers to one very spectacular archeological find." She laughed between gasps for breath. "Come on, girl. We're almost there."

A wide, wooden board had been placed across the divide from the trail to the entrance to the formation, and Kate followed Tasha across to it, waiting for her to disappear behind it. Taking another look at the colorful scenery as she waited, Kate reached up to grab hold of the rock. Her foot slipped and before she knew what was happening, she slid toward the cliff edge several feet below were the trail turned to the right and the canyon wall remained on the left. Her fingers grasped for anything that would hold her, but she continued to slide.

Tasha's voice rang out in fear. "Kate! Grab onto something!"

Kate's heart lodged in her throat even as she slid toward the edge of the cliff. While she scrabbled for a handhold, her mind screamed the words: *Lord, help me!*

Chapter Two

What seemed an eternity must have been only seconds before Kate came to a sudden halt mere inches from the cliff edge. Had her jacket snagged on a rock? It felt like she was hung on something. Glancing above her shoulder, she expected to find a sharp rock holding her steady. Instead her gaze met a pair of slate gray eyes filled with fear. Strong hands held the back of her parka and her daypack.

"Come on, ranger lady," a gruff voice ground out between clenched teeth. "I can't hold you for long. Grab hold of a rock and push yourself up."

Not waiting for a second command, Kate slid her hands along the ground until she found a large enough rock protruding from the dirt. Flinging both arms around it, she scuffled her feet along until she found a foothold to steady them against.

"Great," the man acknowledged, his breath coming in heavy gasps. "Push yourself up toward me. That's it. Good. Now give me your hand."

Kate stretched as far as she could until her fingers slipped into his strong grasp. With his feet wedged against two rocks, he pulled her up toward him. Painstakingly inch by inch, he worked until they both were back on the trail. With each tug, she progressed upward until she sat on the ground beside him.

Panting with exertion, he reached over and righted her ball cap that had nearly been unseated during her fall. "I thought you were a goner for sure, ranger lady."

"That makes two of us." Kate laid a hand over her heart as she gasped for breath. "Thanks for not letting that happen. I don't know who you are or where you came from but thank you."

Tasha squatted down behind and between them and laid a hand on Kate's shoulder. "Well, it wasn't the introduction I had in mind, but Kate, this is Dr. Ethan Wagner, one of the archeologists. He stepped out of the tunnel just as I was heading in. And it's a good thing he did, girl. I couldn't have gotten to you quick enough and I doubt I could've stopped you anyway. We're too close in size, and I don't think I have the strength. Thanks, Ethan."

"Yeah, it would've been pretty tough for Tasha to explain losing a ranger on the first day," Kate chuckled then gasped for breath, holding out her hand. "I'm Kate Fleming."

"Nice to meet you...ranger lady." Ethan Wagner shook her hand and flashed a grin, revealing a devastating dimple in his left cheek. He climbed to a standing position, and reaching out a hand, tugged her to her feet then reached his other hand out to Tasha. "Come on. I'm sure Tasha brought you to meet the crew."

This time when they reached the rock formation, Ethan again grasped Kate's hand and helped her inside the tunnel, then did the same for Tasha. As Kate waited for them inside, she glanced around the tunnel and noticed it disappeared around a bend from where light emanated. Moving slowly forward, Kate was eager to see the city that had been discovered. No one who didn't know about it would ever realize a city lay along this area of the Grand Canyon. She'd never seen an archeological discovery before and excitement prickled down her spine in anticipation. This would look good on her resume for sure.

The tunnel opened into an enormous room filled with stone living spaces built on various levels. The ceiling was at least ten stories high. She gasped at the vastness before her. It wasn't just a little city. It was a huge city.

"Well, what do you think?" Tasha spoke from beside Kate.

"The Grand Canyon is sure full of surprises." Kate's voice was hushed with awe.

"You have no idea, ranger lady." Ethan brushed past the women and led the way toward a group of people near the city's center. "These are the rest of the crazies who climb down here every day to do research.

"Prof. Rosenberg." Ethan raised his voice. "We have guests."

A sixtyish man with longish gray hair, a neatly trimmed gray mustache and a gray Van Dyke beard was stooped over, viewing an item that another team member held out for his inspection. Prof. Rosenberg straightened and walked toward them.

"Ah, Tasha, my dear. Who have you brought with you today?"

Kate noticed that in spite of the Professor's neatly trimmed beard, his clothes looked like they hadn't been changed in days and he'd slept in them every night. However, when he approached, she was happy to confirm that he smelled clean. She bit back the laugh that nearly slipped out at the thought.

"This is Kate Fleming, Prof. Rosenberg. Kate, Prof. Dietrich Rosenberg is the head archeologist on the team."

"What a wonderful thing to have you here, my dear." The professor drew Kate's hand to his lips. With barely a whisper of a kiss he lowered it. "You will make a splendid addition to our team. I know you are not an archeologist, but your presence will contribute much, I'm sure."

Was that a slight hint of an accent? Possibly German?

As he spoke, two other team members joined them. Tasha made introductions.

"Kate, this is Carl Young, Prof. Rosenberg's assistant." The young man who had been discussing the item with the professor was tall and clean-cut with brown short-trimmed hair and brown eyes. Nice looking in a collegiate sort of way. He nodded but said nothing. His tan slacks and work shirt were meticulously pressed and displayed an obvious lack of dirt considering where he was working.

The second team member was a young woman who Tasha introduced as Anna Kelly.

"Nice to meet you, Kate." Anna's smile barely lifted the corners of her lips and definitely didn't reach her cold blue eyes. Her blond hair was arranged in a short braid. Petite and slim, she didn't seem to mind getting dirty, Kate noted. Her khaki slacks and heavy flannel plaid work shirt over a red top were liberally spread with the stuff. An archeologist's hand brush dangled from the gloved fingers of her right hand while the left hand propped against her hip, her work-booted toe tapping with impatience. Did she realize she displayed a disgruntled attitude? Or was that her intention? She obviously didn't care.

"Both Carl and Anna are working toward their PhDs," Tasha

continued, seemingly unaware of Anna's signals. Either that or Tasha was ignoring Anna's attitude due to introducing the new girl. "And you've already met Dr. Ethan Wagner who has his PhD in archeology and anthropology."

Kate's eyes met Ethan's slate gaze beneath dark brown hair. He tossed her another quick salute and his eye dropped in a wink. Her cheeks heated at the impertinent action and she turned away to survey the vast room. Concentrating on the amazing find, she was able to control the warmth and get her focus back on track. Kate was here to work with these very intelligent people, and that included Dr. Ethan Wagner. She would be professional with all of them, and hopefully it would be a beneficial experience.

"This is Michael Pierce," Tasha indicated a tall young man who stood to the side of the group. With a muscular build and clean-cut, light brown hair, Michael's ready smile lit his face as he was introduced. He stepped forward to shake Kate's hand then stepped back. "He's a second-year archeology student, so he's a junior team member, but he's invaluable to the team, isn't that right, Professor?"

"Absolutely. Mike is our heavy-lifting man and jumps in to assist wherever he can. There's one other team member who is not present," Prof. Rosenberg lifted his pointer finger. "Our other rookie archeologist is Paul Schmitz. You will meet him at another time, I'm sure."

Kate returned her gaze to him. "I look forward to it. Mind if I look around? This is fascinating."

"Not at all, my dear," the professor smiled pleasantly and waved a hand toward the vast room. "Ethan, why don't you give our new ranger a quick tour."

"With pleasure." The slate-eyed archeologist grinned, his dimple flashing. He cocked his head toward the stone structures. "Follow me."

Well, that wasn't exactly what she'd intended. Kate had hoped to just wander around a bit and peak into holes or descend a few ladders. A guided tour by this ruggedly handsome man was not what she had in mind. His slate gray eyes and quick grin were a little too unsettling.

"Thanks." Kate followed Ethan from one area to the next listening to his explanation of who they surmised may have occupied these ruins.

"We've only really begun to investigate," he was saying, "but we think an ancient Anasazi tribe may have lived here. We've found various artifacts indicating that anyway."

"So how old do you think this city is?" Kate's gaze wandered upward to the higher dwellings.

"Possibly as old as fifteen-hundred years. We're still trying to determine that, though. We know as many as eight different Indian tribes lived in this region. The Navajo, Hopi and Pueblo to name a few, but this is the most in-tact village that's been discovered in the Grand Canyon. Pretty amazing, actually. Come take a look at this."

Ethan led her toward the front of the immense cavern where a craggy overhang covered the whole upper half of the cavern from one side to the other like a huge stone awning. It protruded beyond the lower edge of the cavern floor which had a natural craggy rock ledge with vegetation growing up from below. Plenty of natural light entered between the two formations allowing the archeologists to move around the cavern without artificial light.

"That overhang has prevented the cavern from being discovered from the air," Ethan pointed along the upper rock formation. "Helicopter tours of the canyon, helicopter rescue flights, and planes pass over this all the time. This cavern has never been seen from above."

"I can understand why it's never been found from the trail," Kate said. "Unless you know it's there, you can't tell anything's behind that rock formation at the entrance. But what about from below?"

Ethan motioned her to the rocky ledge and pointed down. "Look at the drop off here."

Kate's gaze swept the rocky cliff face, a sheer drop with several rock formations here and there blocking the view. Areas of the trail could be seen occasionally hundreds of feet below, but it was doubtful if anyone looked in this direction they would see anything in the landscape indicating a cavern.

"I see what you mean," Kate nodded. She turned and swept her gaze over the whole city. I'm just amazed these people found this place to begin with and then built a city here."

"Yep, it is pretty amazing."

Kate noted the awe in his voice. "What are the holes in the floor?"

"Those are pit houses. Come on. I'll show you."

Ethan led her to the nearest hole big enough for one person to descend at a time. The top of a pole ladder protruded from the opening. He held out his hand.

"Be my guest. The ladder is perfectly safe."

"Not a thousand years old, I'm guessing?" Kate grinned before stepping on the ladder and backing down into the hole.

"Nope. Made just last week by the NPS maintenance department. Very sturdy, I assure you."

Kate continued down into the hole lit only by the light from above. Since the hole was only about ten feet deep, Kate could make out the floor below and stepped easily onto it and away from the ladder. Ethan descended, joining her and flipping on a small flashlight which he pulled from his hip pocket.

The space was round and about fifteen feet across. The floor was dirt but the walls had been plastered with mud. The stacked rock underneath was visible in places where the plaster had flaked off.

"What was this room used for?" Kate propped her arm on a ladder rung. The plastered walls and floor absorbed the sound of her voice. It was so quiet down here.

"We think it was a place for religious ceremonies. It's called a kiva. There are several of them in the village. We've found a few artifacts in here that may have been used in those ceremonies."

"That's interesting." Kate scuffed the toe of her hiking boot in the dirt. "So, there's only the five of you on the team?"

"Yeah. You know how government funding goes. Professor Rosenberg is from the Boston University archeological department. He was invited by the National Park Service to head up this dig. He handpicked his team from his department and from the University of Illinois."

Kate decided it was time to head back to daylight. As interesting as this enclosure was for historical purposes, the closeness of the pit caused it to lose its appeal for standing around in. "I'm heading back up."

She climbed the ladder and waited for Ethan to join her. "So, are you from the professor's department at Boston?"

Ethan shook his head and ran a hand through his dark hair, shoving it back from his strong brow. Kate's breath caught at the gesture. *Wow. He really is a good-looking guy.* She mentally shook herself. *Concentrate on his words, not his face.*

"No, I'm not."

Not what? Oh, yes. Not from Boston University. Right. Get hold of yourself, Kate. "Where do you hail from then?"

"I teach at the University of Arizona and was hired by the National Park Service to join the team." Ethan turned and led the way toward the nearest structure. Patting the side of the enormous sandstone and adobe mortar wall, he then pointed up with his other hand. "This is a tower house. It's about eighty feet tall."

Kate craned her neck to look up at the tall, square building. What once must have been a couple of small rectangular openings adorned the hand-crafted side that was visible to her, but had long ago been blocked up. "Is it built into the back of the cavern?"

"Yep. It sure is." Ethan pointed along the back wall. "All eleven of them are built right onto the wall. Those openings were once windows. Unfortunately, someone sealed them up eons ago and we can't go in them. They're as thick as the walls. And the original door? Who knows why, but it's completely sealed as well."

"Is that odd?"

"Very." Ethan pointed toward the ceiling. "We've never seen anything like it. We'll have to go over the top. There should be wooden floors about every eight feet or so. It'll be fairly easy to cut an entrance through the roof and go in that way."

"This tower," he slapped the stone wall, "we estimate to have nine or ten stories and may be the tallest in the village, but there are a couple towers that have crumbled more, so it's hard to tell how tall they were."

"Kate," Tasha's voice reached them before she did. "We should head back. I have a meeting to attend in a while, and I have to pick up my daughter from daycare before I can head home. Pretty interesting stuff, huh?"

As she halted beside Kate, she flashed a smile. "Ethan's a great tour guide, girl. He can tell you everything you could ever want to know about 'the ancient ones'."

"Who are 'the ancient ones'?" Kate glanced from Tasha to

Ethan and back again.

Tasha waved a hand toward Ethan. "Ask the expert."

"Ok, I'll bite. Who are 'the ancient ones', oh guru tour guide." Kate grinned but wasn't prepared for the sudden flare in Ethan's gray eyes. But no sooner had she seen it than it was gone. Vanished. Had she been mistaken? Was it her imagination? Surreptitiously she considered him again, but his gaze was fixed on the village. She must have been mistaken.

"The ancient ones are thought to be the Anasazi tribes that predate the Pueblos who were also cliff-dwellers. They were nomadic until they settled down to agriculture and built cliff-cities. They're a little harder to pin down in history. That's why we were so excited about this find. A lot of artifacts were left behind that may tell us more than we've been able to glean before now."

"Come on, girlfriend." Tasha tugged playfully on Kate's daypack strap and glanced at her wristwatch. "We still have to climb back up that trail. And daylight's burning."

Kate chuckled and resettled her daypack. "Ok, boss. Lead the way. I'm right behind you.

"Thank you for the tour, Dr. Wagner." Flashing a smile at Ethan, she waved a hand to include the village. "I appreciate your time, and I look forward to learning more about.... all of this."

"My pleasure," he grinned then winked. "See you soon."

~

As Kate Fleming strolled with Tasha toward the entrance to the tunnel, Ethan shook his head. Yep, she sure was cute. Her hazel eyes held laughter in their depths but she constantly tamped it down while at the same time avoiding his gaze, especially when he'd winked at her. As much as she'd attempted to prevent him from seeing, he'd noted the color that flamed in her cheeks in response. And what was *he* thinking? Flirting? Not exactly but certainly something he shouldn't be dabbling with. He had no desire to start a relationship with anyone, much less the cute Miss Fleming. There was no way he would invest his heart in another woman. Nope. Absolutely not.

Chapter Three

S o, what do you want me to do tomorrow?" Kate accompanied Tasha into the visitor center. "Do I go back to the dig and hang around?"

"Oh, I'm sure there's one archeologist who wouldn't mind you doing that," Tasha chuckled as she reached for the door handle of one of the double glass doors into the building. She held the door for Kate to enter then followed her inside.

"Tasha…," Kate began.

"I'm just saying, girl." Tasha held up a hand to halt her words. "He couldn't keep his eyes off you."

"I'm pretty sure you're mistaken about that," Kate shifted her daypack further up onto her shoulder. "He was all business and talked about the dig with enthusiasm. Had your eyes checked lately?"

"Nothing wrong with my eyesight, girlfriend. And they saw plenty. Anyway, I'll let you know after my meeting in half an hour. I'm heading over to the admin building in a couple minutes. Professor Rosenberg will be attending, and I'll find out more of what's expected of you. As for me, I want you there as much as possible. I'm not so sure about these people."

"What do you mean?" Kate halted in her steps. "Is something going on?"

"Oh, I don't know." Tasha let out a heavy sigh and stopped walking too. "Can't really put my finger on it, but I just want you to keep an eye on things. I'll be there when I can, but unfortunately, I have two other projects I'm overseeing right now. The renovation of the Desert View Watchtower at the east end of the canyon is underway and the Tusayan Ruins Museum is also being renovated. I'll be at all three locations. Unfortunately, both of those jobs are at the opposite end of the park from the Anasazi dig, and I'll be on the road a lot."

She laid her hand on Kate's arm. "Why don't you go familiarize yourself with the park? Take a drive through or something. It's already three-thirty and the day's nearly done. I'll meet you here in the morning at eight o'clock. I'll let you know what's happening then."

"Sounds good, Tasha. Thanks for taking me down to the dig. It really was fascinating. I'm looking forward to being involved in this project. It's quite an opportunity, and I don't take that lightly."

"Happy to do it. See you in the morning, Kate."

As Tasha walked away, Kate felt excitement warring with uncertainty within her. She was on the brink of the job of a lifetime. Who got to work with archeologists on an ancient dig on just any old day? Not too many people, and she was fortunate. But at the moment the uncertainty part seemed to grasp hold, and she felt more like she was hanging at a loose end of a rope flapping in the breeze. Dragging in a deep breath, she turned and exited the building, heading for her car. She had the job. Now what was she going to be doing with it?

~

Glancing into the fridge of her one-bedroom apartment, Kate spotted the only contents: a package of ham, another of cheese and a small carton of orange juice. A half loaf of bread sat on the counter. That's what was left from her drive cross-country.

That wouldn't suffice. She needed groceries. Her hike to the dig site today had left her ravenous. Shopping while hungry wasn't recommended, but she wanted something more substantial than what she had.

Closing the near-empty appliance, she walked into the bedroom and rummaged for something comfortable to change into. Donning a blue and white plaid button-down shirt and blue jeans, Kate tugged on her cowboy boots. With a quick glance in the mirror, she brushed her just-below-shoulder length auburn hair till it was smooth. It still took some getting used to. Once she'd had it halfway down her back, and Craig had always liked it long and loose or pulled back in a long ponytail. The thought brought a pang to her chest. Why did something as mundane as brushing her hair lead to pain? Why couldn't she just get over it?

Kate tossed the brush into the sink drawer and slammed it shut. Spinning on her boot heel, she grabbed her blue jean jacket and shoulder bag and headed out the door. She'd occupy herself with some grocery shopping.

Climbing into her little copper-colored Festiva, she headed into Grand Canyon Village and parked in front of the general store in the market plaza. As she climbed out, Kate glanced around the shopping area. Still not at the height of the tourist season, the number of shoppers was few. Few cars were parked in the parking lot. Good. She'd get what she needed and leave without competing with tourists. That would happen soon enough.

Wandering up and down the aisles of the grocery section, Kate dropped items here and there into the cart. As she reached for a box of donuts, someone else reached for the same box.

Her gaze swung up to meet a pair of slate gray eyes. Furrowed brows suddenly lifted in recognition.

"I believe those are my donuts you've grabbed," Ethan Wagner grinned, flashing his charming dimple.

"Umm, I don't think so." Kate tugged on the box, trying to look fierce. She doubted she was pulling it off since she felt her lips tilting upward. "Unhand my donuts, sir."

Ethan chuckled then attempted to look serious. "What do you say we call a truce and we both put it back? Then we each get a different box. No harm. No foul."

Kate considered him for a moment then nodded. "Very well. On the count of three?"

"Of course. What else?" He rolled his eyes with an exaggerated "tisk." "It's the only way to do these things, you know."

"Ok, then. One. Two." Kate paused momentarily. "Three."

They both replaced the box on the shelf then each reached for a different box. Kate placed hers into her shopping cart and Ethan placed his into his hand basket.

"Whew. Glad that's over." Ethan wiped a hand across his brow. "Good thing such tense situations like that don't happen every day."

"You're telling me," Kate nodded and turned to leave.

"Where you going?" Ethan grabbed the side of her cart bringing it to a halt.

"I wouldn't want to cause another tricky situation, so I'm going to grab the rest of what I need and vacate the premises." She pushed past him and headed toward the dairy department to grab some milk.

He followed her.

"You're following me." She reached for a half gallon of milk.

"Well...I...need milk for my donuts, too, you know. Who ever heard of eating donuts without milk?" He shook his head and rolled his eyes again like it was an unheard-of notion.

"No one, I suppose." Kate couldn't help but chuckle at the whole silly scenario. She leaned on the handle of the shopping cart. "So, I guess I assumed wrong that you and the other archeologists are camping at the dig site?"

"Yes, you assumed wrong." Ethan chuckled and added a block of cheese to his basket. "We live in a trailer court of sorts, but we're pretty spread out. We're not the only ones who live there. Seasonal park personnel and other staff do as well. We live in camping trailers. I'm in a fifth wheel. Pretty nice, actually. Our office is in a small double-wide trailer behind the Hermit's Rest Gift Shop, and we hike down to the site every day. Good exercise, that's for sure. Keeps us in shape."

"I'll bet." Kate laughed. "Well, I'm going to take my donuts and head for home. It's been a long day. Tomorrow promises to be just as long, so...I'll be seeing you. Probably tomorrow. Bye."

She tossed a quick wave of her fingers and headed for the checkout line. Ethan Wagner was too good-looking for his own good and certainly too charming and witty. All characteristics she was definitely not looking for.

~

The next morning Kate leaned against the visitor center information desk waiting for Tasha to meet her. The center was not yet open to visitors but a few rangers were milling about preparing for the day.

"Hi, you must be new here," a male voice spoke from Kate's right.

Turning, Kate met the smiling blue gaze of a tall, dark haired young man. Leaning back against the information desk, his arms were linked across his gray uniform shirt, the muscles in his chest and biceps well-shaped. One black oxford-clad foot was crossed over the other. He wore green uniform dress slacks as opposed to her green uniform jeans.

"Yes, that's right. Only been here a couple of days," Kate replied.

He straightened and held out his hand. "Well, welcome to the Grand Canyon. I'm sure I'm not the first to tell you that. I'm Gage Hampton."

"It's nice to meet you, Gage." Kate shook his outstretched hand. "My name's Kate Fleming."

"Pleased to meet you, Kate. Will you be working here at the visitor center?"

"Not completely sure what my duties will be yet. Awaiting orders as we speak." She wasn't sure if it was public knowledge yet that she would be assistant liaison to the archeologists. She'd have to ask Tasha about that. Speaking of which….

Tasha walked in from the back of the visitor center and headed their way.

"Good morning, Gage. Good morning, Kate." She greeted them with a cheerful smile. "It's a beautiful day. And it looks like the number of visitors are picking up out there. Of course, it's Friday, so it's going to."

"Yep," Gage agreed. "They'll be opening the doors shortly. And I need to get going. It was nice meeting you, Kate. I'm sure I'll be seeing you around." With a self-conscious backward walk for several feet, he smiled, nodded then turned and hurried away.

Kate turned to find Tasha grinning at her. "What?"

"Kate Fleming. What are you doing to the young men in this park? First the archeologist, then Gage? Who's next?" Tasha raised her hands and shrugged in question.

"What do you mean?" Kate had no idea what she was talking about.

"I mean you're turning heads, girl." Tasha flashed her a wide smile and chuckled.

Kate shook her head and drew her brows down. "Tasha, please. You're mistaken. They're just being nice to the new girl. Nothing more. Now, what instructions do you have for me? Gage wanted to know what my job here is, and I didn't know if I'm allowed to say or not. I told him I was waiting to find out."

Tasha leaned against the information desk. "Probably best to keep a low profile about the dig for now. The park hasn't announced the find to the public or to the staff yet. Even though they've been working for a month, it's being kept on the down low until more information is discovered concerning the ancient ones. When there's more concrete evidence, they'll make a big announcement and hopefully get additional funding. The Hermit's Trail has been officially closed to prevent hikers from heading down and stumbling on the dig. The park is using a rock slide as the reason for closing the trail. You probably noticed the sign yesterday."

"And my official job?"

"As the National Park Service Natural Resource Liaison, I am in need of an assistant and you are officially it," Tasha grinned. "You are the Natural Resource Assistant Liaison. Just don't mention the job on Hermit's Trail. You are officially assisting me on my other jobs as far as anyone knows. The higher ups are fully aware, so don't worry about that."

"Yes, ma'am," Kate saluted.

"Tasha," a booming male voice reached them before a tall African-American man in NPS uniform did. "Good. Caught you before you left."

"Lance, sweetheart!" Tasha turned and flashed her pearly whites in his direction. "Mmmmm, mmmm. It's wonderful to have you back, darlin'."

Kate glanced from one to the other and back again, a question in her eyes.

The man called Lance pulled Tasha into his arms and planted a long kiss on her lips. Tasha wrapped her arms around his neck and returned his kiss with equal fervor. Kate waited for them to come up for air and grew concerned that they may not make it. Just as she was sure they'd run out of air, Tasha pulled away slightly and smiled up at the man.

"Oh, my darlin', Lance. You know how to make a woman's heart pound for sure." She sighed like a love-struck teenager. "I have missed you."

"I've missed you, too, honey," Lance rumbled in reply, tugging Tasha close again.

Kate shuffled uncomfortably. She didn't know whether to slink away, drop down beside the information desk out of sight and crawl way or just run away. Anything was preferable to the love scene that played out in front of her. Turning away, she picked up a brochure from the information desk, perusing the pictures inside.

"Oh, Kate. I'm sorry," Tasha's apologetic words pulled her back around. "This is my husband, Lance. Sorry about that. Lance has been gone for the last week. He's been in the Everglades National Park on an experimental park police exchange program and has just returned."

Tasha held up her thumb and forefinger with a tiny space separating them. "As you can tell, I missed him. A little."

"Yeah, I picked up on that," Kate chuckled and held out her hand. "Nice to meet you, Lance. And welcome back."

"It's nice to meet you, Kate. Welcome to the Grand Canyon."

Kate determined Lance to be at least six feet five inches. His muscles had muscles and his waist was lean. Fine, curly, close-cropped, black hair covered his head and his dark eyes between long black lashes were bright with laughter. His nose was long and wide while his full lips spread in a broad smile.

"Thank you."

"Well, as much as I'd like to spend the day with you, sweetie, I need to get to work. And so, do you." Tasha tapped his muscular bicep. "But I'll see you this afternoon. Why don't you pick up Ariel and we'll grab a bite before we head home?"

"Sounds like a plan." Lance leaned in for another slow kiss. "See you later, honey."

He released his wife and turned to walk away. "See you around, Kate. Y'all have a good day."

"Come on, Kate" Tasha said. "We need to get this day going."

Chapter Four

A re you sure, Professor?" Tasha asked. "You're positive the artifacts are missing?"

"You can see for yourself." Prof. Rosenberg waved both hands with open palms toward the heavy safe. The open door of the four-feet-tall by three-feet-wide storage device revealed a few papers littering the shelves inside but nothing more. "We had yet to find high-priced artifacts, but what we had found was in there. And now they are gone. This is how we found the safe. Open and empty."

A few minutes earlier Tasha and Kate had arrived at the archeologists' office to find the whole team assembled around the safe discussing what might have happened.

"Can you tell if it was actually broken into or if someone used the combination?" Kate bent down to visually examine the door. "I don't see any damage, but then I don't really know what I'm looking for. Tasha?"

"I'm no expert either. I'll call park police. They'll send someone down to investigate and to fingerprint the safe." She glanced around the room at the assembled archeological team. "No one leaves this room until the park police releases you, understood?"

Amidst mumbles and grumbles from the team, Tasha waved Kate outside.

"Wait here and observe the group. I'm going to radio in. I'm serious about no one leaving. Okay?"

"Right," Kate agreed. "I'll be here."

As Tasha headed to her SUV, Kate stepped back inside and

propped against the wall by the door. As unobtrusively as possible she attempted to note each team member's reaction to the situation.

Professor Rosenberg paced back and forth while ranting at Carl Young who stood with arms folded across his chest, a frown on his lips and his brow furrowed. Anna Kelly sat in a chair against one side of the room and watched them while smacking gum and occasionally rolling her eyes at something the professor said. Her legs were crossed at the knees and the top leg bounced impatiently. Was she eager to disappear from this scene? Ethan Wagner sat behind the desk, legs propped on its surface, ankles crossed and hands clasped behind his head, eyes lowered. As if sensing Kate's gaze on him, his eyes lifted to meet hers and he…winked? Warmth heated Kate's cheeks as she jammed her hands into the pockets of her jacket, shifted her stance and forced her gaze to move on to the last team member.

She hadn't yet met Paul Schmitz. That must be the stocky young man with longish brown hair. She noted his worn button-down shirt with exposed shirttails beneath a stained and faded hoodie, torn blue jeans and worn hiking boots. A pair of ear buds plugged his ears and were plugged into the cellphone in his hand. If he was supposed to be listening to the professor's rant, he was definitely missing it.

Michael Pierce leaned against the side of a book case with arms linked over his chest. His brow was furrowed and his eyes moved from one team member to the next, taking in everything that was going on.

It wasn't long before Tasha returned, a park police officer on her heels. "Ok, everybody, this is Officer Blake Hunter. He'll be in charge of this crime scene. Please cooperate with him in every way possible. If you want your artifacts found, you need to help him find them."

Officer Hunter placed his crime scene tool kit on the desk and opened in. "I'll start by fingerprinting each of you. Tasha, give me a hand, will you?"

Kate continued leaning against the wall and observing the proceedings and responses but wasn't sure she was gleaning much.

"Well, I don't think that wall's going anywhere." Ethan approached Kate and leaned against it as well, crossing one foot over the other. "Not the most comfortable place to be. Why not sit down?"

"Just trying to stay out of the way." Kate shifted from one foot to the other. He was right. She was getting a little tired of just standing here. "Any idea what might have happened to the artifacts?"

"Not a clue. Nothing of great value yet, but there were a few nice pieces that we'd discovered. Arguably more valuable."

"Well, I might suggest the team come up with a more secure means of protecting the artifacts, especially after you start finding things that *are* more valuable. That safe wasn't a very good one."

"Good idea. I'll suggest that to the professor."

Kate turned to peer up at him. Was that a hint of laughter in his voice? "You're laughing at me, aren't you? You've already talked to him about it."

He shrugged. "Yeah. Well, I'm not sure he sees the need. But hopefully after today he will. We'll see, won't we?"

Ethan glanced at Officer Hunter who waved him over. "I do believe it's my turn to be printed. See ya." He saluted, pulled himself away from the wall and strolled over to the desk.

Kate glanced around at the occupants of the room. Everyone looked pretty much the same as before except Professor Rosenberg who caused her to pause in her perusal. He was chewing his nails, and she figured at the rate he was going he'd be down to the first knuckle in about a minute. A lot of people chewed their nails. Nothing out of the ordinary about that. But the intensity with which he chewed? Yeah, that was out of the ordinary. Was he that nervous? And for what? Had *he* taken the artifacts? Was he afraid of being discovered? But he'd seemed genuinely upset they were gone. Was it a ruse to cover up for something?

~

"I have them," the voice spoke softly into the phone, "but there isn't much here. One or two pieces might be worth something."

"Get them to me as quickly as possible. All of them." The man with the accent demanded. "I'll have them appraised. My courier will meet you in the Tusayan Village Airport at noon sharp. Don't be late."

"I won't," came the soft reply. "Will he have my money?"

"But of course. Fear not. You do your part, and I will do mine.

29

You fail me at any time, and you will regret it."

The phone clicked in a final manner. There was absolutely no doubt who was in charge.

~

"A lot of people chew their nails, Kate." Tasha smiled. "I think it was more a response to the stress of the situation. But, girl, that's a good eye you have there. Very good observation."

Kate sighed. "Thanks."

Tasha patted her shoulder then looked back at the office. The archeology team members were coming out with their gear and making their way to the Hermit's Trailhead. "You did fine. Look, Blake will process the fingerprints and the prints he lifted from the safe. Hopefully he'll come up with something helpful. You go on down to the dig site with the team and be a presence like I need you to be. I hope to be down later today if I can. But if not, just stay on till they head back up. As soon as we get the results I'll let you know. Keep your radio handy. Remember, cell phones don't work down there. Radios aren't reliable but they're better than phones. And whatever you do, watch your back. I'm not saying someone on the team is responsible, but I'm not about to say they aren't either. It's possible word has leaked out about this dig, and we may have a black-market thief on our hands. As hard as we try, it's almost impossible to keep the lid on these things. Remember the two guys who found the city to begin with? Who knows who they've told in spite of signing paperwork saying they wouldn't."

"Understood." Kate nodded, hefting her daypack onto her back.

"Oh, and don't worry about food," Tasha turned back from heading to her SUV. "A team of caterers brings meals down for the team for lunch and they leave snacks as well. You eat when they eat, and don't be shy about it. Help yourself. The caterers have been notified you'll be there."

"Wow. That's nice. Thanks." Kate grinned. Her tummy would appreciate that for sure. And someone else would be hiking it in. Even better.

"See you later, Tasha."

"Bye, Kate. Remember. Watch your back."

Kate turned and proceeded down the precarious trail, but had only gone a dozen steps when she heard her name called.

"Kate! Wait up!"

Turning, Kate spotted Ethan jogging toward the trailhead. She waited until he reached her. "Heading down?"

"Yep."

"Like some company?"

"Sure." Kate shrugged. "That way there's a witness if I go over the cliff this time. It'll be documented rather than a mystery as to what happened when Kate Fleming disappeared and her body was never found."

"Now I'd never let that happen," Ethan chuckled as he came alongside her. "I saved you before, didn't I?" He winked and continued on down the trail, leaving her standing there, cheeks flaring warmth.

"Yes. Yes, you did. Thank goodness." Kate followed him as they carefully made their way to the dig site.

~

Throughout the day Kate spent time with each of the archeologists as they worked in their various areas. Except for Anna Kelly, who seemed put out at the prospect of a "non-professional" spending time in her presence, most of the team didn't seem to mind having Kate around. They answered her questions good-naturedly and encouraged her enthusiasm when they found something, no matter how small. After lunch Kate approached Prof. Rosenberg as he worked in one of the underground kivas and asked if he minded if she observed.

"Oh, not at all, my dear girl. Please, come sit and watch." Surrounded by a halo of electric light run by a site generator, he patted the ground beside him. He'd unearthed a stone structure buried in the dirt at the rear of the kiva, approximately four by four feet square in size. A large, flat stone lay across the top of the structure. He was brushing the last remnants of dirt from around the edges of the stone.

"I'm just about to remove this stone to see what might lie beneath. I was going to call one of the others to come assist me, but I think you might be able to do the job. If you'd be willing, of course."

The professor cast a questioning glance at her over the rim of his glasses. One corner of his mouth lifted slightly in a grin and he challenged in almost a whisper, "You might not ever have another opportunity to participate in what could be the most astounding archeological find of all time, my dear."

Allowing that statement to hang for a few seconds, he then added with a slight shrug, "Or you could fetch one of the others and move out of the way while we work."

Kate laughed softly. "Well, Professor, you don't think I can really pass up an invitation like that, now do you? I'd be happy to help you. Even if I pull a muscle, I'll help you get that rock out of there."

He chuckled as he climbed to his feet. "I don't think you'll have to worry about that. Between the two of us, we can handle it, I should think. Besides, I have pry bars to help us get it started."

Slipping on gloves, they worked together, sliding the pry bars behind and beneath the back edge of the rock and with slow rocking movements, were able to edge it upward. Then once they had it loose and moving, they slid their fingers in, gripping the smooth, flat surface. Amongst grunts and groans, they heaved it toward them, pulling it up and out of the hole. They slid the heavy flat stone onto the ground, then panting, they both dropped heavily back to the ground.

"Are you...alright, Kate?" Gasping for air, Prof. Rosenberg eyed Kate with concern as he withdrew a bandana from his hip pocket and wiped his sweaty brow.

Kate shed her jacket and panted, fanning herself with her hand. "Oh, I'm fine. I think I'll feel that in the morning, though. You?"

"No. No, I feel it now." The professor shoved his glasses up on his nose. "Perhaps we should keep going rather than think about it. What do you say?"

"Probably a good idea."

The professor stood and moved the electric light on a stand closer to the hole then they knelt down on either side.

Kate gasped at the same time the professor said something in German that she didn't understand.

"What is that?" she asked in a whisper.

A fragile cloth of fine weave covered a bundled object wrapped with decayed and crumbling bindings. Holes throughout the cloth revealed small peeks of what looked like bone fragments, bits of a golden colored object and more cloth. These small windows into the bundle only gave rise to a myriad of possibilities, but the bone fragments looked the most promising.

Excitement gleamed in Professor Rosenberg's eyes and tilted his lips upward beneath his mustache as he peered at her. His tone was conspiratorial when he spoke. "Shall we see what it is?"

Kate's heart pounded and her palms grew sweaty. Was this what every archeologist felt when they found something? Then she could see why they did what they did. There was definitely something thrilling about finding this object even though they didn't know what it was yet. Her head bobbed in acknowledgment because words failed her.

"Reach into that box and pull out that stack of trays. We'll put the items in those as we begin to investigate the object. But before we do that, we must photograph everything. Bring the digital camera as well, please." Pulling a pair of rubber gloves from his pocket, he tugged them on then carefully probed the object without disturbing anything. No telling how old it was. Whatever it was.

Kate returned with a foot-high stack of plastic trays and the camera.

"Do you know how to use that?" The professor never lifted his head but continued to explore the object with meticulous care.

Kate examined the camera. "Ummmm. Doesn't look too complicated. I think I can figure it out."

"Take a few shots and see what you can do. If you cannot, then I will."

"Oookay." Talk about adding things to your resume. She was adding them by the minute. By playing with the settings and then snapping a few pictures, Kate figured out the lighting, focus and zoom. After showing him what she took, he was happy. She snapped pictures of everything as he disassembled and opened the object.

Suddenly it dawned on her what the camera lens was focused on. A darkened face with two closed eyes, a flattened nose and a mouth with lips stretched thin and revealing broken and missing teeth lay within the fragile confines of the torn cloth fibers. Broken bits of dried, dark hair haloed the face. A leather strap encircled the forehead.

"Professor?" Kate whispered as she lowered the camera. "What...? How...? It's not big enough to be a full mummy, is it?"

Professor Rosenberg's intent gaze beneath his furrowed brow met hers. "Until we open the rest, we won't know, but I assume the rest of the body is folded up inside of the bundle. But look at this."

His rubber-gloved fingertip pointed to a golden object that lay at the throat. It was about two inches by three inches, carved in the form of an ancient figure.

Kate knelt for a closer look and zoomed in with the camera, snapping a photo. She studied the display on the back of the camera. "What is it?"

"I believe it's a royal amulet," the professor whispered. "This is most likely an Anasazi tribal chief."

Glancing up at the hole where the ladder led out to the main floor of the city, he placed his finger over his lips and shook his head. "Don't say anything to anyone. With all our artifacts disappearing, we can't afford for this one to disappear. I believe it to be a one-of-a-kind artifact, and I don't want anyone to know yet. It is invaluable."

Kate's brow furrowed in question. "Not even your team members?"

"No, not even my team members. Not until we find out who is behind the theft. Promise me, Kate Fleming. You must promise me."

Kate spotted the angst in his expression. Sweat beaded on his forehead and trailed down his cheeks. It was not hot down here considering it was a cold April in the Grand Canyon. The professor was actually pretty anxious right now. She remembered him chewing his nails earlier that morning when he reported the theft of the other artifacts. Apparently, it hadn't been because he was afraid of being discovered for having stolen the artifacts like she'd first thought. He was afraid of further thefts.

Prof. Rosenberg reached down and extracted the amulet from the mummy, then taking a small plastic zip-bag from his supplies, he dropped it in and zipped it.

"I want you to take this, Kate Fleming, and hide it somewhere safe." The professor reached over and placed it in her palm, folding her hand closed around the small plastic bag.

Kate tried to give it back. She shook her head adamantly, her voice barely above a whisper. "Professor, no! I can't take this. It's way too valuable. It won't be safe with me."

"It won't be safe with me or in the office either. I don't know who is behind the theft, but I don't trust anyone. And neither should you."

"Professor Rosenberg!" A voice called from the main floor. It sounded like Carl Young. "Professor Rosenberg."

"Hurry," the professor whispered urgently. "Put it into your backpack. You must hide it."

Kate cast one more desperate glance at him then noticed the lower half of a figure begin to descend the ladder. Reaching for her daypack, she unzipped it, dropped the amulet into an inside zippered pocket, zipped it, then zipped the outer zipper and tossed the daypack by the supplies. What in the world was she doing? And what in the world was she going to do with the amulet? Was she crazy? She would have to talk to Tasha about it. But what had Professor Rosenberg said? Don't trust *anyone*. Surely she could trust Tasha. She was the NPS Liaison after all. She could trust *her*. Couldn't she?

Chapter Five

F ind anything interesting down here?" Carl Young stepped off the ladder and into the light. Kate's palms were sweaty and she gripped the camera to control their trembling. Could he see right through her daypack to the amulet? That was ridiculous. Of course he couldn't see through it. Upon casual scrutiny it didn't appear that he'd even noticed the bag. She didn't realize until she dragged in a deep breath that she'd even been holding it. She released it slowly.

"Yes," the professor was saying with enthusiasm, "come see what we've found."

He tugged Carl's arm, pulling him toward the hole where the mummy lay half uncovered. Carl stooped down on his haunches and examined the mummy.

"Wow, now that's fascinating, Professor. That's the first human remains that have been discovered in the village. Perhaps that's a good indication there'll be others." Carl twisted his fingers together and cracked his knuckles.

The sound grated on Kate's fragile nerves. At the moment she just wanted to climb that ladder, hike back up the trail, catch the shuttle bus to the visitor center, forget waiting for Tasha to arrive, and get back to her apartment. Then maybe jumping in her car and leaving the area would be a good plan. Leaving the daypack where it sat would be a great idea too. Why, oh why, had this day gone *so* far south? It had only taken a skinny second for it to happen. And what was she going to do about it?

Lord, I know I haven't talked to You in a while. I've been sort of angry at You. Maybe I still am. I don't know. But I do know I've got a problem I didn't ask for, and I don't know what to do about it. Could You help me out here!

"What do you think, Miss Fleming?" Carl turned toward Kate.

Kate froze. He'd asked her something. She rubbed her temple, not having to pretend to have a headache. "I'm so sorry. I was wool gathering. What did you say?"

"No problem, my dear," Professor Rosenberg chuckled. "Carl just asked what you thought of our find."

"Oh, I think...I think it's amazing. I've never had part in an archeological find before and this one is...really something." She mentally slapped herself on the forehead. What a lame answer. "So how will you preserve this mummy? Won't you have to treat it carefully?"

"Oh, sure," Carl said. "We have a temperature-controlled room at the rear of the office and we'll photograph, catalogue and store it in there. The fabric, the bones, the skin and hair. They're all very fragile. My estimation is, oh... say," he paused to consider, "at least eight hundred years old. Wouldn't you agree, Professor?"

"Oh, most definitely." The professor gave an affirmative nod. "If not older. But we will test to determine that."

"Really? That's incredible. Could there be others?" Kate shifted from one foot to the other.

"Certainly," Ethan Wagner spoke from just outside the circle of light. Stepping forward, he stopped beside the hole with the mummy, crossing his arms over his chest. "Where there's one mummy, there's a good likelihood there are others. Great find, Professor."

"Thank you, Ethan," Professor Rosenberg bowed from the waist and clicked his heels. "Miss Fleming was of particular assistance to me. She helped me remove the stone that covered the remains. And I don't believe you strained any muscles, did you, Miss Fleming?"

Kate tried for the most casual smile she could muster but it still felt stiff and contrived. "No. No muscles strains, Professor. We were very careful."

Kate sensed Ethan's gaze on her and resisted the urge to meet it. Instead she glanced back at the mummy and snapped a few more pictures.

"Here, let me get pictures of all of you kneeling beside the mummy," she suggested.

After snapping a few, Ethan offered to snap a couple of her and the professor with the mummy. She baulked at first but with the professor's urging she finally agreed.

With great care, the mummy was removed from the ground and placed in a sturdy acid-free, cushion-lined crate and carefully carried up the ladder. It was late and time to call it a day. As tempting as it was to leave her daypack at the dig site, Kate picked it up and settled it on her back. The additional weight of the amulet was nothing, but mentally it weighed a ton. The heaviest thing she'd ever carried. Her gut churned. How would she ever deal with this? Where would she put it for safekeeping? She'd have to talk to the professor and get it back to him at some point, but the safe in the office was obviously not a secure place to keep it.

The team hiked up the trail, Carl and Ethan carefully maneuvering the mummy between them. They placed it in the climate-controlled unit where the professor and Paul immediately began photographing and cataloguing it.

"Everyone, it's been a long day." The professor stood in the outer office doorway and waved his hands in a shooing motion. "Go home. Get some rest. Paul and I will begin the cataloging process for the mummy then we will also go home. Now, goodnight."

As the team muttered their goodnights and headed to their cars, Kate hesitated as she watched the professor head back inside and close the outer door. She'd hoped to talk with him about a secure method of storing the amulet, but it seemed he'd already forgotten its existence in the need to get to the processing of the mummy. She knew it wouldn't do any good to put it in the safe in the office. It had already been breached and would no longer be viable for keeping the amulet or any future artifacts secure. For now, she and the professor were the only ones who knew of the amulet's existence. Until she could find a way to secure it, she would just have to take it home and keep it there.

Kate wondered how she was going to get home. So far no one had offered her a ride. Tasha hadn't returned and the shuttle buses from Hermit's Rest Gift Shop and overlook a half mile away had stopped running an hour ago. She stood in front of the office with her daypack slung over her shoulder. The sun had dipped below the upper edge of the western canyon but the colors it left on the canyon walls were spectacular. Pinks, yellows, oranges and reds blended into purples and blues. Simply gorgeous.

"God paints a pretty picture, doesn't He," Ethan spoke from beside her.

Kate glanced at him and nodded. "He certainly does. No one is more talented, that's for sure."

"Need a ride?"

"Is it that obvious?"

"Well, the fact everyone left except for the professor and Paul, who are still inside? And me, of course. Yeah." He chuckled.

"Well, it *would* be a long walk back. And I'm pretty sure there are coyotes and maybe wolves. And mountain lions. And probably tigers and bears. And rhinos and elephants and…"

"Whoa, whoa, whoa." Ethan held up his hand. "I don't think there are tigers and rhinos and elephants in the Grand Canyon."

Kate looked at him in the dying light as the colors faded. "Prove it."

Ethan opened his mouth to say something then closed it. He grinned, flashing that wonderful dimple. "Come on. Let's go before something strange and wild comes out and grabs us."

~

Kate had just settled down with her microwave pasta dish and a side salad when her cellphone rang.

"Hello?"

"Miss Fleming?" Professor Rosenberg's voice was faint and hoarse. "Can you hear me?"

"Barely, Professor. Where are you? Can you speak up?"

"No, I cannot. You must meet with me tomorrow morning. Early. Come to the office. I have had a new safe installed. Before I went to the dig site this morning, I spoke with Officer Hunter and he gave me the name of a safe company in Flagstaff. I called them and told them it was an emergency. Officer Hunter escorted them to the office, and they installed it while we were at the site today. Please bring the amulet. We will put it in the safe in the morning."

"What?" Was that a squeak in her voice? "Why didn't you tell me that today? Why did you make me go through such agony over keeping that thing with me?"

"I am so terribly sorry, my dear. In the moment of finding the mummy and the amulet, I forgot I had ordered the safe. It wasn't until we returned and everyone left that I saw it had been installed. Please. You mustn't worry any longer. Just bring it in the morning, and we'll put it where it will be secure."

"But what if someone on your team is the thief? Won't they still have access to the artifacts?"

"*Nine.*" Hmmm. His German was slipping out. "I'm the only one with the new combination for now, but I will give it to Ethan when I see him. It is a much better safe, and I have been assured by the safe company that it is much harder to break into. Please just bring the amulet and meet me at six a.m. The rest of the team will arrive about seven. That will give us plenty of time."

As irritated as she was that she'd had to agonize over having the amulet with her, she was relieved she'd be getting rid of it. And soon. Tasha had given her the gate code to the access road, so she could drive herself out. If Tasha still wanted to meet with her, she could drive back after securing the amulet.

"Very well, Professor. I'll see you at six."

"Thank you, my dear. I'll see you in the morning. Goodnight."

"Goodnight."

She doubted she'd get much sleep with the amulet in her possession. Maybe tomorrow night.

~

Ethan parked his pickup truck in front of his trailer and climbed out. In the years he'd studied to become an archeologist and since he'd received his PhD, he'd never lived in quiet as nice a place as this trailer while on a dig. Some of his quarters had been real dives but this fifth wheel was fairly new and quite comfortable, to say the least.

Opening the trailer door, he was greeted by a white German Shepherd. She planted her paws on his chest and licked his cheeks in greeting as he climbed the steps.

"Well hello, Haley, girl." Ethan scratched behind her ears and fluffed the ruff around her neck and shoulders. "You've been waiting for me all day, haven't you? Didn't Jill show you enough attention today?"

The teenage daughter of one of the rangers came by during her school lunch and let Haley out, walking her for ten minutes as well.

Ethan grabbed Haley's lead and clipped it to her collar, then shoved a plastic bag into his pocket. "Come on, girl, let's go. I'll take you for a nice long walk."

They soon settled into their afternoon routine. Ethan enjoyed walking Haley. It gave him time to think, and today his mind shot right to the person that had been uppermost in his mind since she'd nearly fallen off the cliff a few days before.

As much as he wasn't looking for a relationship of any kind, he couldn't seem to shake Kate Fleming from his mind. She'd done nothing to encourage him either. As a matter of fact, she seemed to be doing everything she could to discourage him. Was she avoiding him? It sure seemed like it.

Well, that was probably a good thing. Ever since his breakup with Jodi, he hadn't dated anyone and had no intention to. At least not anytime soon. He attempted to shove the painful memories of Jodi from his mind. They weren't worth remembering. Too much deceit. Too much heartache. He was trying to move past it, and if he kept dredging it up, he'd never move on.

Although he wasn't ready for another relationship, it was more fun thinking about Kate. He recalled her at the dig site today. She really seemed to enjoy working with the archeologists, except Anna who didn't work well with anyone. Kate seemed to enjoy it until she and the professor discovered the mummy, then she seemed oddly nervous. Or preoccupied. Something was bothering her. She didn't seem as happy about it as the professor was. She acted happy but her happiness seemed forced. Why was that?

Ethan loved his job. He loved archeology. It wasn't the best paying job in the world by any means, but it was certainly one of the most fascinating. He wondered what Kate would do if she knew about his second job. One no one knew about it. Well, almost no one. And no one could know.

~

Early the next morning, Kate parked in front of the archeologists' office beside Professor Rosenberg's vehicle and jogged up the three wooden steps to the door. Hmmm. The door wasn't closed all the way. The professor must not have closed it when he arrived and went inside. Shoving it open with her jacketed elbow, she went inside. The fluorescent lights were on but no one was in the outer office. She glanced at the new safe. Good. It was shut and looked secure. Surveying the room, she found that everything, other than the new safe, pretty much looked the same as it had the day before.

The door into the climate-controlled room was ajar and the lights were on in there as well. She smiled. Professor Rosenberg had been so excited about the mummy, he was probably continuing where he and Paul had left off with cataloging it last night. Shoving the door open, Kate's smile slipped when she didn't find him bent over the remains. They weren't even on the waist-high counter but were still in their crate on the rack of shelves on the back wall. Kate stepped slowly into the room, concern gripping her stomach and twisting. The buzzing from the fluorescent lights was the only sound besides her heartbeat. Where was the professor? He'd told her to meet him here and his car was outside.

Perusing the counter, she noticed papers scattered haphazardly across the surface and a plastic tray of small examination tools had been overturned. A few had fallen to the floor and lay beside a pair of glasses next to the counter leg. More papers were strewn across the floor beneath them and beyond. Kate knelt to look closer at the glasses but touched nothing. They were the professor's and the lenses were starred and cracked, the frames bent. Her heart picked up its pace and her stomach churned. What had happened here? And where was Prof. Rosenberg?

Climbing to her feet, she left the office and returned outside. She scouted the yard around the building thinking perhaps he'd fallen inside and was injured. Had he stumbled outside and sat down somewhere, waiting for her or someone to arrive? It was still too early for the rest of the team to be here. She circled the building, calling his name, all to no avail. She listened but the only sounds she heard were distant birds singing and a strange muffled sound coming from about forty feet behind the office, back in a stand of Utah juniper trees.

"Professor Rosenberg? Are you back here? Are you okay?" Still no answer. The hair stood up on the back of Kate's neck, apprehension stirring in the pit of her stomach.

Was that snarling? She stopped in her tracks and listened. Snarling and…what? She wasn't sure what the other sound was but it was definitely strange. Possibly an animal of some kind? Kate removed the small flashlight from her utility belt, and shone the light on the ground, spotting tracks. Something had been dragged into the juniper stand and animal tracks intersected the drag marks. Had they possibly killed something and dragged it into the trees? Was that the sound? They were eating their kill?

Kate moved cautiously closer, unsnapping the sidearm holster on her utility belt. She rested her hand on her sidearm grip and stepped closer, her rubber-soled hiking boots muffled on the desert terrain. The snuffling, snarling almost slurping sound grew stronger as she approached the trees and underbrush.

When she was nearly ten feet away, Kate stooped to peer beneath the low hanging branches of a juniper and met the faint gaze of two coyotes intent on their meal. In the early morning light, it was hard to see beneath the shadows of the trees but the reflection in their eyes cast an eerie warning that raised the hair on her neck as did the gleam of their red-tinged teeth. She attempted to make out what it was they were eating.

As she cast the powerful beam of the flashlight beneath the juniper branches, Kate drew her sidearm from its holster, creeping a little closer. The teeth bared further and the growls grew louder. Kate spotted a pair of blue jean clad legs and two hiking boots protruding from beneath the shadowy edge of the tree branches. Her heart clenched and bile rose in her throat leaving a sour taste in her mouth. She thought she was going to be sick. Swallowing several times, Kate attempted to force down the bile.

One of coyotes stepped towards her then the other followed suit. Lifting her sidearm, Kate fired off a round above their heads. The echoing sound startled the animals and both halted, looking momentarily confused. Kate waited them out, and when they attempted another approach, she fired another round. This time they ran off through the juniper stand.

Kate tried to swallow back the dread that filled her as she approached the body. She already knew it was Professor Rosenberg. She glanced around the open area between the office and where she stood. Had he fallen and the coyotes dragged him back here or had someone killed him and the coyotes had simply scavenged his body?

When Kate pulled back a couple of branches, the sour taste of bile filled her mouth and throat. Before she could prevent it, she leaned to the side and lost her breakfast. It was the professor alright, but the coyotes had done a number on him. Covering her mouth, she stumbled back to her car, then yanked her cellphone from her pocket and called Tasha.

Chapter Six

Ethan climbed out of his pickup truck and eyed the park police cars haphazardly positioned in front of the office at Hermit's Trailhead. With strobe lights flashing and police officers coming and going with a purpose, it looked like something serious was going on. What in the world had happened?

He spotted Tasha Johnson talking with Kate Fleming who sat on the front steps to the office. Kate was pale, her gaze fixed on the ground.

Tasha glanced up as he approached.

"What's going on?" Ethan pointing a thumb over his shoulder at the police cars.

Tasha looked grim. "Kate found Professor Rosenberg this morning. Dead."

Ethan's heart stammered at the news. "What?"

He knelt beside Kate and clasped one of her cold hands between his. "Kate? Are you alright? What happened?"

Kate dragged her gaze from the ground to his face. "I found him under a stand of junipers out back. He was breakfast for a couple of coyotes."

Ethan sat on the step and put his arm around her shoulder, tugging her gently against his side. "I'm so sorry."

He looked at Tasha. "And the coroner?"

"He's on his way. He's coming from Flagstaff."

"Can the park police give you a preliminary?"

"They'd rather not in case they're wrong, and I don't blame them. Besides, there was a lot of damage done by the coyotes."

"Mind if I take a look?"

"I'll take you back." Tasha rubbed Kate's shoulder. "Will you be okay here for a few minutes, Kate?"

Kate nodded then shivered. "Of course, but why in the world would you want to see... to see that? It's... it's horrible."

"You forget I have a degree in anthropology as well as archeology. I might spot something that may be of use." Ethan stood from the step.

"I don't understand," Kate shook her head.

"My area of expertise is forensic anthropology." Ethan gave her shoulder another squeeze.

"You are just full of surprises, aren't you? Is there anything you can't do, Superman?"

Ethan thought for a second. "I make terrible coffee. Sit tight. We'll be back shortly."

~

Ethan and Tasha headed back behind the office, avoiding the markers that the park police had placed at various locations indicating where they'd found possible evidence. The branches above the body had been cut away, giving a clear view of the professor's body.

Ethan had seen dead bodies before in various stages of decay and had tried to prepare himself. But seeing someone he'd worked with closely just the day before was harder than he'd realized it would be. He'd liked the little German man, even as temperamental as he could be at times. Prof. Rosenberg genuinely loved his profession and had a passion for finding evidence for the Anasazi city hidden on the wall of the Grand Canyon.

Ethan listened as Tasha told him what the evidence so far indicated. Apparently, someone had surprised the professor that morning when he had come in early. There had been a struggle in the climate-controlled room, the professor had lost his glasses and apparently either been killed there or dragged outside and killed. That hadn't been determined yet. Either way, he'd been dragged outside and back here where the coyotes found him.

"Wow, that's awful." Ethan knelt down to examine the body as best he could without actually turning it over or moving it. "He was an odd little man, but he sure loved archeology. He was determined to get to the bottom of the Anasazi city."

"I know," Tasha sighed. "He was in it for the long haul. Do

you know if he'd found anything of significance that would have led to his death?"

Ethan shook his head. "I don't know. Makes me wonder. Did you see the size of the safe he had installed yesterday? I saw it when we came up last night. He must've planned on something big after all the other things went missing."

"Yeah. Did he share the combination with anyone? Is there anything in there now?"

"He didn't share it with me, and I have no idea if he put anything in there. It would be a good idea to have the park police question the others and get statements to see if he gave any of them the combination, particularly Carl, seeing as how he was the professor's assistant. It would be kind of reckless to be the only one with it, but at the same time reckless to give it to any of them."

"Agreed," Tasha nodded.

"Look at this." Ethan pointed at bruising and contusions on the professor's upper cheek that had not been made by the coyotes. "That should be checked out. It looks like blunt force trauma. And from the sunken-in depression, I'd say it was quite a blow. Looks like that part of his face was crushed. But it could be missed amongst the facial rips caused by the coyotes. How many coyotes did Kate say were feeding?"

"Two."

Ethan shook his head. "They definitely didn't drag him back here. He was dragged by a human or humans."

He stood and shoved his hands into his pockets. "What are you going to do about the dig? It would be a shame to close it down, Tasha. This is too big of a discovery and we've come too far."

Tasha stood and walked a short distance from the body. "No, we won't close it down, but I want to keep these folks close, Ethan. The National Park Service has too much invested in this dig. We don't want to lose this opportunity. It's too big to let go. We'll probably have to shut down for a few days to let the park police do their investigation, but we'll keep going after that. I need to think and seek some advice. Hang tight. I'll let you know."

~

"That was a stupid thing to do." The voice on the phone berated. "Why would you do that? He was in charge of the dig and the one who could find the artifacts for us. No one else on the team is as capable unless Dr. Wagner is."

The soft voice spoke in self-defense. "I couldn't stand dealing with him another moment. I hadn't meant to kill him. I only wanted to threaten him, to tell him to ease up on me. But he made me so angry. All he ever does is berate me for everything I do. I could do no right in his eyes. I saw red and lashed out at him."

"I don't care about Prof. Rosenberg, but you should hope the good Dr. Wagner will continue his work until he finds more artifacts. We have made a contract, and I want *the* artifact. The one that will set the black market on fire."

"But they'll stop the dig if artifacts continue to disappear," the voice continued softly.

"Let them accumulate until something of monumental value is discovered. Then you will contact me." The line went dead.

~

Kate sat on the couch in her apartment, chin on her hands, elbows on her knees and stared at her daypack as it sat on the coffee table. Now what was she supposed to do with the amulet? The professor was dead, and he'd said not to trust anyone. Well, that pretty much ruled out...well, anyone. Tasha, Ethan, everyone on the archeological team. And that was everyone she knew at the Grand Canyon.

Professor Rosenberg had installed that fancy new safe at the archeologists' office, but she had no way of putting the amulet inside and securing it. Now the golden object was burning a hole in her daypack, and she didn't know what to do about it. She half expected it to burst into flame as she sat staring at it.

Then an idea popped into her head. She'd opened an account at the bank in Grand Canyon Village the day after she'd arrived. Did they have safe deposit boxes? It would be safe there. But was that stealing? Was it hers to put there? Well, no, not technically. But it had been put in her care for safekeeping and until a solution to the problem presented itself, perhaps it was the best solution. She'd be more than happy to hand it over when the time came. At least it wouldn't be rattling around in her daypack waiting for something to happen like accidentally falling over the edge of the Grand Canyon as had nearly happened her first day on the job. Yeah, that would be her luck. Neither would it be where someone could steal it and sell it on the black market. That's what the professor assumed had happened to the other artifacts.

Kate glanced at her watch. Tasha had sent her home early due to the morning's circumstances. Circumstances? Was that what she referred to the professor's death as? Bile once again rose in her throat as memories from the morning returned. Rushing to the kitchen, she grabbed a glass and drank some water, striving to flush the sour taste from her mouth even as she shoved the memory from her mind.

There was plenty of time to get to the bank to find out if they had safe deposit boxes.

Digging the plastic-wrapped amulet from her daypack, she placed it into her purse, grabbed her car keys and headed out the door. Kate wanted to get this thing as far away from her as she could. Now.

The bank was only a small branch but they did have a few safe deposit boxes. Once she'd arranged for one, had the amulet safely inside and locked away in the bank, she breathed a huge sigh of relief and walked outside, feeling as if a huge weight had been lifted from her shoulders. *Thank you, Lord.*

Had He really arranged all that for her? She'd like to think so. She once had trusted in Him more than she did now. Shame washed through her as she thought about how far she'd drifted from Him. Life hadn't gone quite the way she'd anticipated, and she'd turned her back on the Lord. Hadn't He caused it to be that way? Hadn't He taken Craig from her? Wasn't He to blame for how things had turned out?

Turning to her right she walked into the Yavapai Lodge to the coffee shop and bought a cup of coffee and a muffin. She'd missed lunch. Her appetite had deserted her since finding Prof. Rosenberg that morning, but she needed to eat something. Now that the amulet was safe, she could move on. Tasha had given her the day off. She'd told her she would be in touch, and she'd let her know what she would be doing tomorrow morning.

After eating her muffin, Kate grabbed the remainder of her coffee and strolled around the village with no destination in mind. Eventually she reached the general store and stopped beneath the covered walkway to gaze in the window at the display of merchandise. Nothing in the display seemed to register in her mind.

"So, you're at loose ends, too, I see," a familiar voice said from beside her.

Kate turned to find Ethan, a crooked grin on his face as he held the lead to the most beautiful white German Shepherd.

"Yep. Who's this gorgeous lady?"

"This is Haley. She doesn't know what to do with herself since I'm home early today. I've gotta be careful. She'll get spoiled."

Kate held out the back of her hand to let Haley sniff before petting her. Haley ran her damp nose along Kate's skin before licking it, giving her approval. Kate rubbed between her ears.

"Oh, now that's not fair." A half scowl crossed Ethan's face but didn't reach his gray eyes. "You'll win her over and have a friend for life."

Kate laughed. "Good, I need all the friends I can get."

She spotted the curiosity in Ethan's eyes, but he remained silent. Kate dropped her own gaze to the dog as heat warmed her cheeks. What was it about this man? She was not interested in him. *Yeah, keep telling yourself that and you just might believe it.*

"What have you got planned for the rest of your afternoon?" Ethan roughed up Haley's fur. Kate could tell the dog reveled in her master's touch.

She shook her head. "Not much. Just trying to get this morning's events out of my head, waiting to hear from Tasha as to what I'm doing tomorrow. She said the site's closed for a couple of days while the investigation's going on, but she's got some things she wants me to do. Busy work, I'm sure."

"Probably best. Staying busy is a good thing when you want to forget something."

More than you know.

"Well, I'm at loose ends, too, so how about dinner?" Ethan's question was tossed out with a shrug. "My treat."

Kate wanted to go with him. She really did, but she needed to set some parameters. "I'd like that. Very much. But Ethan, we can only go as friends, okay? I mean, I know that sounds weird and all for me to say, but...well...I can't go into details. Just try to understand. We can only go as friends."

Something flashed in Ethan's eyes that Kate didn't understand then it was gone. "Of course. Just friends. Nothing more."

"Thanks for understanding."

"No problem. Look, I'll meet you at the Yavapai Lodge at six. Okay?" Ethan pulled up on Haley's lead and took a step back. "I need to get Haley home, and I need to take care of some things before I meet you."

"Yeah, I need to go, too. I'll see you at six." Kate turned and stepped into the street, waving over her shoulder.

Out of nowhere a plain navy-blue car sped toward her as she started across the street. It accelerated, engine gunning loudly.

Kate heard the sound and looked to her right just as she heard Ethan's command for Haley to "stay." Then she was knocked forward and to the ground as the car swerved at the last second missing her completely and veering down a side isle in the parking lot, tires squealing as it sped away.

Kate saw stars for a moment as her head hit the pavement.

"Kate, are you alright?" Ethan rolled away from her and to her side. "Are you hurt?"

She gingerly touched the side of her head as she tried to sit up. "I hit my head when I hit the ground, but I'll be okay. Some drivers have no care when it comes to pedestrians. Thanks for keeping me from getting smooshed like a pancake."

Ethan helped Kate to stand and plucked her purse from the pavement, handing it to her. With his hand at her waist, he urged her back to the sidewalk where Haley waited patiently for them to return, her head cocked sideways, ears up and alert. Then he clasped Kate's shoulders, forcing her to look at him.

"Kate, that was no careless driver. He was aiming for you."

"What? But...but why? Why would someone do that?" Kate couldn't comprehend why someone would deliberately try to hit her with a car.

"I don't know, but they didn't want to hit you. They swerved away at the last second."

"It doesn't make any sense." Kate shook her head then pressed her fingers to the goose egg forming on the side of her head. "If they didn't want to hit me, then why swerve away?"

Ethan turned to look in the direction the car had fled. "I'd say it was a warning."

Chapter Seven

A warning?" Kate sat across from Ethan in the Yavapai Lodge Restaurant. "What kind of warning? What would anyone want to warn me about?"

Their food had come and Ethan had eaten, but Kate had mostly picked at her food.

Ethan shook his head, hands spread wide in a question. "I don't know, Kate, but I'm pretty sure it has something to do with the professor's death. You were with him when he discovered the mummy. You found him dead. Can you think of any reason why someone would target you?"

Kate's mind filled with one big reason--the amulet. She dropped her gaze to the table. Could he read her thoughts? Should she tell him? What if he were the black-market thief the professor was afraid was stealing objects?

"Kate. Look at me, Kate."

Kate raised her eyes warily to his gray gaze then watched as he pulled his wallet from his hip pocket and held it in his hand.

"Kate, have you ever been in a place in your life where you felt like you couldn't trust anyone? Anyone at all?"

Kate nodded with slow deliberateness, a pucker between her brows. Oh, yeah. She was there now. And did he know? Where was he going with this?

Ethan opened his wallet, glanced around the room then slipped out an ID card and placed it in front of her.

"Please don't read it out loud. Just to yourself then hand it back."

National Park Service Special Agent Ethan Wagner. Really?

Kate certainly hadn't expected that. She handed the card back to him. "Why are you telling me this? You obviously hadn't planned to before now or you would've sooner."

"Because someone delivered a deadly warning to you this afternoon for a reason, and you need someone you can trust. Tasha hired me for this dig, Kate. Tasha's trustworthy, too, by the way, but you can start with me. The fewer who know the better. Is there anything you can tell me?"

Kate heaved a huge sigh and closed her eyes for a minute then she nodded and opened them. "Yes, I didn't know what to do. Prof. Rosenberg told me not to trust anyone."

"He didn't know who I was."

"So, you're not really an archeologist?" Kate propped her forearms along the edge of table and leaned forward.

"Yes, I really am. I have my degrees in forensic anthropology and archeology just like I told you, but I don't really teach college. That's the only falsehood in this whole thing."

"Didn't the professor check all that out?"

"Well, I think Tasha took care of all that." A grin lifted a corner of Ethan lips, displaying that amazing dimple.

Kate chuckled. "I'm sure she did.

Ethan grew serious. "So, tell me why you think you may have been targeted."

Kate spent the next few minutes explaining about the amulet and where she'd placed it for safe keeping.

"Am I wrong for having placed it in the safe deposit box?"

"Under the circumstances, I'd say that's probably the safest place you could've put it." Ethan shoved his plate aside and leaned forward on his elbows. "I'd leave it there for now. We have no way into the new safe. Tasha has indicated that I'll be taking the lead on the dig for now, so I'll call the safe company and have them come out and change the combination. I'll have it and give a backup to Tasha."

"So where do we go from here?"

"Watch your back, Kate. I couldn't see into that car. The windows were tinted. Did you get a look in through the front windshield?"

Kate shook her head, her shoulders dropping as she leaned back in her chair. "I was in too much shock that a car was coming at me. I didn't see a face. It was all more of a blur."

"That's what I was afraid of." Ethan's expression was grim. "Please be careful. I don't know that anyone is aware of the amulet so much as the fact that you're the one that found the professor's body, and someone is afraid you may have recognized something incriminating. Perhaps they're missing something and are afraid they dropped it at the murder site."

"I didn't find anything except the professor and his glasses."

"But they don't know that. Just watch your back."

~

Ethan unlocked the door of his camper and was greeted by his faithful companion. Haley accepted him no matter what. Faults and imperfections? Accomplishments and failures? She didn't care. Humans tended to judge one another on those things but give a dog some attention and fulfil their basic needs, they'll love you forever.

Ethan dropped his keys on the kitchen counter and tossed his jacket on the couch. Unfortunately, his needs weren't the same as Haley's. He longed to find a woman of like faith to share his life with. He thought he had once, but he'd been burned. Badly. Jodi had attended church with him faithfully for a while, then she'd started coming up with reasons not to. Then just before the wedding he'd found out she'd been unfaithful to him, with someone he thought had been his best friend.

Attempting to shake the painful memories from his head, he walked to the fridge, grabbed a bottle of orange juice and poured a glass. That was all behind him. He needed to forget and move on. *Please, Lord, help me move on. Life is too short to dwell on the past. If You have someone else out there for me, then help me to trust You to bring her into my life. In Your time, not mine.*

Unbidden, the face of Kate Fleming formed in his mind. He didn't know about Kate. She certainly was easy on the eyes. Cute to say the least with that silky-looking auburn hair, but she'd made it pretty plain this afternoon she wasn't looking for a relationship. She only wanted to be friends. Made it clear she had her reasons. Had she been burned in the past as well? If so, he could sympathize. It was just as well. Jodi had left a scorch mark on his heart that would take some time to heal. He couldn't help but wonder if Kate was a Christian. He'd surely find out.

Ethan had enjoyed spending time with her this evening,

although much of it was discussing Prof. Rosenberg's murder. Not a delightful discussion, but at least he got her to open up and trust him. It was a start.

~

"Kate, this is Cassandra Rosenberg, Prof. Rosenberg's daughter." Tasha introduced the flashy young woman as they stood in Tasha's office.

Kate shook the young woman's outstretched hand that was adorned with neon-pink and black checkerboard nails. "It's nice to meet you, Cassandra. I'm so sorry for your loss. I had the pleasure of working with your father at the dig, and I enjoyed it very much."

The young woman flipped back her dyed-white, hot pink, black and neon-green hair. It was unevenly cut short from one ear down to a longer shoulder length on the other side. She laughed pleasantly. "Thank you, Kate. You may call me Cassie. I'm glad you enjoyed digging in the dirt with my father. He always wanted me to become an archeologist, but these nails were never meant to dig in the dirt."

Kate noticed a slight German accent but it was less pronounced than her father's.

"My forte is fashion, and that is what I'm studying." Cassie waved one manicured hand in the air.

Kate glanced at her hot pink, black and white zebra-striped ski outfit and black hiking boots. A white long-fur jacket topped it off. It was a definite fashion statement. Kate was afraid the Grand Canyon would leave the white a dusty tan by the end of the day.

"Cassie arrived two days ago for a visit with her father," Tasha explained.

Kate nodded. "Oh, I'm sorry that this happened while you were here, but I'm glad that you were able to spend some time with him."

Then she realized what she said. "I'm sorry. That sounded bad. It's terrible that it happened at all whether you were here or not."

Cassie placed a hand on Kate's arm. "It's alright, Kate. I understand your meaning. Yes, it is terrible that he died while I'm here. While I'm here. Before I come. It does not matter. Either way. He is gone. I shall miss him."

Kate noticed that her words seemed a little too sterile and not at all like she'd really miss him. Hmmm. Interesting.

A knock sounded at the door.

"Come in," Tasha called.

The door opened and a familiar-looking ranger stepped into the room. Kate knew she'd seen him before.

"Kate, you remember Gage Hampton?" Tasha asked. "He's one of our park police. Good morning, Gage. How are you?"

"Good morning, Tasha. Kate. Miss." He nodded to all three women.

"Oh, yes," Kate smiled. "It's nice to see you again, Gage."

He no longer wore his dress slacks and oxfords but had exchanged them for uniform green-jeans and hiking boots.

Tasha introduced Cassie to Gage. "Cassie, you've shown an interest in seeing the dig site that meant so much to your father. Since we don't know why your father was killed, I've asked Gage to escort you to the dig sight for added security. Kate and Ethan, one of the other dig team members, will also be accompanying you there this morning. The other dig members have been given a few days off due to the investigation that's underway. However, the dig site itself is not part of the investigation."

"Thank you, Tasha," Cassie cooed, her eyes locked on Gage. "I look forward to seeing it. I hope that I can make the hike. I'm not much of a hiker. I'm more of a flat sidewalk kind of a girl."

"We'll be with you the whole way, and we'll take it nice and slow," Gage reassured her.

Cassie flashed him a seductive smile. "Thank you, Gage. You are a sweetie."

Tasha met Kate's amused gaze with a grin as red rolled up from Gage's collar. He coughed and turned toward the door.

"We'd better get this hike underway." He grabbed the doorknob as if it were a lifeline.

~

By the time the small expeditionary party reached the opening to the tunnel, Kate felt sorry for both Ethan and Gage. Cassie had demanded their full attention all the way down the Hermit's Trail. She'd twisted her ankle and leaned first on one then the other. That had miraculously healed itself, then she'd slipped on a rock and ripped her ski trousers. After breaking a nail on another "accidental fall" she had needed Gage's immediate attention. Water. She must have water, which Ethan had provided for her with reddened cheeks.

Was that his teeth Kate heard grinding? She chuckled inwardly. Both guys were good-looking and well-built, and that was the price one paid, Kate supposed, when a woman like Cassie came around. Apparently, she had no shame when it came to men. Cassie had pretty much ignored Kate the whole trip down.

Once inside the Anasazi city, things were no different. Cassie wasn't interested in the dig at all, although she glanced around with bored attention.

Kate wondered why she even asked Tasha to have them bring her down here. Cassie never descended into any of the kivas, she barely glanced at the ceiling and she pretended to listen when Ethan explained the history of the city. What were they doing here?

"Well, this is all very nice," Cassie nodded, looking bored out of her skull. "I know Father enjoyed what he did. He must have been very happy here. This is a big site compared to some of the ones he used to show me pictures of."

"He was very happy here," Kate agreed.

"Well, I'm ready to return." Cassie shrugged her shoulders in a careless manner. Turning, she headed for the entrance, calling over her shoulder as she went. "Thank you all for bringing me."

Kate met Ethan's glaring gaze. Was that steam escaping from his ears?

Without a word, the trio followed Cassie through the tunnel then helped her back up Hermit's Trail to the top. Slightly more subdued on the return trip, she still pulled a few stunts, much to Ethan and Gage's dismay. Kate, on the other hand, silently chuckled all the way to the canyon rim.

~

When Kate and Ethan returned from their expedition with Cassie, Tasha invited them to dinner that evening along with her husband, Lance, and their little girl, Ariel.

"You have got to be kidding me," Tasha laughed as she set plates around the dining table. "Kate, you had to have been laughing your way down the canyon and back up again. Poor you, Ethan."

"And poor Gage too." Kate followed Tasha with the napkins and silverware, placing them next to the plates. "Cassie didn't let up on either of them."

"All I know is it was one of the worst days of my life." Ethan sat on a barstool leaning his elbows back against the counter behind him. "If I never see Cassie Rosenberg again it'll be too soon."

"Oh, you'll probably see her again, honey," Tasha chuckled. "Like tomorrow. She'll be around for a while. At least until the investigation is over and arrangements can be made to have her father's remains sent back to Boston. But this is a murder investigation. No one is going anywhere anytime soon."

"But she's his daughter," Kate said.

"Doesn't matter." Tasha handed a bowl of salad to Kate to place on the table. "She was here when he was murdered. I can't really say much more because I don't know much more, but I know they'll start interrogating the team members soon. Both of you can expect to be called in."

Kate hadn't thought of being questioned in a murder case, but having discovered the body, it stood to reason. It didn't bother her to help however she could. She certainly hadn't killed the professor, and although she hadn't known him long, he'd treated her kindly and included her in the dig. That was nice and she'd appreciated it.

"Lucy, I'm home," a booming voice attempted an imitation of Ricky Ricardo but failed miserably. Lance Johnson strolled in the front door carrying the cutest two-year-old sporting four tight braids and a bright purple sweat suit beneath a pink coat. Rosy-ebony cheeks bracketed a sweet smile that shot straight to Kate's heart.

"There's my Ariel girl." Tasha swept the little princess from her daddy's arms and, hugging her, covered her face with kisses, eliciting giggles and squirms. "Let's take off that jacket and meet my friends."

After hanging up the coat, she walked Ariel over to Kate and Ethan. "Ariel, these are my friends, Kate and Ethan. Can you say hello?"

"Hewwo," Ariel's voice was soft.

"Hi, sweetie," Kate said. "It's nice to meet you."

"I not sweetie. I Awiel." Ariel placed her hands on her hips for emphasis.

Kate was taken aback. "Well, I'm terribly sorry, Ariel. I won't make that mistake again. Let's start over. Hi, Ariel. It's nice to meet you. Was that better?"

"Yes," Ariel nodded one big nod and turned away.

Ethan covered his mouth with a hand to hide his chuckle.

"Wow," Kate mouthed silently.

"That's my girl," boomed Lance, "she'll be a go-getter one day."

"What are you talking about? She already is," Tasha turned and headed back to the kitchen.

Chapter Eight

Whata do you mean she was nearly run down by a car?" Tasha's gaze swung between Ethan and Kate as she waited for further explanation.

Ethan glanced at Kate for a moment and knew she wasn't going to say anything. He'd have to finish what he'd started. Fortunately, supper was over, Ariel had been put to bed and the four adults relaxed with mugs of coffee by a warm fire in the huge fireplace in the living room. He sat on the other end of the couch with Kate while Lance and Tasha blatantly snuggled on the opposite couch.

While Kate's gaze remained fixed on the brew inside her cup, Ethan described how the car had deliberately sped toward Kate then swerved at the last second. "I believe it was a warning to Kate of some kind."

"Why a warning?" Tasha lifted her mug of coffee to her lips.

"If they wanted to harm her or kill her, they wouldn't have veered off at the last second," Ethan pointed out. "Seems more like they wanted to get her attention."

"Well, they got it." Kate shifted in her seat, tucked her socked feet beneath her legs, and curled up, holding her mug between her hands.

"To what purpose, Ethan?" Lance placed his empty mug on the coffee table in front of him. "Why would they warn her?"

"Possibly several reasons. Someone's aware that Kate was working with the professor before he died. They know she was with him when he found the mummy. Perhaps the mummy itself is important." Ethan deliberately withheld the information about the amulet for now. "They also know she found the professor after he was murdered. Maybe they think she found some evidence that would link the murder to them. If they dropped something at the murder scene, they may be concerned she found it. There are any number of reasons they're warning her."

Tasha nodded slowly. "That really concerns me, girlfriend. How are we to keep you safe if someone is after you?"

Kate stood and walked to the fireplace, turning her back to the flames. "Y'all are scaring me, you know that? What if it was just some stupid driver who was careless and inconsiderate enough not to stop and see if I was okay? Couldn't that have been the case?"

Ethan shifted his gaze to meet Tasha's. He'd have to talk with her later. Kate was in denial and he could understand why. She didn't want to believe that someone meant her harm. He got that. But he didn't want to see anything bad happen to Kate. He'd have to be extra vigilant and they'd have to come up with a plan of some kind to keep her safe.

Tasha stood and came over to Kate's side, placing an arm around her shoulder. "Kate, you may be right, but it's better to play things on the safe side until we know for sure. All I ask is just be careful, okay? Watch yourself and don't take any chances. Keep your firearm on you at all times, even when you're off duty."

Tasha glanced across at Ethan then continued. "Ethan told me that he explained to you who he really is. Now you know you can trust him. And you know Lance is park police. You can always call any of us if you need to."

Kate nodded and slid her hair behind her ear with trembling fingers. "Thanks, Tasha. I don't want to believe someone out there has their eye on me for nefarious reasons. It's unsettling. I feel like my world just went topsy-turvy and I can't do a thing about it."

Tasha squeezed Kate's shoulder again. "We'll get you through this. Try not to fret. Are you a believer, Kate?"

Ethan noted Kate's hesitation then she nodded. "Yes. I haven't been very faithful lately, but I've put my trust in Christ."

"That's good, then now would also be a good time for you to have a talk with Him. Maybe renew that relationship. He's looking out for you whether you're talking to Him or not."

A look of surprise crossed Kate's face and Ethan felt a grin lift the corners of his lips. Maybe he should be praying for Kate. She seemed to be struggling with something. Yeah, he'd pray for her that she'd get whatever it was straightened out. The Lord was already on her side. She just needed to rely on Him again and not herself.

~

"I noticed you didn't mention the amulet when you were listing the reasons someone might be warning me," Kate said as she and Ethan left Tasha and Lance's house and walked out to their cars.

"Thought I should keep that quiet for now. Is it a reason someone could be warning you? Possibly. Is it likely? Who knows. After all, how would they know you had it?"

Kate shook her head as she reached into her purse for her car keys and unlocked the car door. "I don't see how they would."

Ethan reached for the door handle and opened the door for Kate, but before she could slide into the driver's seat, a car drove past, its engine roaring. A loud bang filled the night air just before the front windshield of Kate's car shattered. Ethan grabbed her and with his body shielding her, pulled her to the ground. The tires of the car screeched as its engine roared into the distance.

Fear gripped Kate's heart even as Ethan held her securely beneath him. Someone had just fired a gun at them. How had they known where she was? They had to have followed her here, waiting for her to come out. Who were they and why were they doing this? Had they meant to warn this time? Or had they meant to kill?

~

Tasha showed Kate to the guest room. "I know it's not the best of circumstances, girlfriend, but you're not going home alone tonight. And while Lance and his buddies work the scene outside, you need to get some rest."

"Do you really think I can sleep after just getting shot at?" Kate couldn't stop the ridicule that filled her voice. "There is no way."

"At least try." Tasha handed her a pair of jersey knit PJs and an unopened toothbrush and a travel toothpaste tube. "I'm a little bigger than you so these may hang on you, but it'll be better than sleeping in your clothes."

Kate accepted the sleepwear and released a heavy sigh. "I'm

sorry, Tasha. I shouldn't have snapped at you, and I certainly shouldn't be ungrateful for your hospitality. I appreciate you opening your home to me and giving me a safe place to sleep. Please forgive me."

She wrapped her arms around her newest friend, tears threatening to fill her eyes, but she fought them back. "I'm just a little rattled, I guess."

Tasha gave her a hearty squeeze then held her away and looked her in the eye.

"But of course. Kate, I know you're scared. I would be, too, if I were in your shoes. Tonight's event kind of clarified the other incident. Now we have to do everything we can to keep you safe, but not sleeping isn't going to help you any. Please try and get some sleep. Okay?"

Kate nodded. "I'll try. Thank you."

"Good night." Tasha headed for the door and closed it behind her.

After changing into the borrowed PJs and brushing her teeth in the guest bathroom, Kate slid between the sheets on the bed and pulled up the comforter and blankets, snuggling into their softness.

As comfortable as the bed was she couldn't shut her mind off. It ran in every direction, chaotic to say the least. Kate couldn't make sense of anything. The more she thought about things the more confused and frustrated she became. Past hurts became entwined with the professor's death and her own current dangers. She tossed and turned, until the nice neat bedding became a huge tangled mess. Finally, she sat up in the darkness, tears streaming down her cheeks, her heart aching.

Lord, I can't do this. Not alone. I'm not strong enough. I never have been, have I? That's why You want me to lean on You. I guess I need to talk to You more and trust You more. But I haven't wanted to talk to You. Why did You take Craig away from me? Did You take Craig away? And why are You letting these people come after me? I don't understand any of these things?

As sobs ripped from Kate, she muffled them with her pillow and cried it out before God. She still didn't understand it all but she tried to put things into His hands. Tasha seemed to be a wise Christian woman. Perhaps she could seek advice from her.

In the wee hours of the morning, Kate finally dropped into an exhausted sleep amongst the tangled soft bedding, weary both in spirit and body. But she was a little closer in trusting her Lord.

~

"Your eyes are a little puffy this morning, Kate. Are you okay? Did you get any sleep at all?" Tasha poured a mug of coffee and set it on the counter for Kate.

Kate touched the bags beneath her eyes as she sat on a bar stool at the kitchen counter. Apparently, the cool water she'd applied from the bathroom sink earlier hadn't worked well enough. It was just the two of them in the kitchen. She nodded as she reached for the coffee and doctored it. "Sort of and sort of. My mind wouldn't shut down, and it took a long time to fall asleep. I did some soul searching and talking with the Lord. I'm not there yet, but I'd like to think I made some progress."

Tasha set the coffee carafe back on the coffee maker and leaned on the counter. "Oh, I like the sound of that, girl."

Kate smiled "I have a question for you when you have some time."

"What's wrong with right now?"

Kate shrugged. "Okay. Does God make things happen? Bad things, I mean."

Tasha tapped a finger on the counter. "No, sweetie, He doesn't make bad things happen. He tells us in His word that the plans He has for us are to prosper us and not to harm us. They're to give us hope and a future. He has our best interests at heart, girlfriend. When bad things happen, it's because of the sin in this world. Yes, He allows them to happen to us for reasons that sometimes only He knows. Sometimes it's to help us to grow closer to Him, to make us stronger Christians. Possibly to help us help someone else. There are lots of reasons. Look at Job in the Bible. That poor man went through more than any man on earth ever went through. God didn't make those bad things happen to him. Satan did. But God allowed Satan to do it to prove to Satan that Job would never curse God."

Kate had read the account of Job once. Perhaps she should read it again. "I had forgotten about Job. I guess my troubles seem light in comparison."

Tasha placed her hand on Kate's arm. "Unfortunately, man lets Satan have his way in his life and sinful man does bad things.

That's why there's so much bad stuff going on in the world today and all through history. Man has let Satan rule in his life instead of God. Look, if you ever want to talk about your troubles, I'm here."

Kate patted her hand. "Thanks. I may take you up on that sometime."

Ariel and Lance joined them and they were eating breakfast when the doorbell rang. Lance answered it. Ethan walked in dressed in blue jeans and an open tan button down shirt with a dark green t-shirt underneath.

"Morning, Ethan," Tasha called from the kitchen. "Come have some coffee. Have you eaten yet?"

"Coffee sounds good. Yes, I've eaten." He occupied the stool beside Kate.

"Morning, ranger lady," he winked and gently elbowed her arm. "How'd you sleep?"

"Not so well. Is it obvious?" Kate chuckled.

He tugged her short auburn braid. "Not at all. Looks to me like you slept well."

"Liar." She lightly punched him on the arm.

"Here, drink that before you stick your foot in your mouth." Lance handed Ethan a mug of coffee. "Cream and sugar's on the tray."

"What did I say?" Ethan spread his hands imploringly.

Kate giggled and sipped her coffee.

Tasha laughed. "Ethan, I'd like you to take Kate home so she can shower and change clothes if she wants to, then she's up for questioning today by the investigators. So are you, by the way. Cassie Rosenberg is as well. I wish I could allow you both into the listening booth during that interrogation, but I can't. Even with being the NPS Special Agent, Ethan, you now are under investigation.

Tasha shook her head. "This whole beast has taken on a different form since the murder. But your job stays the same. You're now lead on the dig and will continue to keep an eye on things. You have the National Park Service's interest at heart."

"What about Carl Young, Anna Kelly, Paul Schmitz and Mike Pierce?" Kate cupped her coffee mug in her hands. "What's going on with them?"

"Carl will continue as Ethan's assistant just as he was to Prof.

Rosenberg, and the other three will continue to work as usual. Officer Blake Hunter has already questioned all of them."

"And?" Ethan's eyebrows raised hopefully.

"Now, now, Ethan," Tasha tisked tisked, "you know I can't tell you anything, but it was a nice try."

Ethan chuckled. "I thought it wouldn't hurt to ask."

"When do we go back to work at the dig site?" Kate sipped her coffee.

"Probably tomorrow, but you go nowhere without Ethan at your side. Understood? I mean nowhere. And you may as well pack a bag while you're at your place, because you'll be staying here for a while."

Kate nodded, a wry expression settling on her face. "Seems like rather a burden to put on Ethan, you and Lance."

"As for me, you let me worry about that." Ethan set his cup down, crossing his arms on the counter. "I don't mind at all. Besides, following a beautiful woman around all day may just help my image. What do ya think, Lance?"

"Sure couldn't hurt it." The big man collected breakfast dishes and picked up his little girl. "Look where following a beautiful woman around got me."

Tasha stood on tiptoe and kissed him on the cheek. "I thought I followed you around, love."

Kate's gaze tugged to Ethan's and the spark she found there kindled into a flame sending warmth up her neck into her cheeks. For a long moment she was unable to look away. Then Tasha cleared her throat and her next words broke the connection.

"You two should get going. Lance has to get Ariel to daycare, and I'm headed to the interrogations. Blake asked me to sit in the observation room."

"Right," Ethan stood and downed the last of his coffee.

Kate hurried to grab her daypack and jacket.

"Stay safe. Both of you." Tasha came around the counter. "I don't want to hear any more reports of incidents."

Kate slipped her arm around her waist and gave her a hug. "I'll see you later. And don't worry. I'm in good hands. Both God's and Ethan's."

Tasha hugged her back. "You got that right, girlfriend."

Chapter Nine

The interrogations took place at park police HQ. Ethan's interrogation hadn't taken long, but to Kate it seemed hers dragged on interminably. Since she was the one to find Prof. Rosenberg's body, Officer Hunter had so much more to ask her. Apparently, the investigators had found some evidence from the murderer, but she hadn't seen anything except Prof. Rosenberg's body and his glasses.

"Did you notice footprints in the dirt in back of the archeologists' office?" Officer Hunter scanned his notes before lifting his gaze to Kate.

She shook her head. "All I saw were drag marks that I assumed were made when the murderer dragged the body to its final resting spot. I remember seeing animal tracks intersecting the drag marks. I assumed they were coyote tracks."

"Your footprints were found amongst others discovered near the professor, Miss Fleming."

"Well, of course, they were. I found him. I was looking for him." Dread filled Kate. Was she going to have to disclose about the amulet? Or could she evade that and just talk about the safe?

"Why were you looking for him?" Officer Hunter's brows furrowed.

"We'd discussed the previous evening about the safekeeping of artifacts. Remember some had been stolen from the old safe? Then the professor called and asked me to meet him at the archeologists' trailer at 6 am. He wanted to show me the new safe and reassure me that artifacts would be secure. He'd had it installed the day before. He told me you had accompanied the men who had installed it."

Officer Hunter looked at Kate for a few moments considering her words. Then his brow cleared as he looked down at the papers in front of him. Kate wished the problem of the amulet didn't hang over her head. Thankful Ethan knew about it, she just wished it would go away. She hated deception, but she had to protect it. She had a feeling the golden object lay at the bottom of what was going on, but if so, how did whoever was after her know about it?

"Miss Fleming, what happened when you went to the archeologists' office the next morning?" Officer Hunter jotted notes as she spoke.

"When I arrived, the front door stood ajar, like someone had tried to close it but hadn't and it swung open a little or they had entered in a hurry. It seemed odd so I used my elbow to push it open and went inside. The lights were on but nothing seemed out of the ordinary in the main office. However, when I went back to the climate-controlled workroom, it was in shambles. Papers were scattered over the desk and onto the floor, and I noticed the professor's glasses lay broken on the floor. There were some tools scattered on the desk and floor as well. The professor wasn't in the room, so I went back outside and called for him. I walked behind the building calling for him. I heard a strange noise further back so I followed it, continuing to call the professor. That's when I heard the coyotes, only I didn't know that's what it was at the time."

Kate described the scene and what her actions were.

"Thank you, Miss Fleming. I know it must've been difficult." Officer Hunter gathered his papers and tamped them against the table, straightening them.

"It's almost the worse thing I've ever seen," Kate mumbled, bowing her head.

"Almost?" Officer Hunter's voice was low.

Kate shook her head and spoke louder. "Probably the worst. It was horrible."

"Yes, it was. I believe that's all I have for you now. You can go. If I have anything further, I'll be in touch." Officer Hunter stood, effectively closing the interrogation.

Kate stood and exited the room when he held the door for her. Ethan stood in the hallway leaning against the wall. He pushed away and stood straight, coming to meet her.

"Wow, he must've enjoyed your company. That took a while." He joined her as she headed toward the exit.

"Yeah, well I'm not so sure he doesn't think I didn't kill the professor." Kate hated the glumness in her voice but it was the emotion roiling through her being, and she was struggling to reign it in.

"What do you mean?" Ethan took her arm, effectively halting her.

"He wanted to know why Prof. Rosenberg wanted to meet me the morning I found him dead. I told him he wanted to show me the safe. Which was true. What I didn't tell him was the professor wanted me to bring the amulet to put in the safe. I told him the professor wanted to reassure me that artifacts would be secure in the safe. He also commented that my footprints were all over the area where the professor was found. Duh! I was the one that found him."

Kate started forward again, frustration in every step. How did she end up in this horrible mess? It just got more complicated by the minute. And she was afraid to walk out the door for fear of being run over by a car or shot at.

Lord, why is this happening? I really need Your help here.

"Kate, wait up." Ethan again halted her progress. But before they could go further a flashy blur of hot pink, purple and leopard burst through the front entrance.

"Oh, Ethan, darling," Cassie's voice called in syrupy tones from across the main lobby where Kate and Ethan stood. "Oh, and Kate, how sweet to see you too."

Feeling like a second fiddle, Kate heard a disgruntled rumble emanating from Ethan then he mumbled, "Great. I forgot she's being interrogated today as well."

"It's alright, Ethan. She's heading in and we're heading out." In spite of the emotions threatening to overwhelm her, Kate plastered her best smile on her face as the professor's daughter approached. "Good morning, Cassie. How are you today?"

"Oh, I'm not so good." Cassie's expression was one of blatant glumness as she placed her hand on Ethan's arm. "I'm sad that I haven't seen Ethan very much. Why haven't you called me, Ethan darling? I've been waiting to hear from you?"

Ethan lifted her hand and dislodged his arm all the while

shaking his head regretfully. "I'm not interested in a relationship right now, Cassie. I have some things going on that prevent it. I just can't get involved."

"Oh, you don't know what's good for you." Cassie latched back on. "We German girls are the best in the world to have a relationship with. I will treat you well, darling. Don't worry."

"Won't you be late for your interrogation, Cassie?" Kate pointed in the direction of the interrogation room. "I think Officer Hunter is waiting."

Sure enough, Blake Hunter stood in the hallway near the interrogation room waving in their direction and pointing toward Cassie. Then he propped his hands on his hips and lifted his chin looking very stern.

"Oh, yes, of course. I must go, darling Ethan. But I will see you later." And with a blown kiss and a wave of her hot-pink tipped fingers, she toddled off toward the interrogation room on her purple and leopard high-heeled shoes.

"Not if I see you first," Ethan mumbled through clenched teeth. "Come on, let's get out of here."

Before Kate walked outside, she slipped on a pair of large sunglasses, tugged her uniform ball cap low and lifted her jacket collar up just a little higher. "Think they'll recognize me?"

Ethan chuckled. "Well, I do and you're with me, so yeah, probably. Sorry."

Kate released a huge sigh and shook her head. "I just wish this would stop."

"You and me both." He slipped on his own work-worn ball cap.

"So now that these interrogations are over, at least for the present, what's the plan? Did Tasha leave orders?"

"We're to go to work at the dig site. The other team members are already there." Ethan pulled his car keys from his pocket. "The investigators wrapped up at the archeologists' office yesterday. I called the safe company this morning. Someone should be out this afternoon to change the combination. So, let's go to work."

~

By the time Kate and Ethan arrived at the dig site the team was just breaking for lunch, so they joined them.

"How did your interrogations go?" Paul grabbed two

sandwiches and filled his plate with potato salad, chips and baked beans. "Did they act like you'd killed the professor?

"I think they're supposed to do that so they can try and trip you up, Paul." Carl sat on one of the low stone walls where the group had gathered to eat. "They want to see if you make any mistakes in your answers, you know. I think I did fine with my interrogation. How about you?"

Paul shrugged his shoulders. "Yeah, I guess so. They try and make you nervous."

Anna sipped at her soda but didn't eat anything. "I've lost my appetite after the pictures they showed me of Prof. Rosenberg. What those coyotes did to him....It was horrible. How can they even tell he was murdered? He could've just wandered back there and been attacked for all they know."

"They know." Ethan watched Anna and the others carefully as he spoke. Was one of them the murderer? He noticed that Mike hadn't said anything. Just sat eating his lunch and watching the others. "They have evidence: on the body, in the building and in the yard."

"Really?" Was that concern on Anna's face? "That's amazing. It just looked like he was...was...mauled. It was you that found him, wasn't it, Kate? How horrible for you."

Ethan watched as Kate sat a little off to the side drinking a bottle of water.

"Yes, it was horrible, Anna." Kate's voice was soft and low, her gaze on the ground.

"I think I would've just fainted dead away had it been me." Anna's laugh seemed forced. "I do fine with ancient bodies but not so well with freshly dead ones."

"So, what's going to happen with the dig, Dr. Wagner?" Paul returned for seconds. "This was the professor's baby. It's what got him up in the morning."

Ethan glanced around to see all eyes on him. "This is possibly the most important dig in the US at this time and certainly to the National Park Service. They want us to continue just as if nothing has happened. We have to keep going even without the professor. They've asked me to take the lead. Carl will continue as assistant just as he was with Professor Rosenberg. Paul, Anna and Mike will continue in the same capacity as before. Nothing else changes. The safe company is coming out today to change the combination on the new safe so we can secure new artifacts when they're found. So we still have a job to do, folks. Let's give it our best, okay? It's what the professor expected and it's what I expect."

As he glanced around at the team members they all agreed.

"Great. Let's get back to work and find some artifacts."

As the team moved back to their work areas and the caterers began packing up the food for the return climb up the trail, Ethan started to approach Kate as she stood but was halted by a voice behind him.

"Dr. Wagner? Could I have a moment, please?" Mike called as he jogged toward Ethan.

Ethan glanced from Kate to the young man headed his direction and blew out a breath. Okay. What was this all about? "Sure, Mike. What's up?"

Mike stopped when he was a few feet away and seemed hesitant to begin what he wanted to say. "Well, could I maybe call you sometime soon, and...um...well, I need to talk to you."

Ethan noticed he kept glancing over his shoulder toward the other team members who were disbursing to their work areas. He jammed his hands into his pockets and seemed unusually nervous.

"Mike, are you alright? Do you want to talk now?"

Mike's gaze swung back to Ethan's. "No, not now. That's probably not a good idea."

His eyes darted back to the others then returned to Ethan, his breathing accelerated. "I'll call you if that's alright."

"Sure it is, whenever you want."

"Thanks, Dr. Wagner. I'll be in touch."

Ethan watched as he disappeared into a kiva to begin his work. Odd to say the least. Something was definitely bothering Mike. He sure hoped he called soon.

Ethan shook his head and turned back to Kate who stood waiting for him. She seemed unsure what to do.

"You okay, ranger lady?"

"Yeah. Just not sure what to do with myself down here now. I worked with the professor before. He welcomed my help. Not sure the team will be so welcoming."

Ethan reached over and twined his fingers with hers. "I'll be happy for you to work with me. I can always use help, you know."

He made his eyes as puppy-dog pleading as he could, drawing a grin from Kate.

~

Kate knew Ethan poured it on thick for her sake, and the touch from his fingers sent a zing up her arm. Trying to ignore it, she laughed. "Wow. You missed your calling. You should be in Hollywood with that bit of drama."

"Did it work? Will you help me out?" Ethan's lips lifted in a grin. He didn't release her fingers when she tugged at them.

"Well, seeing as how you're first in a long line of so many requesting my assistance," Kate pointed at no one behind him, "sure, I'll be happy to help you. Lead on. What shall we do?"

Releasing her hand, Ethan pointed to the top of the tallest square tower near the ceiling. "See that? We have to climb up there and check it out. For some reason that tower was blocked off eons ago and there's no other way in. We may have to cut an entrance through what we hope is a wooden beam ceiling when we get up there. Once in, we'll start at the top and work our way down."

"Really? Hmmm. Sounds like fun." Kate couldn't quite muster enthusiasm as she looked up at the stone tower. It brought back too many bad memories, but she wasn't about to mention them to Ethan.

"You don't sound like you mean that," Ethan chuckled, leading the way to the tower.

"I'll reserve judgement till later." Kate followed him over to where a couple of nylon equipment bags lay by the stone foundation. "Have you been up there yet?"

"Nope. This'll be the first time."

"So...how are we going to explore this monstrosity?"

"Have you ever rock climbed before?"

Kate's heart stalled in her chest and her lungs seized up. Leaning against the rock wall of the tower as casually as she could, she attempted to suck in air. Had Ethan noticed? Had her face paled or anything else obvious?

"Yeah. A few times." Was her voice shaking? Jamming her hands into her jacket pockets, she hoped Ethan hadn't noticed they were trembling.

"Good, so you're familiar with the general operation." Ethan's gaze roamed over the back wall of the cavern and across the ceiling. "I'll climb the back wall of the cave to the top of the tower and attach the proper anchors to the ceiling above then clip ropes in. As we descend into the tower, if a floor gives way, we'll be secure. Also, as I climb up, I'll drive some hand and foot grips in the back wall since we'll be using it for a path. We'll need something more secure to get in and out than using the wall of the tower. It might crumble if we climb on it."

Kate was thankful he was looking elsewhere and attempted to focus on his words. *Breathe, Kate. Just breathe. You can do this. It's not that high.*

Ethan turned his attention to her, so Kate leaned over the nylon bag to hide any telltale signs of fear. "Okay. How can I help?"

Chapter Ten

K ate's silence hadn't gone unnoticed by Ethan. She followed his directions in preparing the equipment but when he teased her about something, she never responded. It was as if she were a thousand miles away. Her gorgeous features were ashen and her hands trembled. She attempted to hide it, but he could tell. Standing back, she watched anxiously as he drove in the hand and foot holds then climbed to the ceiling where he positioned the anchors. As he glanced at her below, he realized her face had grown paler if that was possible.

Was this the right job to ask her to help with? Why was she afraid? Had something bad happened to fill her with fear?

When the ropes were clipped in, Ethan easily descended to the cavern floor and approached Kate's side. "Hey, are you okay? You look like you've just seen a ghost?"

Kate's tortured gaze met his and she attempted a half smile. "A ghost? That's funny."

"Kate? What's wrong?" Ethan tossed a thumb over his shoulder toward the tower. "You don't have to do this if you don't want to. Are you afraid of heights?"

"Nope," Kate denied and headed for the equipment bag. "I'm just fine. Let's go."

Ethan wore his baseball cap backwards but pulled a climbing helmet from the nylon bag and held it out to Kate. "Here. Put this on. I'll help you adjust the straps."

Removing her NPS ball cap, Kate slipped it on and Ethan adjusted the straps along her cheeks. Wow, her cheeks were soft. The sudden urge to run his fingers along her cheeks and over to her lips to see if they, too, were just as soft was almost more than he could stand. There was no doubt in his mind they would be. His gaze dropped to them and he swallowed. Hard. What would she do if he kissed her here and now?

His gaze lifted to hers and found a question there even as her soft cheeks flamed. She ducked her head and turned away. How long had he been holding his breath? Air filled his lungs as he breathed deeply. This woman who held him at arm's length was drawing him in without even trying.

"Ok, so let's go." Kate headed for the ropes. "Remind me what to do. It's been a while."

Ethan noticed the color that had just filled her face had completely drained away, leaving her pale, but she was determined. "Okay, ranger lady. Let's go exploring. You first. I'll be right behind you."

After giving her a quick refresher, they climbed the back wall of the craggy cavern and headed toward the high ceiling.

~

As Kate climbed, she tried to think of anything and everything except Craig's crumpled and broken body as he lay at the bottom of El Capitan in Yosemite National Park. No, this climb didn't compare in any way to that one, but the fact she was climbing brought it all rushing back. She hadn't climbed since that day. Ethan had noticed that something was wrong, but she wasn't going to go into it with him. Not now.

Ethan was a nice guy. Nice? No, Ethan was more than nice. And his touch did things to her. She couldn't deny that anymore. When he'd helped with the straps of the helmet and his fingers had grazed her cheeks, wow, they'd sent sparks down her spine. And the look in his eyes? Well, that had stirred her insides for sure, sending a warmth through her that she'd rather not think about.

Was she being unfaithful to Craig's memory? They hadn't yet been married. Just engaged and planning a wedding when he had died. Would he want her to remain single and mourning his death for the rest of her life? Probably not. Craig had been such a life-loving guy, and he'd loved the Lord most of all. If Kate were to face facts, she knew Craig wouldn't want her to go through life unhappy and filled with regret. He would want her to be happy and most of all, he would want her living her life for the Lord.

Kate's foot slipped and she floundered for a footing. She felt her fingers slipping.

Ethan's hand grabbed her foot, guiding it back to the foot grip. "It's okay, ranger lady. I've got you." His voice drew her back from the past, reassuring her.

"Thanks, Ethan," Kate gasped, stopping to make sure she had a good grip.

"No problem. Take your time. We're in no rush."

Kate sucked in a deep breath and grabbed for the next handhold. Yes, there was a safe rope but she had to pay attention. Glancing up, she realized she was nearly at the top. Refusing to look down, she kept her eye on the next handhold and then the next footrest and kept climbing.

Once at the top, she climbed over the top of the tower and onto the roof and waited for Ethan to join her. Pulling her rope along with her, she kept it tight, then stepping carefully, she found what seemed to be firm flooring and stood still. Reaching up, she turned on her helmet headlamp and shone it around the darkened space. Very little light from the canyon reached this far up into the cavern, and with no effort she could touch the roof of the cavern above the tower. The cold but dry surface was mere inches above her head. Ethan would likely have to duck to prevent knocking his head on it. Shining her headlamp on the roof of the tower, it looked rotten and very unstable. Again, she checked her harness and climbing gear, tightening her rope securely.

As Ethan climbed over and tightened his rope, he lowered himself to the roof, ducked beneath the cavern ceiling and turned his head sideways. "Well, this doesn't look at all secure, does it?"

"Not really. Please be careful. The roof has a spongy feel to it."

As his feet settled onto the ancient wooden beams, they suddenly gave way and Ethan slipped through.

"Ethan!" Kate screamed, her hand reaching for him, but she couldn't move far enough or fast enough. Her heart hammered in her chest and her breath hung in her throat as dust swirled around the hole he'd disappeared into.

Kate edged toward the hole feeling her way with her feet, trying to find a sturdy foothold. As the dust began to settle, she spotted Ethan's pale but grinning face staring at her from the hole.

He coughed a few times from the dust as she realized he'd tightened his rope and caught himself before he could fall more than a few feet. His head was the only part of him sticking out of the hole he'd made.

"How clever of you to make us an entrance," Kate chuckled.

"I thought you'd like that, ranger lady." He coughed again as the dust began to settle. "Just be careful of that first step. It's a doozy."

Ethan tore off what pieces of loose timber he could to widen the hole and make access easier. Kate watched as he lowered himself, then she put her hand over her heart and patted her chest. Sucking in a deep breath, she puffed out her cheeks in a huff of air and closed her eyes. *Thank you, Lord, that he wasn't hurt.*

Following him through the rough new entrance hole, Kate settled near him on the level below and glanced around, examining the room with her headlamp. Cobwebs hung in the corners and the air was stale. Whole clay pots sat amongst broken shards in one corner. A thick layer of desert dust covered them. A long, flat, gray stone lay along one wall covered in the same dust. A rectangular hole cut in the floor in another corner had a broken ladder leading down to the next level.

"Well, I'm not so sure I trust that ladder." Doubt tinged Kate's words.

Ethan shook his head. "I wouldn't."

Removing his pack from his back, he removed two full-face mold remediation respirators and handed one to Kate.

"I was going to give you one of these up top, but my unexpected entrance nixed that. It'll prevent mold and dust from getting into your lungs. Unfortunately, we may have already been compromised. I'd get it on quick to prevent further possible issues."

Once the masks were in place, they examined the clay pots, and finding nothing, Ethan gingerly stepped toward the hole and lowered himself to the level below.

"Come on down but be careful. Part of the floor is missing."

Kate tightened her rope, carefully stepped over the edge and lowered herself down through the opening. Her helmet light illuminated the rotted edges of the hole as she descended then swept the interior of the room below. Ethan carefully stepped aside to make room for her but as he'd said, parts of the floor were gone. Choosing a place to land was going to be difficult.

"Give me your hand, and I'll help you swing over here." Ethan's hand reached toward her as he steadied himself against the rough sandstone and adobe mortar wall. "It seems fairly stable."

As she followed his suggestion, her light swept through the holes in the floor to the level below and she caught a glimpse of something...interesting? But she couldn't tell what it was.

"Ethan, there's something down on the next level." Kate gasped as she caught Ethan's hand and worked to get stable footing. "I only caught a glimpse, but it looked pretty large."

"Right." Ethan avoided looking directly at her so as not to blind her with his light. "There doesn't appear to be anything on this level except more cobwebs. Let's work our way down there."

Stepping gingerly, he made his way over to the largest hole and descended. His weight on his rope against the old floor supports broke right through them, sending large pieces of timber raining down around him.

"Ethan!" Kate yelled. "Are you okay? Ethan? Answer me!"

Particles of dust danced in the light beam from her helmet as she waited what seemed like an eternity for him to answer.

"Ethan!" Kate made her way to the edge of the hole. Had he been knocked out by the fallen timbers and couldn't answer? He wasn't wearing a helmet, the idiot. Why hadn't he worn a helmet? Men! Their bravado and macho egos got in the way of their common sense and sometimes got them killed. Was that what had happened to Craig? No of course not. Craig was a by-the-book kind of guy. He didn't pull any punches.

"Ethan, answer me, you...you...," Kate nearly jumped out of her skin when Ethan's head reappeared through the hole in the floor.

"You what?" A huge grin lifted the corners of his mouth inside the clear respirator mask. "You weren't about to call me anything bad, were you, ranger lady? Now that wouldn't be very nice."

Kate dropped her head to her hands as they gripped the edge of the hole, her heart in her throat. She lifted it again, glaring. "You scared me. Again. I thought... I thought, well... I thought you were conked out down there somewhere, and I wasn't sure I was going to be able to get to you. I thought you might be seriously hurt this time. I thought… well, I thought a lot of things, Ethan, and none of them were good."

Ethan had the grace to look repentant. "I'm sorry, Kate. I didn't mean to scare you. But I found the thing you saw, and it's kind of cool. Want to come see?"

"Well, maybe after I jumpstart my heart again, yeah."

"Want my help?" Ethan waggled his eyebrows in a suggestive manner. "I have a few ideas."

Kate shook her head. "I think we'll just go straight to me coming down to see what you found."

Ethan snapped his fingers. "Shucks. Could've been fun."

He descended with a reminder. "Be careful. You saw what happened when I came down."

"Right." Kate swung her legs over and sat on the edge of the hole, and after tightening her rope, lowered herself down.

This level seemed a little more stable than the last and when Kate joined Ethan, she relaxed a bit. By the time she got there, he was already down on his knees examining a cloth-wrapped object sitting in a corner. It was approximately the same size as the mummy that Prof. Rosenberg had discovered in the kiva.

"Do you think it's another mummy?" Kate knelt beside him.

"I don't know but there's a good chance."

"It's amazing how they've been so well preserved out in the open like this. I mean, think about it. If this is a mummy like the one the professor found, both were never buried. They were just left above ground, left to the elements."

"You have to remember the desert is so dry. High temps and no humidity. It's like an oven. It pretty much dries out and bakes the dead body, then preserves it. Even the cold weather is a dry cold."

"Amazing." Kate couldn't prevent the excitement that scooted up her spine. "Are you going to open it up?"

"You sound like a kid on Christmas morning, Kate." Ethan chuckled. "Yeah, but we have to do it carefully. I didn't bring the digital camera. I have my cell phone, though. Want to take pictures?"

"Sure." Kate accepted the phone and found the camera app.

Ethan pulled a pair of rubber gloves from his pocket and

slipped them on, then began meticulously removing the dark, brittle cloth covering the object. Kate found acid-free zip bags in his backpack along with acid-free tissue paper.

The cloth, a dark thin fabric, tended to break off as Ethan pulled it back. It was no longer a supple fabric but brittle fibers that snapped off.

"That's the kind of thing that breaks an archeologist's heart." Ethan shook his head. "Let's hope we get better results the further in we go."

Ethan was able to remove some larger intact patches of the outer fabric and placed them in plastic bags, but most disintegrated. When the outer covering was removed, they found another thicker blanket lay beneath. Now a mere shadow of its past due to fading from centuries of age and neglect, this blanket must once have been a vibrant and beautifully decorated piece of thick linen with tribal designs and desert colors. It had been chosen as the final resting place for whoever this individual had been.

Ethan set about opening up and removing this layer, only to find it much sturdier, and remained intact for the most part. Flecks shed off the edges but he was able to carefully fold back most of the blanket to reveal a skeletal face. Its skin stretched tight across high cheekbones, a flat forehead and a sharp chin. Eyelids had long ago dried up and one had partially fallen off. That eye socket was hollow. Bits of gray hair still remained attached to the scalp and a leather strap was wrapped around the forehead. Thin lips had separated and a few darkened teeth remained in place.

All the while Kate snapped pictures recording the evidence as Ethan revealed it.

As he gently tugged the blanket away from the body, they saw it was arranged in a sitting position, legs crossed and tucked close to the body, the arms folded close across the chest.

"Is it odd that they would've left what appears to have been an elder in their living quarters?" It sure seemed odd to Kate.

"Remember the Anasazi's were nomads. It's possible he was left here when they moved on. If they moved on." Ethan pointed at an object just inside what once was probably a bright yellow shirt. "He was probably a very important person in the village, and it doesn't mean that he was important at the same time as the one that you and Prof. Rosenberg found. I'd say the one you found was at least a couple hundred years older. And he was buried in a kiva."

He carefully slid aside the brittle fabric and lifted a golden object with his fingers. It was held around the mummy's neck by a leather strap.

"Ethan," Kate whispered. "That's very similar to the one Prof. Rosenberg and I found on the other mummy."

She snapped several more pictures with the phone camera.

"I suspected as much." A grim note slipped into Ethan's voice. He glanced up through the holes where they had descended.

Kate followed his gaze. Surely no one was watching their discovery right now. Yes, the others knew they were heading into the tower, but they had no way of knowing what they'd find.

She glanced back at the amulet laying in Ethan's palm glittering in the lamplight. Then she looked at the phone in her hand with the last picture of the amulet still on the display. A thought formed in her mind, then her stomach began to twist and roil. Oh no. No. No. No. Kate had forgotten all about the camera that she and the professor had used that day to record their find. Yes, she'd taken steps to hide the amulet, but she'd completely forgotten about the pictures on the camera.

Kate groaned aloud. "Ethan, I think I know why someone is trying to warn me."

"What?" Ethan, caught up in the moment of the mummy find, was completely thrown off by this change of subject. "What are you talking about, Kate?"

"I think I know why someone warned me by nearly hitting me with a car and then shot at me."

Ethan dropped the amulet back to its resting place. She had his full attention now. "Why?"

"Do you remember when the professor and I found the mummy and the amulet? We hid the amulet, right? But we were taking pictures that day too. Remember you and Carl came down and you all were snapping pictures of us with the mummy?"

Ethan nodded, his brow furrowed as he thought back. "Yeah."

"I just remembered that the professor asked me to take pictures as he unwrapped the mummy, just like you did now. There are pictures of the amulet on that digital camera. What if someone went through the pictures and saw it? Saw the artifacts from that discovery? They know there's a high-value artifact that hasn't been reported and they know I know about it."

In the glow from their helmet lights, Kate couldn't miss the grim expression that settled on Ethan's face. He drew in a deep breath.

"I'll check the camera when we get back and see if anyone's removed them. Even if the pictures are still there, someone could've viewed them and left them."

Kate released a heavy sigh and shook her head. "If only I'd remembered sooner, I could've deleted them."

"What's done is done, Kate. We just have to deal with things as they are." Ethan took her hand and twined his fingers with hers, sending a jolt up her arm and straight to her heart. Why did his touch do that to her?

She'd bumped into Gage Hampton the other day and nothing happened. Officer Blake Hunter had shaken her hand a time or two. Nothing. Ethan? Oh yeah. All he had to do was look at her and her heart went into a tailspin. Touch her hand or her arm and...zing.

What was he saying? Oh yeah. Deal with things as they are. "Yes, you're right, Ethan. Thank you for standing by me."

He still had her hand, she noticed. His fingers tightened ever so gently. His husky voice was almost a caress. "I wouldn't have it any other way, ranger lady."

With what seemed like regret, he slowly released her hand and heaved a heavy sigh. He glanced at his watch. "We need to bag up this amulet and call it a day. I'll put it in the safe where it'll truly be secure. We'll have to finish up the tower tomorrow. I'll also bring the equipment to pack this guy out. He deserves to be in a museum where his history can be recorded and appreciated by millions."

When the amulet was tucked safely inside Ethan's backpack and his phone was in his pocket where no one would see the pictures until he was ready to divulge them, he started his ascension to the top of the tower, Kate following behind him.

Ethan had reached the top level while Kate just broke through the second. She was definitely out of shape where climbing was concerned. She hadn't been to the gym since she'd arrived at the Grand Canyon, and with everything that had been going on, she hadn't had a desire to go out, much less in public where she was a greater target. Perhaps she could start a workout routine at Tasha's. Kate was sure she wouldn't mind. She'd ask her.

Kate reached for the edge of the hole just as she felt her rope shift. Had Ethan bumped it? Looking up, she didn't see him. Perhaps he'd already crossed the top of the tower wall and was on his way down the cave wall. The rope moved again, causing Kate's heart to go into overdrive. What was that? She looked up again trying to decide what to do when she felt her weight and the rope give way, dropping rapidly back in the direction she'd come. Her arms and legs flailed as she grasped at anything to stop her fall.

A scream ripped from Kate's throat as she fell into the darkness hitting timbers and jutting pieces of wood. With a sudden and painful halt, she landed on a flat piece of flooring somewhere deep in the tower. Pain shuddered through her body as her climbing rope landed on top of her. Turning her head away in an attempt to prevent it from hitting her in the face, she closed her eyes. Perhaps she'd just lay here until…would she become a mummy? *Lord, did I scream? I hurt all over. Please send Ethan to find me.*

Chapter Eleven

E than secured himself at the top of the stone tower to wait for Kate. Drawing a bandana from his hip pocket, he started to wipe the sweat from his brow when a scream stilled his hand. It started fairly close and ended deep within the tower by the time it came to an abrupt halt. The horrifying sound of Kate's scream curdled his blood and froze his heartbeat. Had she fallen?

Scrambling back to the tower roof, Ethan called in a frantic voice, "Kate? Kate? Can you hear me?"

A distant groan met his words, but nothing more.

Before he headed down, Ethan looked over the top of the tower to survey the city, but it looked deserted. He yelled, "Is anyone here? Carl? Anna? Paul? Anyone?"

He waited an interminably long few moments with no one answering then eased down into the tower, following his previous route. This time he proceeded further down, finding Kate four levels below where they'd found the mummy.

With his headlamp he spotted Kate sprawled across the timber flooring amongst broken timbers and pieces of wood. Particles of dust still danced in the air. From the looks of it, she'd passed through previous holes, making them wider and busted through rotted flooring, making new holes.

Stepping cautiously to her side, Ethan knelt beside Kate. Removing his backpack, he set it aside and gently touched her shoulder.

"Kate, sweetheart, can you hear me?" Ethan recognized the huskiness in his voice as he spoke and swallowed hard. He tried again. "Kate, answer me."

She groaned and slowly opened her eyes. "I hear you. I don't want to move. It...it hurts too much. The fall was pretty scary but the sudden stop? It hurt. Bad."

Thank God she was conscious. That was half the battle. Seven floors in? Yeah. That was a good thing.

"Ok, ranger lady, let's check you for broken bones. I have to examine you. You okay with that? Not that you have much choice. Everyone else has gone home."

Kate nodded then grimaced. "Ooowww. Nodding was a bad idea. Yes, I understand. Examine away, Dr. Wagner."

"I'm not that kind of doctor, but I'll have to do." Ethan proceeded with checking for bone breaks. "I've taken extensive first aid so I'll do my best. Let me know if I hurt you."

"Oh, believe me, I will." Kate closed her eyes. "And can I say, it hurts to breath?"

"Then let's examine your ribs. You've likely fractured a couple."

Kate gasped in pain as Ethan poked and prodded.

"Yep. Yep, I'd say so." Kate's breaths came in short gasps. "That's pretty painful."

Ethan continued his search for other breaks and found her left collar bone fractured. Everything else seemed intact.

"Let's get you into a sitting position, and I'll strap your ribs and get that shoulder into a sling."

With gentle care, Ethan helped Kate to sit up, but he couldn't prevent the pain that accompanied the movement. He admired her grit as she bit her lip to prevent from crying out. How he wished he could take the pain for her, but he couldn't.

Ethan glanced up through the tower. It was going to be difficult getting her out of here. And unfortunately, all the windows on every level had been sealed eons ago, so they couldn't exit from any of those. Straight up and out was the only way.

Hauling out his first aid supplies, he had Kate's shoulder and ribs securely strapped for the trip back to the top in no time. She was covered in minor cuts, scrapes and contusions which he dealt with as best he could.

"Ethan, how are you going to get me out of here? There's no way I can climb out on my own with one arm. And my rope is down here with us."

Which reminded Ethan, he wanted to know why it was down here with them in the first place. Reaching for the rope, he examined the end that had been at the top. His heart sank at what he saw and before he could hide it from Kate, her eyes went wide and her mouth dropped open.

"Ethan, tell me I'm wrong and the end of that rope wasn't nearly cut through so that when I started to climb it would break." Dismay filled Kate's voice. She shifted trying to ease her ribs and her breathing.

Ethan sucked in a ragged breath and released it all at once. "I wish that's exactly what I could tell you, Kate, but I can't. It has been cut and when you started climbing, your weight broke the few remaining fibers. I'm surprised you got as far up as you did before it broke."

With a dismal expression settling on her face, Kate shook her head. "I think I'll just stay down here for a while. Let them think I died. I'm so tired of this, Ethan. And I know it's all over that silly amulet."

Ethan wanted to wrap his arms around her and pull her into a hug, but until she'd seen a real doctor, that wasn't a good idea. Instead he placed a warm hand on her good arm. "Don't be discouraged, Kate. We'll get through this. Come on. We need to get you out of here and to urgent care. There may be internal injuries that I can't find, and we still have to climb up the trail after we get out of this tower. Let's get out of here and then I'll use your radio to contact Tasha. I'll have her meet us at urgent care."

"How are you going to get me out?"

"Trust me, ranger lady." Ethan patted her helmet, grabbed the rope and stood. "Sit tight. I'll be back in a bit."

~

The next several hours passed in a blur to Kate. Ethan hoisting her out of the tower, assisting her up the treacherous trail to the top, Tasha meeting them at North Country Urgent Care, and Ethan staying by her side except for the actual examination. She'd noticed he'd refused to leave when she'd told him she would be fine and he could go home. Then when they'd released her, he'd taken her to Tasha's where he was invited in to stay for a while.

When Kate was settled on the couch, she rested her head back and sighed. "It's been a long day. Was it just this morning that I was interrogated and nearly accused of killing the professor?"

Tasha handed her a mug of hot cocoa then one to Ethan. "Here, drink that. Chocolate fixes everything. And you're mistaken, girlfriend. I don't think they believe you killed him. But they have to ask certain questions."

"It sure seemed like it." Kate sipped her cocoa.

"I'll agree it's been a long day." Ethan had downed his cocoa and set his empty cup on the coffee table. "I thought I'd never get down to Kate when she fell. Then to find the rope was cut?"

"This seems like more than a warning to me." Kate shuddered, gripping the handle of her mug with her good hand. "I could've been seriously hurt."

"Or killed." Tasha settled on the other couch with her own mug of cocoa. "It had to have been one of the other team members."

"Not necessarily." Ethan leaned forward, elbows on his knees, fingers steepled under his chin. "There were caterers still there cleaning up when we descended into the tower, but I think it would be odd if one suddenly went over and climbed the back wall of the cave and cut a rope. They all saw us climbing up there. As for the team members, yeah, it could be any one of them. They had all gone for the day by the time I climbed out of the tower. I suspect they'll all deny it, but we have to add this to the two previous incidents, right?"

Tasha nodded. "Right. I'll call Lance. He's covered them both."

She reached for her cell phone. "But the rope…"

Ethan waved away her words. "Don't worry. It's in my car. I knew it would be needed for evidence at some point."

Tasha shook her head. "I guess that's why you're an NPS Special Agent, Ethan. You know your job."

"Yeah, well, I'm just not getting to do much of it right now." His expression was grim.

"Yes, you are." Tasha hit speed dial for Lance. "You're the eyes and ears for the NPS, and that's important for the present."

~

While they waited for Lance to arrive, Kate slipped out to the back deck and leaned her good arm on the wood railing. The sling that immobilized her shoulder was awkward but it at least kept her shoulder supported and helped reduce the pain. The pain meds she'd been given had helped dull the pain somewhat. As for her ribs, it was still difficult to breath. She just couldn't draw in that really good deep breath she longed to drag in. Glancing skyward, she found it filled with brilliant twinkling stars and she was reminded Who was in control of everything. Yes, even this horrible mess she was in. Tasha had told her that God didn't make bad things happen. Satan did.

Lord, I need Your strength to get through this. I think someone bad is after me, and it's really getting serious. I don't think it's a warning anymore. I think they're trying to kill me. Please keep me strong. Please send Your angels to look after me and to protect me. Please, in Jesus name.

Kate heard the French door from the house open and close, then Ethan joined her at the railing. She glanced to her left to see him cross his arms on the smooth wood as he took in the bright night sky.

"I see you're admiring the Lord's sparkling handiwork." A chuckle escaped him. "He really does a fine job, doesn't He?"

"Yes, He does. I'm starting to see more and more His hand in nature. I used to not pay attention to that kind of thing, but now I see it everywhere and it's beautiful."

Ethan turned sideways and leaned his elbow on the railing, clasping his hands loosely together. "Yep, it's everywhere. Beautiful."

Something in his voice had changed making it difficult for Kate to breath. And it had nothing to do with her fractured ribs. She got the feeling he wasn't talking about the sky or nature anymore. She could sense his gaze on her. Eyes back on the night sky, she attempted to draw in a deep breath. Gotta keep breathing.

"Kate," Ethan whispered her name.

Unable to help herself, Kate's gaze was drawn to his. With only light from inside the house shining onto the deck, Kate saw the dark shadowed planes of his face softened by something she hadn't seen there before, and it did strange things to her heart. Ethan reached out and placed a hand behind her neck, tugging her closer. Was he going to kiss her? Was she going to let him? She watched in fascination as his lips parted and he drew her ever closer.

The French door swung open and Tasha called, "Lance is here. Oops. Sorry. My bad."

~

Ethan shook his head and ran a hand through his hair. He sighed in frustration as Kate slipped inside. *Thanks, Tasha. Perfect timing if I've ever seen it.* He rapped his knuckles on the deck railing then followed more slowly. Closing the French door behind him, he took a seat on the bar stool at the kitchen counter. Kate sat on one of the couches beside Tasha with her feet tucked beneath her, a throw pillow in her lap and her sling resting on the pillow. She looked vulnerable and refused to meet his gaze when he entered. Great.

Kate had nearly been killed today, was injured and in pain and he'd let his feelings get the upper hand of his common sense. Ethan mentally head slapped himself. Had he wanted to kiss her? You bet he did. He'd wanted to kiss Kate almost since he'd met her, but now wasn't the time. A little starlight and a beautiful woman had worked its magic instead of him reigning in his horses and giving her time. Now she wouldn't even look at him. A heavy sigh escaped him.

Lance began questioning Kate first, getting her side of the climbing incident, then Ethan's. When he had everything they had to give him, he closed his notebook and stood.

"Kate, I know it's been rough for you since you've arrived at the Grand Canyon," Lance's booming voice filled the room as he tucked his pen into his uniform shirt pocket, "but don't give up, girl. God's got a plan for you. He brought you here for a reason. He doesn't take you through the fire unless he's going to refine you and shape you for something better. I don't know where you are on your spiritual journey, and it's none of my business, but I just want you to know I'm praying for you."

"Mmm mmmm," Tasha murmured softly, waving her hand in the air. "Preach it, baby."

Ethan saw tears form in Kate's eyes and slip down her cheeks. Shoving the pillow off her lap, she stood on tiptoes and reaching up, gave the big man a one-armed hug.

"Thanks, Lance." Kate's soft voice was muffled against Lance's shoulder. "That means a lot. I'm trying to find my way back. I'm not there yet, but I know your prayers are helping."

"Girl, you just keep seeking the Lord, and you'll find Him." Lance stepped back. "Now I gotta get back to work. Y'all have a good evening. See ya, Ethan."

Ethan tossed up a hand. "Bye, Lance. Stay safe out there."

Lance pointed a finger at him then toward heaven. "You know it, man. I got the good Lord looking after me."

"Bye, baby." Tasha gave him a kiss as she walked him to the door, leaving an awkward silence as Kate retook her seat on the couch, hiding behind her pillow again.

Or at least so it seemed to Ethan. Maybe it was time he took his leave as well. He'd caused Kate enough discomfort for one evening. He stood from the bar stool just as Tasha returned.

"Where you going, Ethan?" Tasha sat down beside Kate. "You're not leaving us, too, are you?"

Ethan grabbed his jacket from where he'd dropped it on the other couch. "Yep. Afraid so. It's late and Kate needs her rest. As she said earlier, it's been a very long day."

Tasha stood back up. "Well, I understand that. And she does need her rest. She's not going anywhere tomorrow."

"What?" Ethan feigned disappointment. "Who'll help me recover the mummy from the tower and further check it out?"

A slight smile lifted the corners of Kate's sweet lips, stirring Ethan's insides. She lifted her gorgeous hazel gaze to his. "You might have to postpone that little recovery operation for a while if you're expecting my help. A minimum of ten weeks the doctor said, remember? You should probably rethink that and get one of the other team members to help you get the mummy out."

Ethan twisted his face into a scowl. "I'd really rather have you help me, but I may not have a choice. I wonder if Sir Mummy would mind sitting tight for ten weeks while I research elsewhere. I could save the tower until you get that sling off."

"Then there's physical therapy," Kate added the reminder. 'I doubt I can get the sling off after ten weeks and then jump on a climbing rope."

Ethan nodded. "I suppose you're right. I'll ask Carl to help me recover the mummy and finish searching the tower."

Ethan felt his shoulders stiffen as he suddenly slammed his right fist into his left palm. "I'd really like to punch whoever did this to you, simply because they hurt you. That really angers me.

This is the third incident and with each one, it gets more serious."

Surprise crossed the faces of both women as he expressed his anger. Ethan was generally a laid-back sort of guy and this was unusual for him, but he cared for Kate more than either of them knew.

"Sorry, ladies. I just wish we could find out who's doing this and put a stop to it before something worse happens to Kate." Ethan reigned in his emotions and headed for the door. "I'll be going now."

Ethan had slipped on his jacket and was reaching for the doorknob when he felt a gentle tug on his sleeve. Turning, he found Kate beside him looking sweet and vulnerable.

"Ethan," her voice was soft and hesitant, "thanks for everything today. For standing by me at the interrogation, for taking me with you into the tower. Wow, what an adventure that was. Thanks for rescuing me when I fell. I prayed the Lord would send you back for me, and He did. And thanks for staying with me at urgent care when you didn't have to. You took care of me and made me feel...well, you made me feel...special. Thanks for everything. I really appreciate it."

Leaning forward on her tiptoes, Kate supported herself with her good hand on his shoulder and kissed his cheek. Then she hurried back to the living room, leaving him standing there, heart pounding like a jackhammer in his chest. His cheek tingled from the impression of her lips. For a few moments he stood unable to move. Had she frozen him in place with her touch? He needed to get out of here before Tasha came by and he looked like an idiot.

Ethan turned the knob and forced himself out the door. If he didn't know better he'd say he was falling in love. But he knew better. He wasn't going to allow himself to do that again. Right?

Chapter Twelve

W hat a day. Ethan couldn't remember the last time he'd packed so much into twenty-four hours. After leaving Tasha's, he'd gone back to the archeologists' office, started a new and separate inventory log for the amulet he and Kate had found in the tower, then he'd printed pictures from his phone and placed them and the log book in his backpack and the amulet in the new safe. At some point he'd have Kate put the pictures in her safe deposit box for safe keeping.

He was bone weary and ready to hit the sack, but Haley had met him at the door and was ready for her walk when he came home. They'd just returned and he'd shut the door of the camper when his cell phone rang. He glanced at the time. It was too late for anyone to be calling and he didn't recognize the number. Ethan started to let it roll to voicemail, but something made him answer.

"Hello?" The weariness in his voice couldn't be missed over the line.

"Dr. Wagner, I'm…I'm sorry to bother you so late, but I really need to talk with you."

"Mike? Is that you?"

"Yes, sir. It is," Mike Pierce answered. "I know it's late, but I had to talk to you. I didn't know who else to talk to. I overheard the others talking about black market thefts and selling of artifacts. It almost sounded like they knew what they were talking about."

"Did it sound like they're involved in selling the artifacts or were they just talking about the subject?"

"I don't know, sir. But I thought you should know. I don't want to get them in trouble if they're not doing anything wrong, but we've lost several artifacts to theft. All I know is what I heard."

"Mike, can you be a little more specific about what you heard?"

"Well, yes sir." A pause followed as if Mike hesitated then he continued. "All three of them, Paul, Carl and Anna, were talking in the back room of the archeologists' office. I was in the outer office and I heard them talking. They said they bet they could get a lot of money for artifacts on the black market. Then they wondered how they'd go about finding someone to sell to. Then Anna said it was a ridiculous conversation because Prof. Rosenberg would never allow such a thing. Oh, and yeah, this was before the professor was killed."

"Mike, did you tell this to Officer Hunter during your interrogation?"

There was silence on the line. "I may have missed that part."

"Oh, Mike, you have to divulge all information." Ethan tamped down his impatience and continued. "I'll call Officer Hunter and set up another meeting for you. You need to share that information with him. He's probably going to call all of you in."

"Oh, please don't do that. They'll kill me."

The pleading in his voice was heart rending, but Ethan knew that to get to the bottom of the artifact theft case, they needed to know everything.

"Mike, it's the only way we can find out who's stealing the artifacts. Your help is invaluable, and you have to tell Officer Hunter what you just told me. It doesn't mean the others will have to know."

Silence on the phone lasted a full minute before Mike said, "Alright. I will. I want the thief or thieves caught too."

"Thanks, Mike. And thanks for calling me. It took some nerve, and you did what was right. Officer Hunter will be in touch with you. Good night, Mike."

"Good night, Dr. Wagner, and I hope you're right."

~

True to her word, Tasha didn't allow Kate to return to work the next day. She told her to stay in the house and rest. Kate wasn't a "rest" kind of person and staying inside was extremely hard for her to do. She was used to going and working and staying active and busy. So, while Tasha was at work and Lance slept after his night shift the night before, she watched TV, attempted to get involved in a book from Tasha's book stash, took a nap, watched some more TV and read some more. Soon she found she was bored out of her skull. Kate wanted badly to get out of the house and do something. Pacing past the windows and the French door by the deck, she eventually ventured out to the deck, but didn't feel comfortable being out there for long, and returned inside.

This was crazy. She couldn't even go outside the house without fear that someone was watching and would do something to harm her.

Finally, that afternoon Lance left for work and Tasha came home with Ariel. By that time Kate thought she'd go stir-crazy.

"Hi, girlfriend. How's it going?" Tasha and Ariel walked in the door, a bag of groceries in Tasha's arms.

Kate plopped onto a bar stool and dropped her head down onto her good arm along the counter. Rolling her head back and forth, her muffled voice lifted in agonized tones.

"Help me, Tasha. I'm losing it."

Tasha set her purse and the bag on the counter and told Ariel to go put her jacket and shoes away. "I'll make you a snack, baby."

When the little girl had disappeared, she turned to Kate, "What's the matter, girl? Why are you in such despair?"

Kate sat up. "I can't do another day like today. I'm not used to just sitting around watching TV and reading. I don't take naps. I need to go back to work. Please Tasha. Let me go back to work. I was bored out of my ever-loving mind today."

A wide grin on her face, Tasha chuckled and reached into a cabinet for a jar of peanut butter. "Is that all? I thought something else bad happened."

"Believe me, I'd rather be out there taking my chances."

Tasha turned and waved a butter knife in her direction. "Now I know you don't mean that."

"Want to bet." Kate's voice was flat.

Tasha heaved a sigh and turned to spread peanut butter on graham crackers. "Kate, I only want to protect you. I was going to ask you to stay home another day, but I guess that's out of the question, huh?"

Kate jumped up from the stool and rushed to Tasha's side,

"Please put me back in the field, Tasha. If you don't, I'll mutiny. Isn't there something I can be doing?"

"I really do need another pair of eyes on that dig sight. Ethan still has to be lead on the dig while investigating, but he can't be everywhere at once. With the professor gone, he's spread pretty thin now." She picked up one of the crackers and handed it to Kate then she picked up one and took a bite, thinking as she chewed.

"And the team is going to expect me to be there or they're going to get suspicious." Kate offered another reason, hope in her gaze. "If I just stop coming down, they're going to wonder why."

Tasha sighed again. "I know. I just don't know how to keep you safe, Kate."

"Tasha, I go armed every day, and if you want me to wear an armored vest, I will. I won't like it," she scrunched her nose in dislike, "but I will if you say so."

The doorbell rang.

"Good," Tasha hurried to answer it. "That should be Ethan. I have news for both of you. I'll get Ariel settled in her play room with some cartoons then I'll share."

With her good arm, Kate stopped her in her tracks. "Take Ariel her snack and get her settled. I'll answer the door."

~

When the door opened, Ethan turned expecting to find Tasha, but his heart leaped at the sight of Kate, the air stalling in his lungs. The sight of her seemed to do that to him. Her shoulder-length hair was fashioned into a braid that lay along the side of her neck. Dressed in gray jersey sweatpants and an oversized teal jersey t-shirt, Kate's femininity certainly wasn't in question. She looked comfy but adorable.

Ethan sucked in air trying to jumpstart his lungs again. "Hi Kate. Wow. You look great."

Confusion settled on Kate's features as she looked down at her casual clothing. "Really? Well, thanks. Won't you come in? I guess Tasha's expecting you."

"Yeah. She said she has some news for us." Ethan stepped inside and slipped his jacket off, hanging it on the hall tree by the door. "Did she mention anything to you about it?"

Kate shook her head. "Nothing more than that she has news."

As they entered the living room, Tasha joined them from the

back of the house. "Hi, Ethan. Come on in. Why don't we sit around the kitchen bar? Want some coffee, tea or a soda?"

"Coffee sounds good." Ethan settled on a bar stool.

"Make that two." Kate held up two fingers as she sat on the stool beside him.

Tasha prepared the coffee and retrieved coffee mugs from a cabinet. Then she grabbed her soft-sided briefcase from the couch where she'd dropped it when she came in and laid it on the counter. Opening it, she pulled out a folder.

"Blake Hunter loaned me a copy of the medical examiner's report from the examination of Prof. Rosenberg's body. Kate, I have some photos you may or may not want to see. I'm not going to force you to look at them, of course. It's not imperative that you do. It's your choice. I'll just tell you the findings. The photos only corroborate them."

Kate gave an emphatic shake of her head. "I don't want to see any photos of the professor. When you've seen the real thing....Well, it's still fresh in my memory. Just tell me the findings."

"No problem. Ethan?"

Ethan felt for Kate and would make sure he didn't inadvertently let her see them. He was certain it would be a long time before she could get her last view of Prof. Rosenberg out of her mind. "Sure, I'll take a gander."

Tasha set fresh mugs of coffee on the counter along with a tray of creamer and sweetener for them to doctor their brew the way they wanted to.

"The initial blow to the professor was, as we first thought, a blow to the upper cheek just below the temple. According to the M.E., it was likely made by a rounded piece of wood consistent with a thick limb that was probably picked up outside along the edge of the tree line. Bits of bark were found in the contusions leading to that conclusion. His skull was crushed from the blow. Whoever did it likely had some anger behind their swing. It knocked his glasses off too. Bits of tree bark were also found in the climate-controlled room scattered across the floor. They were widespread as if an impact had distributed them everywhere."

Tasha took a sip of her coffee then ran her finger across the report to find her place. "Then the killer shot the professor in the forehead from a distance of approximately five to seven feet. It was impossible to tell that during the initial inspection because of the damage done by the coyotes, but the autopsy shows a bullet went right through the brain and exited out the back of the skull. The exit wound is consistent with that distance. The shot was obviously fired outside after the professor was dragged behind the office and left beneath the junipers. You know, no fuss no mess."

Tasha handed Ethan a photo and he got up and walked away to prevent Kate from accidentally seeing it.

"Does the M.E. suggest whether it was a man or woman who killed the professor?" Kate stirred her coffee slowly.

"He said the killer could've been either. A woman with enough rage could've swung that limb just as easily as a man. A man would probably do more damage, but a woman could certainly do this much." Tasha shook her head. "Someone out there is really disturbed."

"Were they able to find the limb?" Ethan studied the photo in the brighter kitchen light. "And I'm guessing, no gun?"

"Unfortunately, no. The killer likely tossed the limb into the Grand Canyon. And as for the gun? They probably took that with them."

"Any fired shell casings left at the scene?" Ethan handed the photo back to Tasha and sat next to Kate.

"Funny that," Tasha chuckled. "The investigators found one spent 9mm shell casing half buried in the dirt. Apparently, the killer stepped on their own shell and buried it. They missed it if they were trying to clean up their evidence. The M.E. says it's consistent with the size of the round that went through the professor's brain."

"Ok, so either a man or a woman could've killed the professor," Kate said, "but although he was on the short side, Prof. Rosenberg wasn't a tiny man. He was stocky. Do we think a woman could've dragged him out of the office, down the steps, around the building and all the way to the back under the junipers? I mean, if you go back and look at the drag marks in the crime scene photos, can you tell if he was dragged, then they stopped, dragged, stopped and so on? Or was it more of a continuous drag with no rests? Know what I mean? Do you think there was more than one killer?"

Ethan and Tasha both looked at Kate with interest.

"There's always that possibility," Ethan agreed. "Any fingerprints?"

"A couple partials, but so far nothing has shown up in the Automated Fingerprint Identification System," Tasha replied. "They're still running them, but I don't think there was enough of them to trigger a recognition."

"Well, whoever killed the professor must've thought about what they were doing even though they were angry." Ethan paced across the kitchen. "Either they came there to talk to him and hadn't planned to kill him, became angry then killed him, or they came angry with the full intention of killing him."

"I tend to think maybe the second plan." Kate shrugged her good shoulder. "Why else would they come in with a club of sorts and a gun?"

Tasha crossed her arms and shook her head. "There are so many unanswered questions. I just hope Blake can help get to the bottom of things."

She shared the rest of the M.E.'s photos with Ethan while Kate viewed the ones of the drag marks. She couldn't tell from the photos whether the body had been dragged steadily or if it had been dragged with pauses for rest.

"You'd have to go out there and take a look, but it's been nearly a week since the murder, and the scene has been reopened. I doubt it'll be untainted," Kate tapped the photo.

"Doubtful," Ethan agreed. "Although hikers don't generally have a reason to go back there, you never know. I can drive out and take a quick look before the sun gets too low. See what I can find."

Tasha nodded and walked to a cabinet in the living room. "Won't hurt to try. Here, take my digital camera. It may not help to take pictures but take it just in case. It's a point and shoot camera. Not fancy at all."

Ethan accepted the electronic device and played around with it. He pointed it at Kate, much to her dismay and got the feel for how it worked.

"Okay," Ethan headed toward the front door and his jacket. He poked his head back in after he'd put it on. "I'll be back in a while if that's okay. I'll let you know what I find."

"Absolutely." Tasha waved her hand in the air. "We'll be waiting with bated breath."

Ethan winked at Kate enjoying the crimson wave that rose from the teal neckline of her oversized shirt all the way to her hairline. "Take it easy, ranger lady. Be back in a while."

"That's all I've done all day long," Kate spoke through clenched teeth. "I think I'll blow this popsicle stand and go do something. Anything. I've had my fill of taking it easy."

She turned on her heel and headed out to the deck, shutting the French door a little harder than normal.

Confused, Ethan wanted nothing more than to go find out what was eating at Kate, but daylight was burning and they needed an answer to their question.

Tasha waved him on. "Don't worry. She's just been cooped up inside all day, and she's ready to be done with it. I think I'm going to have to let her go back to the dig tomorrow, or I'm going to have a mutiny on my hands."

~

The afternoon sun edged lower above the rim of the canyon and soon it would be impossible to find what Ethan was looking for. He'd have to act quickly. Parking in front of the archeologists' office, he was glad there were no other vehicles parked there. He'd still need to watch his back.

As he searched the ground near the entrance to the office, he noticed that unfortunately a lot of footprints obliterated the drag marks around that area. It was to be expected. They'd all come and gone over the last week since the professor's death. But as he walked around the side of the office, he was able to make out the drag marks. Apparently, no one had been back here. *Thank you, Lord.*

Stepping to the side of the dirt impressions, he followed them all the way to where Kate had found Prof. Rosenberg's body. It was one long drag mark. Yes, there was the occasional animal print in the drag mark where errant creatures had unknowingly ventured through the evidence, but it was obviously one long drag mark. He also spotted human prints here and there, most likely those of Kate, the killer and the investigators. Those within the drag marks were likely the killer's. They were smooth-soled, not knobby like hiking boots would be.

Returning to where the beginning of the drag mark began, he took a succession of pictures with Tasha's digital camera, working quickly before the light faded. He overlapped the pictures and picked markers of rocks, twigs, and such, to ensure they could be pieced together in succession.

When Ethan was satisfied that he had what he'd come for, he climbed back into his pickup and headed back to Tasha's, eager to see Kate. She'd stormed out to the deck just as he'd left. Would she have settled down by the time he returned? He sure hoped so. For someone who had no intention of starting a new relationship he couldn't control the longing to see that woman. She made his heart do crazy things. And his breathing? His lungs tended to seize up when she was near. It didn't bode well if he planned to stay alive for long. He'd have to work on a breathing routine when she was present. He chuckled. Yep. She definitely had an affect him.

Chapter Thirteen

Kate stood on the deck at Tasha's, frustration filling her chest. Whoever was behind these attacks on her life had truly made her miserable. Three incidents on her life had her pretty well banged up but one day stuck inside was all it took to make her see she'd had enough.

Closing her eyes, she took a breath of fresh air, only as deep as she could until it hurt too much. Then she grabbed her ribs and pressed gently against them. Ooowww. She couldn't even take in a good deep breath of fresh air.

Lord, I'm sorry. Forgive me for complaining. I should just be thankful that I'm alive, and that in time I'll breathe deeply again. It's been a long day of doing nothing, and I just want to get out and get away for a while. Is that too much to want? A sigh slipped from Kate. *If so, it's ok. I'm trying to trust You with whatever You think is best. I...I love you, Lord!*

It seemed a bit awkward adding that last part. She'd gotten out of the practice of praying, but she was trying. And she was trying to talk to God more from her heart. More like she was talking to Him not at Him. So, if she was going to have a relationship with Him maybe she should tell Him she loved Him. It only made sense.

"Kate," Tasha called from the French door. "Your cell phone was ringing on the kitchen counter, so I answered it. It's Blake Hunter. Oh, my, it's chilly out here. You need to come inside before you catch your death, girl."

Kate hadn't really noticed until Tasha mentioned it, but it was chilly. Hurrying inside, she took the phone from Tasha. "Thanks, I'll take it to my room."

Once in her room, she sat on the edge of the bed, unmuted the device and held it to her ear.

"Hello?"

"Hi, Kate. This is Blake Hunter." Blake's pleasant voice sounded in her ear. "How are you doing? I heard about your accident. Tasha filled me in."

"I'm doing ok. It's kind of hard to breathe sometimes with these cracked ribs, but other than that, I'm ok."

"Tasha said she didn't let you go to work today. Gone stir-crazy yet?" Blake chuckled.

"How'd you guess?"

"Well, I know I would."

"Yeah, it was a rough day. I'm not used to sitting and doing nothing."

"Well, that's why I'm calling." Kate heard the lilt in Blake's voice and wondered at it. "I thought maybe you'd like to go out with me this evening for a bite to eat. The El Tovar has great food and overlooks the canyon. It should be nice until the sun disappears at least. What do you say? I promise not to interrogate you."

Kate was shocked. Would he invite someone out to dinner if he suspected them of murder? Doubtful. "Wow, that's... really nice. I appreciate the invitation. And you must know that I'm so desperate to get out of the house that of course I'm going to take you up on it, right?"

"I'm under no illusions that it's my fine personality that's drawing you." His chuckle resounded through the airwaves. "But seeing as how we don't really know each other yet, I can live with that."

Kate laughed for the first time that day. "I'm sorry. That sounded terrible, didn't it? I mean, really terrible."

"It's alright, Kate. I understand where you're coming from, and this lowly law enforcement officer will be happy to be the one to get you out of the house and give you a change of scenery. Think nothing of it. I'll pick you up in thirty minutes. Will that give you enough time?"

"Plenty." Kate stood and walked to the closet where three shirts hung. "Is this El Tovar casual or fancy?"

"Casual. Don't dress up. I'll see you in half an hour."

After Blake hung up, Kate decided on a teal print button-up cotton shirt and a pair of blue jeans. She'd only brought a few things with her from her apartment when she'd moved in with Tasha and Lance. The shirt was easier to get on with her ribs and shoulder. She called for help from Tasha.

"So, Blake's taking you out to dinner?" Tasha helped Kate put her bad arm into the shirt and then the good one. "Wow, girl. You just keep turning these men's heads around here."

"I don't know what you're talking about, Tasha." Kate ignored her meaning. "I'm just happy to be getting out of the house tonight."

"I know you are. Just promise me you'll be careful. Watch your back, girlfriend. You just never know when this person or persons is going to show up."

"Well, they say things happen in threes." Kate reached for her blue jeans and stepped into them. "I've already had three things happen. Let's hope they're done."

"They also say three strikes and you're out." Tasha held up three fingers and swiped them with the index finger of the other hand. "Kate, be careful. You've had your three strikes. I don't want you to be out."

A chill ran down Kate's spine at Tasha's words. Would someone try and take her out? Was that the plan? To wipe her out? And to what purpose? Because she'd found the professor? Or because they knew she had the amulet.

~

Ethan rang the doorbell hoping perhaps Kate would answer again. However, this time Tasha responded to the ringing.

"Come on in, Ethan." She stepped back and opened the door wide to allow him in. "What'd you find?"

He hung his jacket once again on the hall tree and followed her to the kitchen counter. "Where's Kate? It was her question that sent me out to the archeologists' office to check out the drag marks."

"Oh, she's gone for the evening." Tasha waved her hand in the air, dismissing Kate's lack of presence as nonessential to the conversation. "We'll catch her up later."

Ethan felt his brow furrow as his heart sank within his chest. Gone? For the evening? Well, of course, she could go wherever she wanted to. He had no say in her movements. He wasn't interested in a relationship after all, right? So why did his heart sink at the news?

"Oh? Where'd Kate go? Is she going to be safe?" He couldn't have stopped the words from slipping from his mouth if his life had depended on it.

Tasha gazed at him deliberately, one eyebrow tilted above a knowing expression in her dark eyes and a smile lifting the corners of her full lips. "Oh, she'll be fine, Ethan. Don't worry about her. She's with Blake Hunter, sweetie. He'll take good care of her. He took her out to dinner to get her out of the house for a while. You know, she was about to go stir-crazy being cooped up inside all day, but really I think he's got a thing for her, you know?"

Ethan swallowed the lump that formed in his throat as something stirred within him. Something he didn't care for. An image of Kate with Blake Hunter formed in his mind's eye and left a bad taste in his mouth. Was it jealousy? There was no reason to be jealous. What did it matter to him? He wasn't starting a new relationship, right?

Then an image of Kate alone filled his mind. Her beautiful hazel eyes and her gorgeous smile that always set his heart to beating faster. Ethan knew he was sunk. Was he falling in love? Why did he keep refusing to accept it? He hadn't planned to start a relationship, but somehow Kate had slipped unbidden beneath his plans and had rooted herself where it mattered. Deep within his heart.

"Ethan?"

A gentle touch on Ethan's arm drew his gaze to Tasha's ebony fingers lying on his flannel sleeve. Glancing up, he met her dark, sympathetic gaze.

"Ethan, I think it's time we had a talk. Have a seat. I'll get the coffee." She turned to grab the carafe.

"But the pictures," Ethan began.

"Oh, we'll get to them, but you need to talk first. Tell me why you keep denying that you're in love with Kate."

"What makes you think I'm in love with Kate?" Ethan plopped onto the bar stool.

"See? You're denying it." Tasha put a mug of coffee in front of him and took the stool across from him. "It's written all over your face every time she's around you, honey. You look like you want to scoop her up and run away with her."

Ethan grimaced then leaned his arms on the counter. Hanging his head, he sighed heavily. "That's because I do."

"Then why don't you tell her, Ethan?"

"Because I decided two years ago I wasn't going to start another relationship." Ethan rubbed his forehead with his fingers as memories flooded back. "I was engaged and headed to the altar. A short time before the wedding, my fiancé was unfaithful to me with my best friend who was going to be my best man. I actually walked in on them."

"Oh, sweetie, that's awful." Tasha patted his arm. "I'm so sorry that happened to such a nice man as you, but it doesn't mean it's going to happen again. Kate is a wonderful woman, and she deserves to be loved by a man who will love her for who she is. But she's been hurt too. I don't know how, but I know it caused her to step away from God. She blamed Him for what happened. She hasn't talked to me about it, but she's asked some questions. Perhaps you can get her to open up about it. Perhaps if you begin to share your love with her, you and Kate can both begin to heal. She's starting to rely on God again and that's the wonderful thing."

Ethan took a deep breath, his heart lifting at Tasha's words. Could he and Kate both let God heal them emotionally? Could love grow between them? He was in love with Kate but what about her? He had no idea what her emotional state was or if she even wanted to be friends. Yes, she was willing to work with him, but beyond that? He had no idea.

"Ethan, I'll be praying for you and Kate. I know you're in love with her, but we have no idea where she is in her feelings for you."

Ethan stared at Tasha. Was she a mind reader?

"We'll just trust God to lead you in this. Kate seems to be vulnerable right now what with everything that's happened to her since the professor's death, in addition to whatever happened before she came here. Look for opportunities to find out about that. Ask God to give them to you. She needs to open up and get some help. And if you think Blake Hunter is competition, ask God to remove him if it's His will. I know I'm going to."

Ethan chuckled. "I think I'm really glad you're on my side, Tasha."

"Oh, you better believe it, honey. Blake doesn't stand a chance. Now show me those pictures."

~

As Kate sat across from Blake Hunter at the El Tovar restaurant, she gazed out the wide expanse of picture windows that overlooked the beautiful scenery of the Grand Canyon. With the sun setting to the west, it cast shadows of varying colors of purple and blue amidst the brighter desert tans and pinks. Would she ever grow tired of that view? As fascinating as it was, she doubted it.

"Pretty amazing, huh?" Blake chuckled.

Kate turned back to her dinner companion. "Sorry. Yeah, I guess I'm still new enough around here I can't help but stare when I see it. Was I drooling?"

Blake laughed and waved a hand. "Not too badly so no worries. I was the same way when I first came here."

"Really? How long have you been here?"

"Nearly five years. I love it here. It's been one big adventure for sure."

Kate smiled. "Oh, I can attest to that."

Blake nodded, a wry expression settling on his face. "Yes, you can. But your adventure has been quite different, hasn't it? How's the shoulder and ribs, by the way? Tasha said you'd be in the sling at least ten weeks for the collarbone."

Kate looked down at the table. "Yeah. I've never had anything like this happen before. The shoulder doesn't bother me that much, but it does limit what I can do on the dig. That is when I go back to the dig, which I'm hoping is tomorrow. The ribs? Yeah, that's more painful. It's hard to breathe, and if someone makes me laugh, it hurts. A lot."

"So, I shouldn't tell you a good joke then, I guess?" A grin lifted the corners of Blake's lips.

"Please don't." Kate pleaded with a smile. "It would just be better if you didn't."

Blake chuckled. "Ok, I'll take pity on you."

Just then the waiter brought their orders, and as Blake began to eat, Kate bowed her head and prayed to her herself, then opened her eyes and began to eat. Blake had taken notice but said nothing.

"I know you can't talk about the case," Kate stabbed a piece of bison on her fork, "and I'm perfect with that, but I have one question. If you can't answer it that's fine. Mind if I ask?"

Blake nodded. "Go for it. I'll let you know if I can't answer."

"During the interrogation, I got the feeling that I'm a suspect in Prof. Rosenberg's murder. Am I, Blake?" Kate felt her brows furrow. Did her voice sound as desperate to him as it did to her? She sure hoped not.

Blake laid down his fork and, leaning his arms on the edge of the table, looked directly at her. "Kate, as you said, I'm not allowed to discuss the investigation with anyone, especially with those that I've interrogated."

She watched his gaze move to his plate as he thought about how to answer her. Then his gaze returned to hers as a grin split his lips. "Let me see if I can say this so you can understand. I'd never take a suspected murderer out to dinner. Is that pretty plain?"

Kate's cheeks flushed with warmth, more from relief and gratitude than attraction. "Very plain. Thank you, Blake."

"You're welcome. Now let's not discuss that again. Ever." Picking up his fork and knife, he dug into his steak with relish.

Kate was more than relieved to know she wasn't a suspect in the death of the professor. *Thank you, Lord.*

But she'd been made to feel she was just as all the other team members were. Did that mean they weren't suspects either? Or perhaps they still were. But if not, then who was?

~

"I thought you'd be dropping me off at the archeologists' office." Kate stirred sweetener into her coffee the next morning. "I'm going to inconvenience someone no matter what since I can't drive my own car. And I just got it back with a new windshield."

"Ethan said he'd stop by and pick you up." Tasha arranged Ariel's hair into braids. "He's headed out there anyway."

Happy to be back in uniform and headed to work, Kate had asked Tasha to braid her hair over her shoulder. She sipped her hot coffee and grabbed half a bagel and a yogurt.

She'd just finished when the doorbell rang. Tasha let Ethan in.

"Morning," he greeted, taking in Kate's appearance. "You look great. And except for the one non-uniform item, the sling, you look very professional and ready to head back to work."

"Thanks," she chuckled, grabbing her olive-drab uniform jacket. "I think."

Ethan laughed. "Hey, good news, ladies. It's actually warming up out there today. Hopefully cool weather will be coming to an end and warmer weather's on the way."

"Well, it's already May. It's about time," Tasha said. "Come on Ariel. Time to go, baby. Have a good day, y'all. And be careful. Especially you, Kate. Don't take any chances. Ethan…"

"I know. Keep an eye on her." He saluted Tasha then winked at Kate. "I've got my orders, ranger lady. Come on, let's go."

Chapter Fourteen

E than drove along Hermit's Road toward the archeologists' office. The road was already busy with shuttle buses and park vehicles that shared access to various Grand Canyon overlooks and was available only to them during this season. The morning access traffic, however, was far from Ethan's mind this morning. The woman beside him seemed to constantly fill his thoughts whether she was with him or not.

"How did your pictures of the drag marks turn out?" Kate turned from looking out the side window of Ethan's pickup.

"Great. For one thing, even though Tasha has a point and shoot camera, it takes pretty good pictures. I was able to capture a succession of drag marks from the side of the building all the way back to where you found the body. It was one long, continuous drag mark. There were no intermittent breaks. I wouldn't think the average woman could drag the professor that distance without numerous breaks if at all. Even some men couldn't do it. It would take a certain physique and strength to handle that job."

"Really? Will you pass those photos on to Blake for his investigation?"

A flash of...of what? --irritation? jealousy? --surged through Ethan. There was no reason to feel either one. He had no claim on Kate, and it was a simple question that had nothing to do with a relationship and everything to do with a murder investigation. *Get a grip, you idiot.*

"Yeah, absolutely. Hopefully they'll help."

Had his voice sounded strained to Kate's ears? They certainly had to his own. Blake was obviously interested in Kate just like he was. But he had some prayer power on his side as he recalled Tasha's words from the night before.

Silence filled the interior of the car for several minutes then Ethan cleared his throat.

"Did you have a good time with Blake last night? When I came back from taking the pictures, Tasha said he'd called and taken you out to dinner. That was a great way to end a very long, boring and frustrating day for you." He hoped his voice came across even and conversational. Had he pulled it off?

Kate nodded. "Yes, we had a nice time. He's interesting and witty but I had to tell him to hold off on the jokes. Laughing is too painful on the ribs."

Ethan released a sigh. Great. Interesting and witty, huh?

"Well, I'm glad you had a good time." Not. His insides roiled at the thought that she might be attracted to Blake Hunter. *Lord, I need some help here. You know my heart belongs to Kate. I need wisdom in sharing that with her. Whatever is standing in the way, whatever is hurting her, help her to open up, at least to You, and give it over to You, so she can heal. I want to be there for her, Lord. For always.*

Ethan parked in front of the archeologists' office right next to Mike Pierce's car. So, he was the first to show up for work today.

"Kate, I also wanted to tell you I got the digital camera yesterday while you were off, but I haven't had the opportunity to tell you what I found." Ethan had mixed feelings about the change in subject. This one would be hard for Kate to hear.

"Really?" Kate turned her attention toward him. "What did you find? Were the pictures I took of the amulet still there?"

Ethan hated to break the bad news to her, but he shook his head. "No, they weren't, Kate. Someone viewed those pictures then deleted them."

The angst written across Kate's face nearly caused him to reach across and draw her into his arms, but he held back. Now wasn't the time.

"Ethan, I was right. Someone killed the professor and now they're after me." Her statement wasn't one made out of fear but of fact.

"Kate, we just have to continue being careful and watch your back." Ethan reached across to grasp her good hand. "Nothing's changed. This just reaffirms what we already knew, right?"

She looked out the front windshield, her brows knit. "Right."

"Come on." He squeezed her hand. "Let's go immerse ourselves in an archeological dig."

A grin lifted the corners of Kate's sweet lips. He could think of other things to occupy their time, but…*Nope, don't go there, Wagner.*

Kate had already climbed from the car and was walking toward the office, her good shoulder slumping at the news he'd just given her. Shoving open his car door, he grabbed his backpack and followed her.

Kate climbed the steps and stopped in her tracks. "Ethan," she turned to him, her face pale beneath her uniform ball cap. "I have a horrible feeling about this."

"About what?" Ethan stepped onto the step below the one where she stood and saw what she pointed at. The door stood ajar. Dread gripped Ethan's heart as he removed a pair of rubber gloves from his backpack and slipped them onto his hands.

"I'll go first." He pushed the door open. "You know the drill. Don't touch anything."

Proceeding into the outer office, Ethan flipped on the overhead light and glanced at Kate to make sure she was alright. Having already experienced this beginning scenario before, was she feeling a sense of de´ ja` vu? She slipped her good hand into her jacket pocket. Her face was pale and drawn, but her chin was up and set with determination. Good. She'd be fine.

"Mike? Are you here?" Ethan called, wondering if he was in the back room. There was no answer. Then he saw.

The room had been ransacked. Ethan's eyes moved immediately to the safe. Good. It was still closed. With only him and Tasha having the combination, it would be difficult for anyone to get in unless they were a professional safecracker. And the safe company had assured him that even then it would be difficult. Supposedly it was the best. The top of the line, they'd said.

"Mike? Mike Pierce, are you here?"

Ethan headed toward the climate-controlled room to see if Mike was there, but as he rounded the side of the desk, he spotted a foot and then a leg. Oh, no. That's not good. He moved further around to get a look at who lay behind the desk.

Mike Pierce. Dressed in a white t-shirt with a blue plaid button-down shirt open all the way down. Ethan's stomach lurched at the huge bloom of red spread across the expanse of the white t-shirt. Three small holes in the center of the blood mass near his heart indicated three bullets to the chest. Mike's face was deathly white and his lips were blue. His eyes were open

Ethan heard a gasp from beside him as he realized Kate had also seen Mike's body. He slipped his arm around her waist and drew her to his chest, being careful of her shoulder and ribs.

"Kate, let's get you out to the pickup while I call Blake." He attempted to tug her in the direction of the door.

"No, I've seen…I've seen far worse than this."

Ethan noted her words, determined they would talk later. Somehow, he knew she wasn't talking just about the professor. He slipped his cell phone from his pocket and called Blake, then they both walked outside together and waited for his arrival.

~

"Shot?" Anna's voice rose in a squeal of disbelief. "Mike? But…but why? All he ever did was the heavy lifting for the team. And of course, sneak around listening to conversations."

Ethan noticed the last sentence was added with rancor.

"In what way?" Blake jotted in his notepad as she spoke.

Anna kicked the dirt in front of the archeologists' office with the toe of her hiking boot. Did she regret mentioning that? Would Blake ask about the conversations? *He* would if it were his investigation.

"Well, he'd always remain in the background and act like he was busy, or he'd be in the other room doing busy work, you know? I wouldn't realize he was there, he was so quiet. He wasn't much of a talker, but it seemed like he was just always around. He acted like he wasn't listening but how could he not have been?" Anna rolled her eyes and plopped her hand on her hip, waving her other hand in the air in a question. "But…dead? Really?"

"What kind of conversations were you having that you're upset he overheard, Miss Kelly?" Blake looked her in the eyes.

Anna flinched and glanced away, shrugging. "I don't know exactly. Just…stuff, you know. Just…conversations."

Ethan remembered the phone call from Mike and how he'd passed Mike's information on to Blake. He wondered if Blake had questioned Mike before his death. He certainly hoped so.

"Thank you. That'll be all for now, Miss Kelly. Once the medical examiner arrives and gives us a time of death, I'll have further questions for you. I think you know not to leave the Grand Canyon area until further notice."

A grimace crossed the young woman's face. "Yes, I know."

She started to stomp over to where Carl leaned against his trendy sports car, but Blake stopped her.

"Miss Kelly, I'll need you to stand over here to the side until I've had a chance to speak with Mr. Young." As she rolled her eyes and stomped over to his patrol car, he added, "Thank you."

Carl had arrived during Anna's questioning. Paul Schmitz still hadn't made an appearance.

"Well?" Ethan turned to Blake. "Anna isn't the easiest person to talk to on a regular basis. Under these circumstances, it's even harder to talk to her. Did you ever question Mike after he called me concerning his eavesdropping on the team and their discussion of the black-market sale of artifacts?"

"Yes, I did, fortunately." Blake turned his back toward Anna. "It was helpful but not conclusive. It's more of his word against theirs. I had planned to bring them in for further questioning concerning it, but now that this has happened, I'll just include it with the questions concerning Mike's death. Should make for an interesting interrogation."

Ethan crossed his arms over his chest. "Oh, that it will. Have you noticed who is conspicuously missing this morning?"

"Yep. Paul Schmitz hasn't made his appearance yet. Is he usually this late?"

Ethan shrugged his shoulders. "It's not unusual. Prof. Rosenberg spoke to him about it on numerous occasions. Looks like I'll have to as well."

"Let me get the initial questioning with Carl going. But before I do, how's Kate holding up?"

They both glanced in the direction of Ethan's pickup truck where Kate sat in the front seat leaning her head back against the head rest. Ethan had convinced her once Blake arrived that she couldn't do anything to help with the situation at present and she should just sit and rest her ribs and shoulder. It hadn't taken much convincing.

"She's okay but two murders in just over a week is taking its toll. The fact that someone's trying to harm her has her understandably on edge, but she wants to go to work. She's a stubborn one."

"Yeah, and a cute one." Blake's eyes were on Kate and missed the look of irritation that crossed Ethan's face. By the time Blake turned back around, Ethan had schooled his expression back to normal.

"Anyway, back to questioning." Blake raised his voice, waving Carl over. "Mr. Young? Step over here please."

The young man stood away from the car and ambled over.

"Good morning, Mr. Young. I suppose by now you've gathered that Mike Pierce was murdered. We've determined that it happened sometime in the last twelve hours. What can you tell me about Mike and his movements recently? Anything odd or out of the ordinary?"

Carl snorted derisively then jammed his hands into his pants pockets. "Mike was a nice enough guy and all, but pretty much everything about him was odd and out of the ordinary. He was strong and our heavy lifting guy. He hauled the heavy equipment for us which was much appreciated, but it seemed like he was always sneaking around. He tried to act like he wasn't, but you could tell."

"Why would he sneak around? To what purpose?"

"I have no idea, except that he really didn't fit in with the team. Yeah, he was an archeology student, but it didn't seem to be what he really wanted to do."

"But wasn't he just a second-year student? He had a lot to learn. Did the rest of the team include him or exclude him?"

An uncomfortable expression flashed across Carl's face before he quickly arranged it in a more benign appearance. "Of course we included him. And the professor took a lot of time with Mike."

Neither Mike nor Prof. Rosenberg was available to dispute Carl's words, Ethan noted. How convenient.

"Why do you think he would have been here at the office?" Blake scribbled in his notepad.

"Who knows?" Carl shrugged his shoulders. "I left straight from hiking up from the dig site. I didn't even go inside yesterday. I went right to my car and left, so I never saw Mike go inside. He was behind me when I left the dig site."

"Alright," Blake jotted that down. "I don't think there's anything else for now, Mr. Young. We're waiting for the M.E. to arrive from Flagstaff. That could be a while. Don't leave the Grand Canyon area. You know the drill. I'll have further questions after he determines the time of death so I'll be in touch."

Carl walked over to where Anna stood, and they began to whisper between themselves.

Tasha drove up in a cloud of dust and parked beside Ethan's pickup truck. Ethan and Blake strolled over as she climbed out and leaned in to speak to Kate.

"Hey, girlfriend," Tasha shook her head and patted Kate's arm on the windowsill. "This is becoming a habit I don't like. You doing ok?"

Kate nodded. "Yeah, I'm fine. Just sitting because it's easier on the ribs than standing. Poor Mike, though."

"Yeah. We gotta catch this killer before he or she takes somebody else out." Tasha spoke vehemently, propping her hand on her hip. "I'm tired of this nonsense."

"You and me both," Ethan said as he and Blake stopped beside her.

She straightened. "Hey fellas. What happened?"

Blake pointed a thumb over his shoulder toward the office. "The place was ransacked. I'll have Ethan go through after the investigators get through processing the office and tell me if anything is missing. There were three taps to Mike's chest in the region of his heart. My guess is he died instantly. The M.E. will tell us more. He'll be here in about an hour. Had a chat with those two."

He tilted his head in the direction of Carl and Anna. "Not overly helpful but both suggest that Mike was an eavesdropper. Liked to listen in on conversations. Wouldn't elaborate on the kind of conversations, but Mike had indicated to Ethan and me that they've talked about selling artifacts on the black market. Whether that was just chit chat or real plans, I guess we have to find that out."

"Wow, that's interesting," Kate said.

"Yeah, and we got the impression there was no love lost between them either," Ethan said. "I don't think they liked him

116

very much.

"I wonder if they realized he overheard their conversation about the artifacts and decided to do something about it." Tasha glanced around. "Where's Paul?"

"Hasn't shown up yet," Ethan said. "It's not the first time. Probably won't be the last. I'll have to have a talk with him. The professor did several times."

"The slovenly type, huh?" Blake shifted his clipboard under his arm.

Ethan nodded.

"Well, I came with a little news." Tasha crossed her arms over her midriff. "There will be a memorial service for Prof. Rosenberg Saturday afternoon. I'm not sure how Cassie managed to get a permit for the Shrine of the Ages so quickly but she did. It usually takes months to get one."

"I do." Ethan yanked his ball cap off and jammed his fingers through his hair. "She has a certain, shall we say, demanding quality about her. It appeals to some and repels others. Believe me."

Kate snickered as she opened the truck door and climbed out, shutting the door behind her. "Yep, I saw it firsthand. If she appealed to the right admin clerk in the right tone of voice and batted her eyelashes just the right way, and if the clerk was male, voila, she had her permit."

Tasha laughed. "That's pathetic."

"But true." Ethan's tone was as dry as the canyon before them. "Don't test her, Blake. Just stay out of her way."

"Too late. I interrogated her. Remember?" Blake lifted one eyebrow. "It wasn't pretty."

"Oh, that's right." Kate snapped her fingers. "No, that couldn't have been easy at all. I'd love to have been a fly on that wall."

Ethan turned his gaze on Kate. Her color had returned and her smile was genuine. He was happy she was among friends and that she was okay. Mike's death had hit her but certainly not like the professor's.

"So, can I count on y'all to be at the memorial Saturday?" One of Tasha's eyebrows rose expectantly. "Cassie obviously doesn't have any family here but she wanted to do something for her father. The body won't be released until the investigation is over, and now that we have another body, that doesn't look like it'll be any time soon."

"Sure," Kate agreed. "I'll be there. What time?"

"One o'clock."

Ethan and Blake were a little more reluctant to agree to attend and it took a look from Tasha at both of them before they responded.

"Yeah, sure," Ethan replied without enthusiasm.

Blake pursed his lips. "I may be on duty, but I'll check and let you know."

Tasha eyed him through narrowed lids. "Ummhmm. You do that."

She checked her watch. "I can't wait around for the M.E. I need to get over to the Desert Watchtower. They've got the renovations going on, and I need to check on things. One of the contractors has been giving me fits about the Navajo designs that they're painting on the walls. He's using cheap paint and charging the park service an astronomical price for it. So, I'm putting my war paint on and going to battle. I'll see y'all later."

"Go get 'em, Tasha," Kate called after her with a grin.

Chapter Fifteen

W e caught him eavesdropping. He overheard everything that was said," the voice spoke softly into the phone, "I couldn't let him go to the authorities. He had to be stopped. Yes, we killed him and left the body to be discovered."

"Do you think that was a wise idea? Why didn't you dispose of the body?" the man with the accent asked, his voice rising.

"If he disappeared, there would have been a search for him and then there would have been more questions. This way they will pin it on one of the others, I have no doubt."

"I don't care about the boy," the man yelled into the phone. "Get me the artifacts. The ones you sent to me weren't worth much. I want artifacts worth millions. You said there's a safe. Get it open and find out what's inside."

"It's a new safe, larger and harder to break into. My accomplice has tried. You told me to let them accumulate, but not much has been found. The team has only discovered several minor artifacts. Nothing of significant value. You know, the ones I sent to you."

When the man spoke again, he had his anger back under control. But barely. "Yes, I know that you depend on the whole team and you are one person. Do your best but remember that you owe me. My patience will not last forever."

Click.

My patience will not last forever either, but I must be careful. This man will kill me if I don't find something to satisfy his thirst for high-value artifacts. The accomplice he sent to keep an eye on me will kill me as soon as look at me. If something didn't break soon, it would be time to escalate the situation.

~

Kate watched three of Blake's park police officers work the office, fingerprinting and searching for evidence. The climate-controlled room would be worked next. They'd be there all day and into the night. Was it just last week since they'd finished processing the crime scene for the professor's murder? At least they were familiar with it.

"The M.E. says Mike was killed last night about six o'clock." Blake stepped away from the coroner and over to where Ethan and Kate stood near the door. "Just like we thought. Three taps to the chest, and he died instantly."

"He must've arrived just after I left from taking my pictures," Ethan shook his head. "I just missed them."

Blake turned a grim expression on him. "For your sake, it's probably a good thing."

He then pointed toward the other side of the room where one of the officers had placed evidence markers beside three shiny pieces of brass. "The shell casings were found over there. What we didn't know was he was shot with a 9mm hollow point. They did a lot of damage."

"Yeah, that seems to be this killer's M.O." Kate's voice was belligerent. "Lots of damage. Poor Mike. Whether he liked listening in on conversations or not, he certainly didn't deserve to die like this. He didn't deserve to be murdered."

"Nope," Ethan shook his head. "What else did the M.E. have to say?"

"Not much until he gets Mike's body on his table, obviously, but he seems to think he saw his killer coming. From his posture, It didn't seem to be a surprise."

"Yeah, I noticed that," Ethan said.

"Nope, I didn't see that," Kate shook her head, "but then I'm not used to finding dead bodies."

"No surprise there, so don't beat yourself up," Blake said. "You're not an investigator. If it's not your job, why would you notice?"

Kate nodded. "True, I suppose. So now what?"

"Not much need for you two to hang around here. The guys and I will process the crime scene. The M.E. will take the body back to Flagstaff and start the autopsy. He'll have a report in a few days. I'm sure the family will be notified, and we'll probably have more family arriving."

Ethan grimaced. "Let's hope he doesn't have a sister like Cassie."

Kate grinned. "I doubt we'll have to worry that two family members show up acting like Cassie, Ethan. At least for all the male population of the Grand Canyon, let's hope not."

~

"Well, we seem to be at loose ends again." Ethan commented as he and Kate climbed into his pickup. "And on your first day back at work too. I know you don't want to go back home, so what do you want to do?"

Kate sighed. "I don't know. I hate being at loose ends. I'm really bad at it."

Ethan started the truck and headed back toward civilization. "Well, since we can't work, let's go play tourist."

After driving back up Hermit's Road to Grand Canyon Village, Ethan parked near Bright Angel Trailhead. "

In no hurry to get out of the car, he turned toward Kate, giving her his full attention. "We've got all day."

Kate looked at him, a wistful smile lifting the corners of her mouth. "This has been the most bizarre job I've ever had. You know, I worked at the Great Smoky Mountains National Park for my first two seasons with the park service, and I absolutely loved it. That's where I met...."

Ethan noted her instant halt as she turned her head away and gazed out the side window. Then she immediately turned back and started speaking again. But what had she been about to say?

"We had a huge poacher problem there, and one of the rangers I worked with, Molly Walker, was kidnapped. It turned out to be bigger than local poachers taking the occasional bear. It was an international black-market poaching problem that nearly cost Molly her life."

"That is pretty bizarre."

"Yeah," Kate nodded, "but I didn't have a big role in that situation. And when I worked in Yosemite...well, there weren't any real issues there. As far as the park was concerned anyway."

Ethan watched Kate closely. Something had happened at

Yosemite. She dipped her head then looked out the side window again completely unaware of the little indicators she was giving away. As a special agent with the park service, he was used to looking for them. Ethan almost felt like he was invading her privacy, but it couldn't be helped. More than anything he wanted to help her through whatever painful memories she was fighting to overcome. His heart ached knowing she hurt deep down over something that had happened. He wished he already knew what it was so he could help. *Lord, give me wisdom and opportunity.*

The opportunity is now. The words rang in his mind unbidden. His heartbeat quickened. *Now, Lord? Help me.*

Peace descended over his mind and heart as he took a cleansing breath and reached across for Kate's right hand. Giving it a quick squeeze, he let go, not wanting to overwhelm her or give her too much personal emotion when he asked his question.

Kate turned a puzzled gaze to his.

"Kate, I don't want to stick my nose where it doesn't belong, but I want you to know you have a friend, and you're welcome to talk if you ever need to. I've sensed something's troubling you, and I want to ask you a question. If you don't want to answer, I understand. Please don't feel like I'm pressuring you to."

He waited for her to respond.

Kate nodded with reluctance. "Ok. Ask away. If I'm not comfortable answering I'll let you know. Is that okay?"

"Absolutely." Ethan took another deep breath. "A couple of times since the professor's death, you've made comments indicating you found someone else who had died in a terrible way. Was it someone you knew? Someone close to you?"

Kate's gaze dropped to her lap. Her fingers moved to the seam on the door handle and she absentmindedly ran her fingernail along the stitching. She didn't speak for several minutes and Ethan didn't rush her. He'd give her all the time in the world if that's what it took.

"You're pretty perceptive, Ethan." Kate returned her gaze to his as she dropped her hand back onto her lap. She shifted in her seat slightly so that she faced him more and leaned her head sideways onto the headrest. "Yes, it was someone very special to me."

Ethan watched as Kate closed her beautiful hazel eyes, most

likely in memory, for a few moments before opening them again. Taking a deep breath, she began her story.

"I met Craig Wilson my first season at the Great Smoky Mountains National Park, during the whole poacher fiasco. Craig and I fell for each other. He wasn't your average guy by any means. He was sort of goofy and cute and hardworking all rolled into one package. Craig was still in college but only had a year to go. We worked summers for a couple of years then went full time after he graduated. We stayed at GSM for two years then applied to Yosemite and were both hired on full time. We'd only been there eight months when..."

Kate stopped and dragged in a deep breath, closing her eyes again and gripping her left fingers inside the sling. She opened her eyes and sat for a moment.

"Kate, it's ok. You don't have to go on if you don't want to." Ethan kept his voice low and reassuring, gently touching her elbow in the sling.

She shook her head. "No, I need to talk about this. I haven't talked to anyone since it happened. Maybe it'll do me some good."

With another fortifying breath she continued. "Craig and I had been taking rock climbing lessons for a while. It was his idea. He thought we should expand our horizons and in so doing, add another certification to our job applications. We had done several small climbs since we arrived at Yosemite. On one, he proposed to me. My mother, who lives in North Carolina, was ecstatic. She thought the world of Craig. We had even set the wedding date, and my mom was arranging everything since we were getting married in North Carolina."

Kate chuckled. "Craig was always looking for the next adventure. The next milestone. It was never boring with him around, that's for sure."

She turned to Ethan. "Have you ever been to Yosemite?"

Ethan nodded. "Yeah. A few years ago."

"Then you know that El Capitan is the Mecca of rock climbers and it's not to be taken lightly."

Ethan nodded again, afraid where this story was going.

"Craig got it in his head that we were ready to scale El Capitan. I didn't want to do it and refused go. I didn't feel we were experienced enough, and we had an argument about it. So, Craig got one of the other rangers to partner with him. A lot of the climbers start at the top and come down. El Capitan is so high it can take weeks to scale it. I talked him into at least starting at the bottom and going up. They agreed that would be wiser. So, they decided to go up one day, spend the night on the rock face and back down the next. Sounds easy enough but, as you know, El Capitan is pretty much a sheer wall.

"I felt horrible about our argument," Kate's voice shook as her good hand rubbed back and forth along her uniform pant leg, "so I camped out at the bottom to wait for him to return the next day. Only he returned sooner than expected. There was a malfunction with one of the anchors and he fell from over eight hundred feet. I heard his yell as he was falling and then the horrible sound as his body hit the ground."

By this time tears streamed down Kate's cheeks as her voice became softer. "I rushed over, but of course there was nothing I could do to help him. I had no idea at that time how far he'd fallen. He was almost unrecognizable. I called the park police. Craig's climbing partner rappelled down, which was much faster. He was the one that explained that the anchor seemed to have malfunctioned."

A soft hiccupping-sob escaped Kate nearly breaking Ethan's heart. "Craig died three weeks before our wedding."

Ethan could contain himself no longer and, leaning over, carefully drew Kate into his arms. "I'm so sorry, Kate. I can't imagine what you've been through. It's never easy losing someone you love, but in this manner would've been so much harder."

"What makes it so heartbreaking," Kate's muffled voice rose from Ethan's jacketed chest, "was that our last words were spoken in anger. We never had the chance to clear the air and make things right."

"Kate, rest in the knowledge that he knew you loved him." Ethan whispered into her hair. "Your heart belonged to him. He had your forgiveness and you, his."

Were his words giving her comfort? Ethan certainly hoped so, because they were ripping his own heart to pieces. Reminding Kate that she loved Craig wasn't going to make it easy to help her fall in love with him, but it was the right thing to do. It was what she needed to bring her peace.

Ethan let Kate cry until she was spent, then he pulled a fresh bandana from his hip pocket and tucked it into her hand. "Here you go."

Kate pulled back and opened the navy and white print square, wiping the sparkling droplets from her eyes and cheeks. "Thanks. Sorry. I didn't mean to blubber all over you. Look, you have drip marks down the front of your shirt and jacket."

She giggled sending Ethan's heart into a tailspin. Oh, how delightful she'd felt in his arms and hopefully the giggle indicated she was headed toward healing. *Please, Lord, let it be so.*

"Ehh. They'll dry." Ethan waved away her words. "What do you say we go get some coffee and take a walk?"

"You don't think I'll be a target out there?" Kate's voice held only a slight hint of apprehension. "I mean, I know it's either that or go home. And I definitely don't want to go home."

Ethan chuckled. "Didn't think you did. Remember, situation awareness always. We just have to be careful, Kate. Keep your eyes open."

Chapter Sixteen

After going inside the Bright Angel Lodge and purchasing two cups of coffee to go, Ethan and Kate stepped back out into the late morning sunlight. Ethan suggested a visit to the Lookout and Kolb Studios to see the beautiful paintings and artwork on display. Kate had not yet visited these buildings and was amazed at how they were built right onto the edge of the Grand Canyon. One, built of stonework, was constructed to look as if it were part of the canyon. The terraces surrounding the building gave visitors plenty of spectacular views of the canyon, and Kate took full advantage of them.

When they left the studios, they meandered from the Bright Angel Trailhead up along the rim walkway taking in the canyon views.

Ethan pointed out a position far down in the canyon. As he stood closely beside Kate, a hand on her good shoulder, trying to point out the tiny destination far below, his cheek came dangerously close to hers, causing her breath to stall in her chest.

"Sometime you'll have to take the Bright Angel Trail down to Indian Garden. It's a great day trek. If you get really adventurous, you can take a mule train down to Phantom Ranch. But that's an overnight trip, and you have to have reservations far in advance."

It wasn't until he moved away that Kate realized she'd been holding her breath. She dragged in a lung full of air. No one since Craig had caused Kate's heart to flutter or her breath to seize up like Ethan did. Just his mere presence did that to her. And when he wasn't around she found her thoughts turned more and more to him.

"Really? That sounds…Oh!"

Kate was suddenly bumped from behind by a man who was taking pictures of the Bright Angel Lodge behind them. She nearly fell forward onto the low stone wall that bordered the rim trail but Ethan quickly put out an arm and stopped her. She banged her shins against the stone wall and dropped her coffee cup, knocking the lid off and splashing coffee on her hiking boots.

"Ah, I'm very sorry," the man's deep voice rumbled in a German accent. He grabbed her arm to help right her. "You ok? *Ja?*"

Kate nodded, trying not to give away the fact that he'd smacked right into her fractured shoulder and ribs. "Yes, I'm fine, thank you."

Extricating her arm from his hand, she took in his appearance. Completely bald with no facial hair, he wore a short black leather jacket zipped low and a maroon turtleneck beneath it. Black jeans and black leather boots completed his attire. A small digital camera was gripped in his left hand. A wide bright smile lit his face, but his eyes…. his eyes were dark and cold, belying the friendliness in his voice.

"*Ja, das gut.*" Reverting back to English, he introduced himself, "I am Claus Von Richter. I vas taking picture of the architecture of dis building. Vas not vatching vere I vas going. Again, I am very sorry. Und may I buy you anozer coffee?"

"No, no, that's not necessary. I was almost finished anyway." Kate inwardly lamented the fact she had over half a cup to go. Oh well.

He nodded first to Kate then to Ethan. "Then I leave you. *Guten morgen.*"

"Good morning." Kate half expected him to click his heels and bow, but he didn't.

They watched as he snapped another picture of the building behind them, then walk away and snapped a couple of the Grand Canyon.

"Are you ok, Kate?" Ethan looked at her closely, his hand supporting her lower back. "He smacked into you pretty hard."

Kate nodded then sat down on the rock wall. "Boy, did he," she said, almost beneath her breath, then plastered on a smile for Ethan's sake. "Nothing a couple of Tylenol won't take care of."

Ethan eyed her critically and bent down to pick up her empty coffee cup. "I'm not so sure about that. He almost knocked you over. And did it seem strange to you that he had a German accent?"

Kate rubbed her shins then glanced up at him. "Not really. I mean everywhere you go around this place you hear foreign languages being spoken. People travel here from all over the world. Everyone wants to see the Grand Canyon."

Ethan sat down beside her on the low wall. "That's true. It just seemed a little too coincidental, what with Prof. Rosenberg and Cassie both speaking German. I suppose I'm a little on edge still with everything that's going on."

"Well you did say 'situation awareness' a little while ago, right? You're probably trying to connect dots where there are none."

"Yeah, and I should've been more alert and watching more closely." Ethan grimaced, his hand balling into a fist in his other palm.

Kate reached over and put her good hand over them. "Hey, don't beat yourself up, Ethan. You're doing the best you can, and you can't prepare for every situation. You were standing on my left where my injuries are. How would we know someone would come at me from behind? Besides, he's just a tourist who wasn't watching what he was doing."

"Well, now we know." He glanced at his watch. "We'll be prepared next time. You stare at the canyon. I'll watch your back and everything behind you. Literally. Want to walk some more? Or have you had enough? You've already admitted you need some Tylenol. It's almost lunchtime. How about we grab something to eat then get you back to Tasha's for a while. You get a little rest then maybe later we'll take Haley for a walk. What do you say?"

"I say that sounds like a plan." Kate smiled. Why should the idea that she would be able to spend more time with Ethan make her inexplicably happy? "I like the idea of spending time with my four-footed friend."

"Oh, I get it." Ethan stood up and linked his arms over his chest. "It's my Haley you want to spend time with."

Kate stood up and grinned happily. "Do you really feel threatened by your dog?"

Ethan's expression turned serious and a flame in his gaze set Kate's heart to racing. He shook his head as he took a step closer to her. "Nope. Not in the least."

~

"Kate, it's Anna. Do you have a minute?" The confidence that usually marked Anna's voice was missing and had been replaced with...what? Anxiety? Fear?

"Anna? Sure. What's up?" Kate looked at Ethan and shrugged.

They'd just walked in the door at Tasha's with takeout. Ethan set it on the counter and waited to remove it from the bag as Kate set the phone to speaker so he could hear the conversation. Kate sat on a bar stool and awaited Anna's reply.

"Kate, I need to talk to you but not on the phone. Can you meet me? I have some concerns, and I don't know what to do." Was this for real? Was Anna's anxiety genuine or was she trying to draw Kate somewhere to set her up? The hair on the back of Kate's neck prickled as she met Ethan's questioning gaze.

"Where did you have in mind and when?"

"A very public place if that's okay. I don't want any of this secret stuff. Too many people ending up dead for my liking. How about in an hour at Bright Angel Lodge restaurant?"

Kate glanced at the takeout bag and then at Ethan. "That'll be fine, Anna. I'll be there."

"Thanks, Kate. See you there." Anna hung up.

Ethan reached for his phone and dialed. Kate stared at him, puzzled.

"Hi, Blake. Yeah, it's Ethan. Got a situation and I need to run something past you. We may need a body wire. Yeah."

Ethan explained Anna's phone call and where Kate would be meeting her, why and when.

"No problem, Blake. We'll meet you there." Ethan clicked off the phone.

"Blake is calling for a warrant for a body wire since Anna is a suspect in the professor's murder. Hopefully he can get it quickly." He glanced at his watch. "We don't have much time. We're to meet him at the far end of the Bright Angel Lodge parking lot. If he can get the warrant, he'll have a body wire for you to wear. If not, you'll just have to get as much info as you can on your own."

"You mean they'll be listening in on Anna's conversation?"

"Yep." Ethan opened the takeout bag and pulled out their sandwiches. "Here, you've got to eat something. An hour is an hour. And I don't know about you but I'm starved."

Kate eyed the sandwich then reached for it. "So am I."

Ethan said a quick blessing over the food with a prayer for wisdom and protection for Kate.

He took a bite, chewed then swallowed. "I know Blake will be listening in but you know I'm not letting you go into this meeting alone, right?"

"Never thought for a minute you would." Kate reached for her drink. "In case you thought I hadn't noticed, except for when I'm here and Tasha is home to stay, you pretty much haven't left my side. I had no doubt you'd be tagging along on this little outing. How are you going to keep from being seen?"

"I'll just hang around on guard outside the door and keep watch. Try to sit facing the door and try to maneuver her to face away from it. Simple."

Kate harrumphed and rolled her eyes. "I am not cut out for this investigative stuff."

"You'll do fine. Just get to the table first. The rest is just a matter of listening to what she has to say and ask as many questions as you can to keep her talking."

"Right." Kate crumpled her sandwich paper and tossed it in the garbage can. "It's going to be interesting for sure. I wonder what in the world Anna is concerned about. She's a suspect, for goodness sake."

"This could shed light on some things. If she's involved in the theft or the murders, maybe she'll be willing to point a finger."

"Then why come to me? Why not go to the police directly?"

"I guess we'll soon find out."

~

Kate waited for Anna by the huge log and stone fireplace in the lobby of the Bright Angel Lodge. Wooden seats were built on either side biding visitors to take a break from their touring and sit a spell. If she'd had the time she'd like to do just that. Glancing around, she watched as the hotel clerks checked in guests behind the log reception desk, its support posts reaching to the high ceiling. The lights hanging from rough log beam supports looked like old oil lamps that had been electrified.

Blake had met Kate and Ethan in the far end of the parking lot and installed a listening wire just under the inside of Kate's uniform shirt. He'd managed to get a warrant faxed from a Flagstaff judge just minutes before he met them.

"Talk about cutting it close," he'd said. "But that's usually how it works around here."

To Kate the wire felt like it was visible to everyone that passed her. In reality it was a micro-wire that was barely there. Blake sat in his patrol car in the parking lot with listening equipment and would be recording her and Anna's conversation.

"Kate, there you are." Anna's low voice came from beside her.

Kate turned to find a white-faced Anna wearing large sunglasses and a ball cap, her hair tucked beneath it, with her back to the room. Grabbing Kate's good arm, she hauled her toward the restaurant. For someone who wanted to meet in public, she was trying desperately not to be seen.

As they moved toward the entrance to the restaurant, Kate glanced around for Ethan. She spotted him near the gift shop leaning casually against the wall, a newspaper in his hand hiding his face. He dipped it just enough for her to glimpse his eyes beneath his ball cap. He winked.

Warmth flooded her face as a smile tipped her lips upward. Barely shifting her head in acknowledgment, she turned her eyes back to the entrance as she and Anna followed the hostess to their table. Just in time she remembered to move ahead and sit facing the doorway. Hopefully Anna was distraught enough not to notice.

When they were seated and had menus in their hands, Anna removed her sunglasses and glanced around the room and over her shoulders. Kate had been doing that out of habit for a while now. After all, someone had been trying to harm her since the professor's death.

"Thanks for meeting me, Kate." A heavy sigh slipped from Anna's lips. "I just don't know who to talk to. I know that you've had your share of...well, misfortunes lately."

"I suppose you could say that," Kate chuckled, trying to put Anna at ease.

"So, I thought maybe you'd be a good person to talk to. Maybe you could tell me what I should do." Anna glanced over her shoulders again.

There weren't many people in the restaurant. It was an hour past lunch and the crowd had thinned. Probably the reason Anna had chosen that time.

A waiter approached and took their orders. Kate only ordered coffee and a piece of pie. She explained to Anna that she'd already had lunch.

When he left to place their orders, Kate asked, "So tell me how you think I can help you, Anna."

Anna twisted her fingers together. "A while back before the professor was killed, Carl, Paul and I were talking one evening after we got back from the dig. We were just being silly, wondering what artifacts would bring on the black market. We weren't serious, but I guess Mike overheard us and said something to someone in authority. They started investigating us. Ok so that's not really the problem although it's not good, because they think we're thieves when we're not. Or at least I'm not. I honestly don't know if they are or not because we now know artifacts have been stolen. But the real problem is that now Mike and the professor are dead. So I'm wondering if one of them, either Carl or Paul might not be the murderer. I'm terrified, Kate. And Paul has disappeared. He never did come in today. It could be him. He could be laying low."

Kate listened and hoped that Blake was getting all of this. Anna was basically accusing Paul Schmitz of murder and either Carl and or Paul of theft.

"Anna, you have to be very careful what you say," Kate advised. "You can't let emotion and fear rule your life. Step back and take a breath before you make accusations."

Anna leaned forward and whispered loudly, "Kate, who else could it be? Mike and Prof. Rosenberg are gone."

Then she gasped and sat up straight as a quick thought hit her irrational mind. "You don't think it could be Dr. Wagner, do you?"

Kate crossed her arms along the edge of the table. *Lord, help me. This woman is losing it. Help me bring her back to rational thinking.*

"Anna, you have to stop seeing the boogie man behind every tree and let the police do their job."

Anna jumped as the waiter made his appearance with a tray of their food. She had the grace to look embarrassed as he set their food before them then walked away, a puzzled expression tracing his features.

"That's what I'm talking about, Anna. Relax. Believe me, I get it. Someone nearly ran me down and shot at me last week. I'm not exactly comfortable being out where everyone can see me. Yeah, I'm vulnerable. But you know what? I'd be a wreck like you're about to become, but I choose to put my life in God's hands. I've decided to let Him take care of me. He can do it a whole better than I can."

Anna cast a skeptical glance at Kate and picked up her fork. "I've never believed in God. I only believe in what I can see."

"That's too bad." Kate stuck her fork into her pie and broke off a bite. "Because the One who created all that we see is the One who wants to have a relationship with us. He wants to give us the strength to help us through the difficulties we face. It's something to think about."

Kate placed the bite in her mouth and chewed it up before asking, "So what makes you think Paul is laying low? Has he disappeared before?"

"Yeah," Anna nodded, pushing her food around on her plate with her fork. "A few times. When he got back he said he'd gone home to visit his mom. Apparently she's got cancer or something."

"But he never told anyone he was going?" Kate asked. Odd that he wouldn't say anything to anyone when he left.

"Nope. He's pretty private. Keeps those ear buds in his ears and listens to his music most of the time."

"And Carl? What's he like? Does he ever leave without saying anything?"

"Oh no, not Carl. Carl is a by-the-book kind of guy. Straight-laced and hard-working as they come. That was one reason the professor chose him for his assistant. But the professor yelled at him a lot. I'm not sure why except that maybe the professor used him for his sounding board and that included using him for his release valve. Carl got tired of it though. It wore on him."

"Do you think Carl would sell artifacts to spite the professor?"

Anna ducked her head. "I don't know. I know he loves archeology, but he'd lost his respect for the professor. He's a hard worker but he'd had enough."

"Did he tell you he'd had enough?" Kate's voice was low. She didn't want Anna to stop talking.

"Not in so many words," Anna fidgeted with her fork, "but he did tell me he was tired of the professor yelling at him all the time."

"Anna, is Carl capable of murder?"

Anna hesitated before answering. "I guess I just don't know him well enough to answer that. I'd like to say no, but I can't. I…I just don't know."

Kate sensed the turmoil in Anna and hoped it wasn't an act. Was all this just a ruse to draw them from her own trail? That was still a possibility.

"Is there anything else you want to tell me, Anna?" Kate slipped the last bite of pie into her mouth.

"I've told you my greatest concerns," Anna held up her hand for the waiter. "Do you mind if I let you know if I see something else that bothers me? Or if I feel in danger?"

Kate shook her head. "I don't mind at all, but I think it might be a good idea if you open a conversation with the park police. It would probably be a better idea if you share this information with them. They can afford you the protection you need. Please consider it, Anna."

Doubt crossed Anna's face as her eyes darted about the room. "I don't know, Kate. I'm not really comfortable going to them."

"But you should be if you have nothing to hide."

"Oh, I don't have anything to hide," Anna said quickly. Too quickly?

"Then go to them," Kate encouraged her. "You'll probably have to in the end anyway."

Anna stared at Kate oddly for a moment. "You may be right. I'll think about it. I have to go."

She stood as the waiter brought the check. She handed him enough cash to cover her meal as well as Kate's pie.

"Thanks again for meeting me, Kate." Anna dropped her wallet back into her purse and slipped on her sunglasses. "You know I came to you because someone's after you, right? I know how vulnerable you are, and I thought you might be sympathetic to how I'm feeling right now. Aren't we a pair, living in fear and dread? Be careful and stay safe, Kate. Hopefully we can get back to the dig and normalcy soon."

Kate stood while Anna paid the waiter and now placed a hand on Anna's arm before she walked away. "Anna, you be careful, too. And I'll be praying for you. Whether you believe or not, I do."

Anna didn't pull away but, removing her sunglasses, she searched Kate's eyes and seemed satisfied at what she found there. "Yes, you do. Somehow, I find that comforting. Thank you."

Chapter Seventeen

W ell, Blake," Kate faced the wall and removed the tiny listening wire. "What'd you think of the conversation?"

She and Ethan had driven straight to park police headquarters and were in Blake Hunter's office.

Kate awkwardly re-buttoned the top two buttons of her shirt beneath the strap of the sling with her right hand then turned back around. She laid the device on Blake's desk. "Here you go. I hope I don't have to use one of those again anytime soon. I was really self-conscious with that thing on."

Blake chuckled. "Yeah, they tend to have that effect on people."

He opened a black, plastic foam-lined protective case with a cut out the shape of the device and laid it inside, snapping the lid shut. "You did a great job trying to draw out information, Kate. I'm still not sure if she's attempting to cast aspersions on her co-archeologists to throw us off her trail or if she's genuinely afraid one of them is a murderer and or a thief."

Ethan linked his arms across his chest and sat on the edge of Blake's desk. "Yeah, she even tried to throw me under the bus."

"You heard that?" Kate sat in the chair in front of Blake's desk. "Way out where you were standing?"

Ethan pulled an earwig from his ear and laid the tiny listening device on the desk. "Courtesy of our most helpful park policeman. Thanks, Blake."

"No problem." Blake sat in his desk chair and leaned back, causing it to squeak. His fingers twined behind his head, elbows extended past his ears. "What's your take on it, Kate? You were there to observe her expressions and to get a feel for her emotions."

Kate shook her head doubtfully. "It's hard to say, guys. The Anna we all know and love is one of absolute superiority, confidence, and disdain. Not once since I've started working at the dig has she ever sought me out in any way. She's always treated me like I was…well, beneath her. I don't come up to her level of existence."

"Don't take it personally," Ethan chuckled. "She treats everyone that way. If her grades hadn't been dependent on Prof. Rosenberg, she wouldn't have given him the time of day."

"I don't," Kate shook her head and shrugged her good shoulder, "and I don't care. My existence doesn't revolve around her approval. But it's just odd that now all of a sudden she's seeking me out and wanting to tell me things and get my advice."

Blake sat forward in his chair, leaning his forearms on his desk in front of him, hands fisted together. "Yeah, that's the thing. Why all of a sudden? What's her motive?"

Kate stood and walked to the window, gazing out. Instead of the parking lot, she again saw Anna sitting across from her at lunch. "She said it was because of the things I've been through, you know, nearly being shot and run down and the accident at the dig site that she met with me. It's like she thinks we're on the same level now or something."

"But you aren't." Ethan shifted one ankle over the other one. "Nothing has happened to her. She hasn't been attacked in any way. At least not that she's told you."

Kate turned around and leaned against the window sill. "No, she didn't tell me about anything like that. Only that she's afraid of Carl or Paul. She no longer trusts them."

"So she says." Blake raised a finger in the air. "I'm not convinced she's not trying to draw a red herring across the trail. We have two murders involving two members of the team that she's a part of. She's one of three prime suspects. What better way than to plant a bug in your ear, no pun intended, and get you on her side."

"True," Kate nodded, "but she seemed genuinely afraid today. Do you think she could've staged all of this on purpose?"

Blake glowered and folded his arms across his chest, leaning back in his chair, eliciting a another squeak. "You'd be surprised how easy it is for some people to put on an act, Kate, when the situation suits them. I interrogated Anna, remember? And I can't go into it, but I have reason to doubt her sincerity."

"Okay."

"Kate, why don't we get going?" Ethan stood from Blake's desk. "You completely missed that whole rest time you were supposed to get this afternoon. We've just about got time to get in a walk with Haley before I have to get you back for supper with Tasha, Lance and Ariel. Then you'll probably be ready to crash."

Kate laughed and stood from her chair. "I might just do that. It's been a…." She stopped and searched for a good word, nothing coming readily to mind. "A day. But I do want to visit with my friend, Haley."

"Then let's go." Ethan reached for the doorknob." See you around, Blake."

"Bye, Blake." Kate waved her good hand and stepped through the door while Ethan held it for her.

"Bye, guys," Blake called. "And try and stay out of trouble, huh?"

~

"Well, don't you look handsome." Kate grinned at Ethan as she and Tasha stepped up beside him. He was waiting for them by the entrance to the Shrine of the Ages looking about as uncomfortable as he could in a black suit, white shirt and burgundy tie.

"Thanks." Ethan ran a finger between his collar and his neck. "I hate wearing suits. Give me my dig clothes any day."

"Too bad you have to stay undercover," Tasha spoke in a soft voice. "I bet you look sharp in your dress NPS uniform."

"Oh, I definitely do." Ethan brushed his fingers dramatically down his lapel. Then he eyed the two women in their dress uniforms with their "Smokey-Bear" hats, dress jackets and smartly creased dress slacks as they stood beside him. "You two look rather sharp and professional."

"Thanks." Kate said.

"Yeah, thanks," Tasha's voice was low. "These togs kind of stymie the feminine side of a woman."

Kate sensed Ethan's gaze on her and before she could stop it hers was drawn up to meet it.

"Oh, I don't think you have to worry about that. Your femininity shines right through." Ethan spoke to both, but the intensity in his gaze was for her alone.

It was difficult to swallow as Kate forced her eyes forward. It was doubtful Tasha could hear Ethan's soft chuckle but she'd heard it loud and clear, and a tingle tap-danced down her spine. Hopefully the wide brim of her "Smokey" hat hid her cheeks. They sure felt warm. She reached up to run her finger around the tightened collar of her shirt, tugging the uniform dress-tie a little looser. Tasha must've tied it too tight making it seem too warm. That had to be it.

Minutes later, Blake arrived in full dress uniform and stood on the other side of Tasha.

"So, you managed to sneak away from duty, I see," Tasha chuckled.

"I figured Cassie didn't have a whole lot of folks to show up, so maybe I should," Blake shrugged.

"How thoughtful of you. Of all of you," Tasha said, a note of pride in her voice. "And look who else is here. Hi, Gage. Thanks for coming."

Gage Hampton stopped beside Blake. "Hey everybody."

Kate focused on the stone-walled entrance to the Shrine of the Ages with its curved archway. Tasha had explained that it was a multi-purpose building that was originally planned to be an interfaith chapel. Somehow that plan went awry years ago, and the building was now used for evening programs and everything from symposiums, training, festivals and office space.

One of the park service chaplains opened the front door and stepped out, signaling for them to come inside. It was time for the service to begin.

Tasha led the way and the others followed her into the stone-walled chapel where individual chairs were arranged in rows. A dais was centered at the front of the room with a podium for a speaker's use. An American and a park service flag were positioned on either side at the rear of the dais. Cassie Rosenberg sat alone on the front row. Carl Young and Anna Kelly sat two rows back beside each other. Paul Schmitz was conspicuously missing. Not good.

The troop of rangers and park police filed in and took seats. A few other people that Kate didn't recognize entered and sat down. Kate puzzled as to who they were. Perhaps folks that Cassie had meet since arriving at the Grand Canyon. She'd been here for nearly three weeks. She could have made friends and acquaintances. After all, she's an outgoing person.

The chaplain went forward and proceeded with the service. Sadly, there were no scriptures read and no message of salvation or no assurance to Cassie that she would see her father again one day. Had Prof. Rosenberg known Christ as his Savior? Kate had barely known him, but she hoped that he had. And how about Cassie? She would pray for her that if she didn't know Christ, she would one day come to know Him.

Kate watched Cassie during the service. Dressed in a highly fashionable outfit as expected, she wore a short black knit dress with leopard cuffs, collar and hem, a black wide-brimmed hat with a matching leopard band, leopard boots and a leopard stole. Though mostly somber, Cassie shed not one tear during the service. She maintained almost a bored expression.

Kate couldn't understand why Cassie had wanted a memorial service for her father if she was so bored during it. Was it for show? Did she want everyone to think she loved her father? Did she love her father? She'd come to visit him before he'd been murdered. It was a good thing she'd been able to spend time with him before his unexpected death.

The service only lasted a few minutes, and before long they were standing to leave.

Kate glanced around and noticed every eye in the place was dry. How sad that no one was really upset that Prof. Rosenberg was gone. Especially his own daughter.

~

"Ethan, darling," Cassie's words followed Ethan out the door. Without a second thought, he reached for Kate's hand and twined his fingers with hers. Her gorgeous hazel eyes looked startled as they flashed to his, but she didn't yank her hand away. He'd never grow weary of the flood of color that invaded her cheeks from his touch or when he looked at her in a particular way. Was she even aware how he affected her? Was she trying to deny it? He'd almost bet on it.

"We can't be rude, Ethan," Kate whispered, tugging him to a stop but not letting go.

Ethan groaned. "I know, but boy, I wish we could just keep walking."

Kate grinned and whispered again as Cassie approached. "It's ok. Let's just get it over with."

"Oh, Ethan, my love," Cassie stopped in front of them and started to grasp his arm then spotted their twined fingers. "Oh, my. . Ethan. I had no idea. Kate, my dear. I'm so sorry. Ethan is *your* man? And all this time I thought he was available."

"It's alright, Cassie. An easy mistake." Kate tried to gently tug her fingers from Ethan's.

"An honest mistake, Cassie." Ethan released Kate's fingers and instead wrapped her whole hand snuggly within his. "Think nothing of it."

"You both are too kind." A shrewd smile lifted the corners of Cassie's lips. "I hope you shall be very happy together."

"Thanks, Cassie." Kate coughed, cleared her throat and smiled. "And Cassie, once again, we're so sorry for your loss. Your father was a wonderful man. I thoroughly enjoyed working with him when I did."

Cassie affected a sorrowful expression, one that she hadn't worn during the service. "Thank you. I shall miss him. He was a...well... *ein gutter Vater*. A good father. At least he attempted to be some of the time. When he remembered and didn't have his nose stuck in the dirt. We didn't have much in common, and we rarely saw eye to eye, but he did tell me he loved me. Sometimes."

Cassie shifted the black clutch purse she held under her arm to her hands. "I must go. *Guten Nachmittag*. Oh, sorry. That's good afternoon."

"How long will you be staying, Cassie?" Ethan asked.

Cassie grimaced then huffed. "Unfortunately, I must remain until this silly investigation is complete. They will not let me go. They say I must stay in the area. So, I stay."

She shrugged causing her leopard stole to slip, then waggling her fingers in goodbye, she marched off on her leopard boots.

Kate tugged at her hand. "The charade is over. You've been rescued."

Ethan held on to her hand for a few seconds longer. "Oh, I

don't know. It fits pretty well, don't you think?"

~

Refusing to answer, Kate glanced around to see if anyone was watching and was relieved when Ethan let go. But was she really? Somehow the warmth of his hand felt good. It was strong and reassuring, like someone she could depend on. Something she hadn't had for a while. A long while. It drew her. But she'd let Ethan use her to thwart Cassie's attentions and it had worked. Mission accomplished.

Sometimes there was something in his eyes or his voice that indicated he might be interested in her. Little comments that he made set her heart to racing. Kate had already come to terms with the fact that Craig would be okay with her moving on. He wouldn't want her to be alone for the rest of her life. But would "the one" be Ethan? Was he who God had in mind for her?

Kate hazarded a glance at him only to find his eyes fully on her face, a question in them.

"You okay?" His voice was low and husky.

"Yeah, I'm fine." She attempted to keep her tone light and cheery.

Ethan grinned then reached into his suit slacks and pulled out several coins. He separated a penny from the others and held it up between his thumb and forefinger. "A penny for them."

Kate giggled and shook her head. "You are incorrigible, you know that?"

"So I've been told on occasion."

With a sidelong glance at Ethan, Kate took the penny from his fingers, dropped it back amongst the coins in his palm, folded his fingers over them and taking his hand, put it into his pocket.

"This one's free." Kate thought for a moment longer as a soft smile settled on her lips. She looked Ethan square in the eye. "I was...I was just thinking about Craig and how he probably wouldn't want me to be alone for the rest of my life. He wouldn't want me to be stuck in the past forever. Craig would want me to move on and be happy."

The flame that leapt into Ethan's gaze sent Kate's heartbeat into double time. She had no idea that butterflies existed in the nether regions of her abdomen until that moment, and how could the flames in Ethan's eyes make them flutter so?

Ethan nodded. "Yeah, I doubt he'd want a beautiful, caring, and special lady like you to remain alone for long. As a matter of..."

"Are you two going to stand here all day or are we leaving?" Tasha sent her voice ahead as she walked toward them. "I missed lunch altogether and I'm starved. Lance said he'd have something for us when we get back to the house. Blake and Gage already left. They had to head back to work."

Tasha paused in her dialogue and observed Kate and Ethan. "Did I interrupt something?"

"Nope," Ethan's gaze remained locked on Kate's.

"Not a thing." Kate felt like she'd been hit by an ocean wave and was trying to fight her way back to the surface.

Tasha's eyes ping-ponged between them skeptically. "Alright. Well, let's go. Come on, Kate. You're with me. Want to come eat with us, Ethan? My Lance is an amazing cook. I think he's making Italian."

"Mmmmm. One of my favorites." Ethan rubbed his stomach. "I'll be right behind you."

As Kate followed Tasha to her car, she pondered over what had just happened. Had she just given Ethan a green light to pursue her if he chose? She took a deep breath. Yeah, she had. Now she'd wait to see what his choice would be.

Chapter Eighteen

T he office has been cleared and is open for our use." Ethan explained to the team Monday morning as they gathered outside the archeologists' office. "We can head back to work. I have a question though. Has anyone heard from Paul?"

Anna and Carl both shook their heads.

"He's never stayed away this long." Carl shifted his daypack over his shoulder. "It's really unusual for him."

Anna rubbed her hands down her plaid-sleeved upper arms. "I'm worried, Dr. Wagner. What if…what if something terrible has happened to him? I'm afraid to go inside the office."

Ethan glanced at Kate then at the door of the office. It looked closed, but maybe he'd better take a closer look before the team went inside for their gear.

"You may have a point, Anna, but don't get too worked up until I take a look, ok?"

Removing a rubber glove from his backpack, he climbed the steps and checked the doorknob. It was locked. Retrieving the key from his pocket, he went inside and searched through the two-room office.

"Everything is as it should be," Ethan reassured the group. "Grab your gear and let's hit the trail. We've missed a lot of days at the dig recently due to circumstances. Let's get down there and get to work. "I'll try calling Paul again and see if I can get ahold of him. Has anyone been to his trailer?"

Anna and Paul both shook their heads as they climbed the steps and entered the office.

"Nope," Carl dropped his pack onto the office desk. "Paul

likes his privacy and never invites us over. It never occurred to me to go check on him. His trailer isn't near mine so, you know, out of sight and all that."

"Same here." Anna was digging in her backpack, adding supplies. "I'd never think to go over to Paul's trailer. If it looks anything like he dresses? Ewe."

Kate entered the office last and leaned on the edge of the desk watching as the others prepped for their day. Ethan met her gaze and smiled. He had a surprise for her today. With her sling still on for several more weeks, she thought she'd be sitting on the sidelines at the dig today, but he had a plan to get her back inside the tower.

Ethan gathered his equipment bags and, when everyone had everything they needed for the day, locked the door behind them.

Carl and Anna headed down the trail while Ethan took a minute to call Paul before he and Kate headed down.

"His phone is ringing," Ethan held his phone to his ear, "but no answer. Yeah, hi Paul. This is Dr. Wagner. When you get this message, please give me a call. We're concerned with your absence, not to mention you have work to do here at the dig. If you're at your mom's I understand that you're concerned for her, but you need to let me know where you are. Thanks, Paul. I hope everything's alright. Hope to talk with you soon. Bye."

He clicked the phone off.

"Ethan, I'm really concerned about Paul. He's been missing for five days. Anna and Carl said it's not unusual for him to take off, but even they're getting worried."

"Yeah, I know." Ethan dropped the phone into his pocket and tugged the backpack over his shoulders, settling it onto his back. "His trailer isn't too far from mine. I'll go by there after work this afternoon. I'll see if he's just skipping work and hanging around since the investigation has been going on. Maybe he lost track of the days. I know he's an avid video gamer. He may have gotten into a game and forgotten what day it is."

"Wow, that would be sad." Kate picked up a bag that she could carry over her good shoulder while Ethan carried the rest.

"Don't overdo," he ordered. "You're going to need your good hand to steady yourself on the way down."

Kate turned a skeptical glance on him as she picked her way

down the trail. "And what about you? You're carrying enough to load a pack mule. How are you going to steady yourself if you fall?"

"I've been on this trail enough that I know where to put my feet to prevent that from happening. Just promise me you'll be careful."

"Yes, dear." Kate's nasally twang teased him.

Ethan came to an immediate halt and turned to face her, causing her to run right into his chest.

"Oofff." Air huffed out of her as she smacked into him.

He dropped an equipment duffle on the trail and with his free hand gently grasped the back of her neck, tugging her toward him. Kate wasn't expecting it when his lips met hers. They were so soft and tasted of the coffee they'd shared earlier. Lingering for a few sweet moments, Ethan regretfully drew back. Was she as affected as he was? His breath had jammed in his chest during their kiss then felt like a motorized bellows as the air raced in and out of his lungs. He swallowed hard as he stepped back.

"That's what you get for teasing. Dear." Ethan's voice was husky as he grabbed the duffle and turning, headed down the trail.

~

Had her heart completely stopped? Nope, it was pumping and fast. Kate felt the blood rush to her face as it left her extremities, leaving them cold. And her lungs were working again. For a couple of minutes there she hadn't been so sure. Wow. So that's how Ethan reacted to teasing? She giggled. She just might have to tease him more often.

Mmmmm. For a short kiss it had been…completely wonderful. What would a really long one be like? No, no, don't go there.

Kate watched as Ethan's back retreated into the canyon. She'd better get her feet into gear and start moving. She glanced upward. Not a cloud to be seen in that light aqua-blue sky and the temperatures had become more spring-like. It was a gorgeous day and she was headed into a cave. What a great way to spend a beautiful day. Oh, well. At least she'd be spending it with Ethan.

~

As Anna continued working in one of the lower kivas and Carl in a pit house with only the lower half of the walls remaining,

Ethan led Kate back to the stone tower where she'd fallen. She set the bag down next to the duffels he'd hauled down the trail and looked up at the tower as if it were her nemesis.

"So, you're going to head back in today, huh?" Kate's eyes scanned the massive rock surface. "See what else you can find?"

"No, *we* are heading back in." Ethan unzipped one duffle and pulled out a motorized winch. He held it up for her to examine. "This will make it possible for you to join me."

Kate swallowed hard and shook her head. "Uuhhh, I don't know, Ethan. Maybe I should just wait out here for you. I brought along a book. I don't mind waiting."

One of Ethan's eyebrows lifted and his lips quirked. "Really? You aren't going to sit here reading when there are artifacts to be discovered, are you? Where's the adventurous Kate I've come to know and love?"

His words hit both of them at the same time. Kate observed the red tide wash upward from Ethan's tan collar toward his forehead, but he didn't drop his gaze. She did however and found it hard to breath. Or move.

Ethan chose to ignore the implications, at least for the present, and reached for the duffle, pulling out another contraption.

"Kate, look. This is a seat that you'll sit in and this is a control box." Ethan demonstrated how it worked. "You'll have it in your hand and you'll lower and raise yourself from level to level. Easy. I'll be right there with you to help if you need me."

As Kate listened, she found her breathing eased and she began to relax. Ethan's words had been just that. Words. She shook herself mentally. *Get a grip, Kate. What has love got to do with anything. It's only a figure of speech. Now pay attention. You're going to have to run this mechanism.*

"So you can do it, right?" Confidence filled Ethan's eyes and voice.

Kate nodded with a shrug of her good shoulder. "I suppose so. I'll give it a shot. But how am I going to get up the back wall?"

"The same way you're going to get down into the tower," Ethan grinned. "I'll climb up and securely mount the winch to the ceiling, then I'll come back down and help you harness into the chair. I'll climb up right beside you. I won't leave your side, okay?"

Kate nodded. "I feel like such a...a baby."

Ethan stepped closer and nestled her cheek in his warm hand. "Not in the least, sweetheart. Unfortunately, your wing has been clipped and you can't fly on your own for a while. I'm just making it possible for you to still be a part of this dig. I don't want you sitting on the sidelines, and most of all I don't want you out of my sight."

Kate dipped her gaze for a few seconds then glanced back up. "Thanks, Ethan. I appreciate your efforts more than you can know. I just hate being so helpless. It's not me, you know? I'm not used to this feeling, and I don't like it."

"I'm sure you don't. I know I wouldn't."

Was Ethan aware that his thumb was caressing Kate's cheek or was it a subconscious action? Either way, it was doing crazy things to Kate's heart rate and to the butterflies that she'd discovered lived in her stomach. They seemed to respond instantly to his touch.

"Just don't fight it when someone tries to help you," Ethan's voice grew husky. He leaned forward. Was he going to kiss her?

His lips landed on her cheek. "Friends help friends every chance they can."

Kate swallowed hard and released a breath. Friends? Kiss on the cheek? It warmed her heart and coming from Ethan she'd be happy to have both.

~

A kiss on the cheek? Really? Ethan had wanted so badly to kiss Kate's sweet lips again, but at the last second he'd chickened out and zeroed in on her soft, smooth cheek instead. He reached for the next hand hold on his way up the back cavern wall to secure the winch, angry that it wasn't Kate that had prevented the kiss but him. The last kiss had been an impulsive response to her teasing. And, oh how sweet it had been.

After Cassie's memorial service for her father, Kate had basically told him that she felt Craig would want her to move on and she was ready. But what about him? Was he ready to move on?

Lord I was wronged, and they never asked my forgiveness. They most likely never will. Can I live with that? Can I move on with life and seek another relationship with that hanging over my head?

Ethan placed his foot securely on a foothold.

Forgive them.

He reached for another handhold.

But they wronged me, Lord.

He reached higher.

Forgive them.

Ethan had read the scripture often where Peter had asked how many times he should forgive his brother if he sinned against him, so he knew this. Peter had asked if he should forgive seven times, but the Lord had told him seventy times seven. In other words, over and over.

You're right, Lord. Forgive me for not forgiving them. Forgive me for my bitterness. It's what's keeping me from moving on, isn't it? Not what they did.

Ethan had started the dig site generator before beginning his climb and had hauled the air hose and impact wrench to the top with him. He pulled the winch from his back pack and the impact wrench from his utility belt along with bolts and proceeded to secure the winch to the ceiling above the tower wall. When the dig was over, he'd ensure that all holes were filled, leaving the cave as close to how they found it as possible.

Lord, You've never withheld Your forgiveness from me. Ever. How can I do any less? I forgive Jodi and Justin, just as You've forgiven me. Thank you for what Your precious Son did for me on the cross of Calvary.

With the winch secured, Ethan repelled down the cavern wall to where Kate stood waiting and unaware of the spiritual battle he'd fought as he worked.

Kate shook her head and a smile lit her face causing his heart to race like a trip hammer. She truly was the most gorgeous woman he'd ever met, and he was thankful God had brought her into his life. Now to trust Him to work out all the details and to clear the path before them.

Ethan turned off the generator and dropped the impact wrench and air hose beside it, then approached Kate. "What? What's that smile for?"

"I'm amazed, is all. You make it look so effortless."

Ethan couldn't help the pleasure her words brought and tucked a playful thumb under his collar. "Why shucks, ma'am. You'll make me blush with them kind words."

Kate giggled. "Ethan, you're crazy."

He watched her smile fade slightly as she asked with some hesitation, "I know you've climbed a lot, but have you ever climbed El Capitan?"

Ethan didn't want to answer her, but knew he had to be honest with her. In reality his words should comfort her knowing not every climber who climbed El Capitan died.

"Yes, I have. All the way to the top."

Kate's fingers moved up to cover her mouth and she nodded. "Thank you for that, Ethan."

He reached over and squeezed her shoulder then tilted his head in the direction of the tower. "Let go exploring. Thanks to you, we have a big hole we can descend almost straight down through. At least to the, what was it? Seventh level? Let's go."

Kate chuckled. "I'm right behind you."

Chapter Nineteen

Kate found it much easier than she'd expected to control the harnessed chair ascending the outside of the tower. The chair was exceptionally light nylon and aluminum, and her arm in its sling was securely inside the framework, safe from bumps. Ethan helped her maneuver it across the top of the tower then she began her descent into its depths, Ethan right below her, leading the way.

He was right. When Kate had fallen, she'd knocked away decayed beams, opening a wider path for their descent. No wonder she'd been so sore and bruised for days and had fractured her ribs and collarbone. It's a miracle she hadn't broken more.

Fortunately, she hadn't disturbed the mummy they'd found. He still sat in his corner awaiting transport to the climate-controlled workroom for further examination. Ethan wanted to bring him out today. Before they left that level and headed further down, he laid the aluminum stretcher-like framework that he would use to haul the mummy out close to the remains. He'd attached it to his backpack with carabiners before scaling the cavern wall.

"There's your landing spot," Ethan pointed out as they arrived at the level where Kate had fallen. Debris lay scattered on the ancient wooden floor.

Kate settled her feet on the floor and halted the chair's descent, glancing upward through her full-face mold remediation respirator then shining her headlamp around the room. "Boy, does this bring back bad memories. It's amazing I didn't break more than ribs and my collarbone."

"You're telling me." Ethan's tone was dry and humorless.

"Wish I'd had that winch the day of the accident. It would've made it a lot easier getting you out of here. Come on, doesn't look like there's anything here. Let's keep moving. On to unexplored territory. Just be careful. It'll be a little trickier from here on out, but I'll be there to help you, so don't worry."

Kate grinned, not even sure he could see it in the lamp light. "I'm not worried, Ethan. You've been very solicitous so far. I doubt you're going to abandon me now."

He glanced in her direction but not directly so as not to blind her with his light. "Never."

They found nothing on the subsequent levels, but when they got to ground level, things were different. Stone "furniture" was built along the walls, some intact but most broken.

"Oh, my." Kate's headlamp beam illuminated a hole in the dirt floor.

Ethan got down on his hands and knees and with his own headlamp looked inside the hole. "I see the remains of an ancient ladder on the ground below. Guess we won't be climbing down."

Ethan preceded Kate through the hole with her following right behind.

"Who knew the ancients had basements in their condos." Kate's feet settled on the sandy surface. "The first day I came to the dig you told me most of the kivas were used for religious ceremonies. Those are larger than this one. What do you think this was used for?"

Ethan glanced around the subterranean interior with his headlamp. "This is different. From the partial strips of wood that remain affixed to the ceiling, I'd say it was some kind of root cellar. They probably hung dried herbs from those. Look at the square holes that were dug out of the walls. Like cubby holes for storing food perhaps. They're arranged all over the walls and they aren't terribly deep."

"Interesting." Kate ran her hand along the wall. "They were definitely dug out for a purpose."

"I'll snap some pictures." Ethan pulled the digital camera from his backpack and took pictures while Kate walked around.

She bent down to examine a pile of clay pots that seemed for the most part intact. They were beautifully painted with ancient tribal symbols and scenes.

"Ethan, when you have a minute come take a look at these clay pots. They're beautiful and seem to be mostly intact."

Ethan knelt beside her and snapped several pictures before putting on rubber gloves and picking up a pot to examine.

"You're right. This is beautiful. Anasazi as we've determined with the other artifacts. What amazes me is how vivid the colors are. I can only assume because it's been down here in the dark and it's so dry down here, it was preserved well."

Ethan set it aside and picked up another to examine. Altogether there were five of varying sizes, each completely intact. He lined them against the wall, and while he was setting the last in place, Kate shone her light on the area where they'd sat.

Odd. It looked like a bit of dark cloth sticking through the dirt at the base of the wall. Then she noticed a couple inches further over another bit of dark cloth. She ran her finger gently over one piece and it disintegrated.

Kate gasped. "Oh, no."

"What? What is it?" Ethan turned back, fear on his face. "Did something bite you?"

Kat shook her head with vehemence. "No, nothing like that. Look. Look closely here at the base of the wall."

She pointed to the first piece of cloth. "There was another piece of cloth sticking out here and I barely touched it. It disintegrated. I'm so sorry."

Ethan reached for his backpack and retrieved a large lighted magnifying glass. "It's ok, Kate. Just be careful and remember not to touch anything before we visually examine it next time, okay?"

"Right." Kate mentally kicked herself. Such tiny evidence of something and she'd destroyed half of it.

Ethan sprawled along the ground and got right down close to examine the piece of cloth. After several minutes, he finally leaned up on his elbows. "I'd say you have a good eye, sweetheart. And we have to dig. There's something under here."

~

With a small folding shovel that he kept for such purposes, Ethan carefully removed dirt until he reached an object, then he switched to a brush and his hand to remove more.

"What is that?" Kate pointed to black fibers that were coming away with the dirt at the same time that something gold could be seen beneath.

"I'm going to hazard a guess and say it's fibers. From cloth. The cloth has disintegrated and as I dig it's coming away with the dirt. Unfortunately, it can't be helped. If we want to find out what's underneath we don't have a choice but to continue on."

Ethan continued to brush away the dirt and fibers, revealing carved objects of gold.

"Oh, my goodness," Kate breathed in awe. "And I thought the amulet was amazing."

Ethan glanced up and through the hole above to ensure that somehow neither Carl nor Anna had managed to follow them down and was watching. As much as he wanted to discover wonderful things at this dig, a weight settled on his shoulders. If word got out about these artifacts, someone would want them. He had to protect them at all cost. So far, the amulets in the safe and in Kate's safe deposit box were both still secured.

That reminded him. They needed to move the one in her box to the safe.

Gazing back at their discovery, he continued to remove the dirt with meticulous care, unearthing more golden objects beneath.

He picked one up in his gloved hand, turning it over and over.

"What is it?" Kate's voice was barely more than a whisper.

Ethan shook his head causing his headlamp light to swivel back and forth across the golden object. "My best guess is it's not Anasazi. I'd say it's Incan gold."

"What?" Kate squeaked. "Incan? How can that be?"

Ethan weighed the object in his hand as he considered it for a few moments, then he studied the hole with the rest of the golden objects. "It's pretty obvious these items were jumbled together into a dark cloth sack. Look here."

Removing several more gold items--bowls, cups, what looked like idols etc.--he set them aside. Ethan pointed to the cloth beneath that hadn't yet been disturbed.

"See the rest of the cloth sack behind and underneath the gold items? I'd say a thief stole these items, which are probably ceremonial in nature and hid them here. Buried them in this cellar then covered them with the clay pots."

"But Incas? Weren't they in South America?"

"Yes, they were, but you have to remember that the Anasazi

were nomads. This city," Ethan waved his hand to encompass more than just the room, "may have just been a temporary dwelling."

"Really? But it looks so permanent."

"Yes, it does. We know that the Anasazi lived down around Mexico at times, too. Apparently, this tribe came in contact with the Incas at some point. Whoever stole this treasure and buried it here may have died and taken the knowledge of its existence to his grave. We'll never know. Just as we don't know if the tribe moved on or not."

"Amazing," Kate breathed in awe. "This has to be the best find at the dig yet."

"Oh, it is." Ethan pulled acid-free paper and zip bags from his backpack and proceeded to wrap the golden objects one by one, then he placed them in his backpack.

"You know, I can carry some of that weight in my lap in the chair, Ethan," Kate's tone was dry. "You still have Sir Mummy to haul out of here."

"Oh, I was thinking of letting him sit in your lap for the ride up," Ethan chuckled, enjoying the glare she cast in his direction.

They searched the subterranean chamber for any other signs of artifacts or other unusual evidence but found nothing else. Ascending to the level where the mummy sat waiting, Ethan carefully laid the ancient remains on the aluminum framework he left there earlier and securely strapped it on.

"I want you to stay here with the backpack while I escort Sir Mummy out of here." Ethan checked the straps one more time. "I don't want to risk taking the gold out and leaving it unguarded while I come back for the mummy. I'd rather take the mummy out and leave the gold here, then come back for you and the gold. It'll be easier to distract Anna and Carl with the mummy and just say nothing about the gold for now. We'll get it back to the office, inventory it, make a photo record then secure it. Later on, we'll share."

Kate nodded and saluted. "Right. I'll stand guard here at Ft. Knox while you escort him out. But don't be too long. I never told you I'm claustrophobic, right?"

Ethan's heart hitched in his chest. "Are you serious? Why didn't you say something? I would never have brought you down here? Today or before."

Kate grinned. "Gotcha. That's what you get for threatening to have Sir Mummy ride out on my lap."

Ethan stood, and being careful of her injured ribs and shoulder, in the same swift movement tugged Kate to her feet. Before she knew what he was doing, his lips were on hers in a firm kiss, his arm around her waist drawing her close.

Thankful it was his habit of turning his ball cap around backwards before donning his headlamp, it made it much easier to lean in and kiss Kate. Oh my, but her lips were sweet. What this woman did to his heart rate. Ethan deepened the kiss ever so slightly before drawing back.

He moved his headlamp sideways and gazed at Kate. Her eyes were still closed as if in a dream. The thought lifted the corners of his lips. He wouldn't mind waking up next to this gorgeous lady every morning.

Kate opened her eyes and drew in a deep breath.

"Claustrophobic, huh?" Ethan's chuckle rumbled in his chest as he gave her another quick peck on the lips then stepped back. "Ready for me to escort this ancient person to the surface?"

"Please. By all means." Kate's voice was unsteady. "I'll just stay here with the gold as you suggested."

With her one-handed help, Ethan strapped the frame to his back and over his shoulders, backpack style.

He prepared to ascend and at the last second turned to Kate and winked. "Don't go anywhere. I'll be right back."

Kate shook her head and rolled her eyes. Ethan couldn't help himself. He loved getting a rise out of her.

~

"Just leave the backpack amongst the equipment bags," Ethan's voice was low. "It looks like the caterers have come and gone but I think they left us something to eat."

"Good. I'm starved." Kate removed the harness for the chair even as her tummy rumbled giving evidence to her words. "See?"

"What did you find in the tower?" Anna's voice reached them even before she did. She'd climbed from the kiva she'd been working in and when she saw Ethan and Kate beside the stretcher with the mummy, she headed in their direction.

"Another mummy," Ethan indicated the stretcher at their feet when she joined them. "I determine it to be a couple hundred years younger than the one Prof. Rosenberg and Kate found. It was sitting on the fourth level down wrapped in cloth."

"Wow, that's great. It'll be interesting to get it back to the workroom and delve deeper into its secrets." Anna was excited but Kate could tell it wasn't over the discovery of their mummy. "But hey, I found something, too, and I want you to come take a look. You, too, Kate. I was hoping you all would've come out of the tower by now. Follow me."

Kate noticed Ethan grab the backpack and put it on his back as he followed Anna toward the kiva. She glanced at her wristwatch and guessed they'd be pushing lunch back a while longer. Her tummy rumbled in disgruntled dissatisfaction.

With no harness chair to assist her, Kate had to carefully maneuver one-handed down the pole ladder into the darkened interior of the kiva. She still wore her climbing helmet with its headlamp but found she didn't need it. Anna had set up several work lamps and was using the generator to run them as well as the winch that she and Ethan had used.

Anna stopped beside a tarp-covered hole. "I've been excavating this every chance I get between times they've shut down the dig. I haven't told anyone yet but...take a look. I discovered it about the time the professor was killed. I was afraid to say anything to anyone. I still am, sort of, but I have to share with someone and I think I can trust you two."

Anna reached to pull back the tarp. Beneath was an elongated, excavated hole where a skeleton lay buried in the dirt. Bits of skin and hair still clung to the scalp and face similar to the mummies. A few bits still clung to the arms and legs.

"As you can see some clothing covers parts of the body but not a whole lot." Excitement filled Anna's voice though she spoke just above a whisper.

"Look at this." She carefully drew back a piece of cloth that she obviously had placed over the chest herself. There lying amongst the ribs and the dirt was another amulet.

"Anna, when did you find that?" Concern filled Ethan's voice.

"Not long after the professor's death. Why?"

"Anna, we need to get that into the safe. Today." Urgency filled Ethan's voice. Did Anna recognize it? "You can't leave that where someone may come down here and take it. Just covering it with cloth won't protect it. Let's bag it and get it into the safe when we get back to the office."

"Sure. You're probably right." Anna slipped on a pair of rubber gloves and picked up the amulet while Ethan pulled out a protective paper and a bag. "I'm sorry, Dr. Wagner. From what I've studied, I believe this to be a female, and when I saw her lying there I wondered if she was perhaps an Anasazi princess or a female chieftain. I didn't want to take away her mark of leadership."

"I understand how you feel, Anna, but if it's found lying around some unscrupulous person will sell it on the black market and it's gone. For good." Ethan marked the bag then laid it in his backpack. "I'll put it in the safe when we get topside. Believe me when I say I'll make sure you get the credit for the find, ok?"

Anna swallowed hard and smiled. "Thank you, Dr. Wagner. I appreciate that."

"What's going on?" Carl's voice spoke from the darkness before he stepped into the light. "What is that?"

"Don't you recognize a skeleton when you see one?" Ethan saw genuine fear in Anna's eyes and tried to make light of the situation. "Kate and I found a mummy in the tower, but this is the first actual skeleton that's been found. What do you think?"

Carl's gaze took in first the dirty bones half revealed in the soil then roamed from one face to the next. "I think you're keeping something from me. Anna looks like a scared rabbit. What is it, Anna? What aren't you telling me?"

Kate's gaze swiveled between Anna and Carl. She looked guilty as charged while he looked angry. Did he suspect she'd found something and he wanted to know what and where so he could sell it? Was he the artifact thief? Was he also the murderer? Unease crept into Kate's middle stirring the butterflies. They didn't feel the same as when Ethan stirred them.

And what about Paul? Where in the world was he?

"I don't know what you're talking about, Carl, but I do know that you concern me lately." Anna climbed to her feet. "You're always snooping around and talking about artifacts and what they bring on the black market. Why do you do that? Are you involved in the thefts, Carl?"

Kate couldn't believe her ears. Had Anna just grown bold because she and Ethan were here with her? And if Carl was the thief, what would happen when they weren't around? Had she just placed a mark on herself? Would Carl hurt Anna?

"Anna," Ethan placed a hand on the young woman's shoulder. "Calm down. I don't think it's a good idea to question Carl like that. Take a step back and think what you're doing."

He turned to Carl then pointed into the hole. "There's nothing to see there but some old bones, Carl. Everyone's on edge because of the professor and Mike's murders. Everything's still up in the air as far as the investigations are concerned, and we have no idea about the artifact theft. Give Anna a break."

Kate watched Carl's eyes as Ethan spoke. Nothing. Not even a flinch when he mentioned the murders and the theft. Was it possible he wasn't involved? She mentally tossed her hands in the air. She gave up.

Carl released a heavy sigh and his shoulders sagged. "I'm sorry, Anna. We started with a team of six before Kate joined us. Two were murdered and one is missing. It's a little nerve wracking."

Anna nodded and rubbed her hands nervously down her pant legs. "Tell me about it. I'm sorry I accused you, Carl."

He nodded. "Understandable. You're going through the same fears and frustrations I am."

"Why don't we call it a day, folks." Ethan grabbed his backpack and slung it over his shoulders and attempted a lighter tone. "We need to get that mummy topside and inventoried. I think I'll work on him for a while when we get back. Kate, want to help me?"

"I'd love to. I've never inventoried a mummy before. I didn't get to help the professor with the last one."

"No, Paul did." Carl turned toward the pole ladder and started climbing.

Kate turned to Ethan and met his questioning gaze. She raised her eyebrows but said nothing.

Chapter Twenty

C arl stowed his gear, said goodnight then left the office first. Anna hung around until he'd gone. Ethan knew she wanted to make sure that the amulet she'd discovered was photographed, inventoried, marked as her discovery and secured in the safe.

"There you go." Ethan closed the safe door and spun the combination dial several times. "Safe and secure."

"Thanks, Dr. Wagner." Anna took a deep breath and shook her head. "I never could understand why Prof. Rosenberg wouldn't spend the money on a larger, more impregnable safe. We probably wouldn't have lost those first relics if he had."

Ethan leaned against the desk and linked his arms across his chest. "You're probably right, Anna, and it's doubtful we'll ever get them back. It's fortunate that we photographed and inventoried them. At least they're traceable."

"True." She picked up her purse and light jacket and slowly moved toward the door. "Are you sure you don't need my help with the mummy? I'll be glad to stay if you need me to."

"Nah, I think we've got it covered. I don't think we'll be here long anyway. The lunch that the caterers left for us wasn't any good by the time we got to it, so we haven't eaten anything."

Anna's face brightened as an idea came to mind. "I'll go get you something and bring it back."

Ethan met Kate's gaze and grinned. "That's thoughtful of you, but it's alright. We won't be long, Anna. We'll see you in the morning. And who knows what you might dig up tomorrow?"

A pleased smile lit Anna's face. "Yeah, who knows?"

When they heard her car engine fade into the distance, Ethan locked the office door and grabbed his backpack then headed into the climate-controlled room.

"I thought she'd never leave." Unzipping the backpack, he withdrew the zip lock bags containing the tissue-wrapped Incan gold.

"Have you noticed a change in Anna lately?" Kate carefully used her left hand to tug a rubber glove onto her right hand.

"Yep, and I'm waiting for the other shoe to drop." Ethan spread a roll of cotton batting and then clean cotton cloth across the waist-high work table then pulled on a pair of rubber gloves from a box on a shelf of supplies. "She's grown rather chummy and nice. Characteristics that are sadly foreign to Anna."

"Yeah, it kind of draws you in, you know?" Kate carefully unzipped the bags and laid them out for Ethan to work with. "I mean, was her former snobby high-mannered personality the real Anna, and this sweeter, friendlier one a ruse? Or has fear and frustration, as Carl put it, made her gentler. And for what purpose? Is she trying to throw us off her trail? She's been trying very hard to make Carl seem like the artifact thief, hasn't she?"

"She certainly has. Today she went all out." Ethan pulled the golden artifacts from the bags and laid them out on the cloth, arranging them to be photographed. He pulled a small, hardbound notebook from his backpack. "Here, log them in this inventory register. I'll tell you what to write. We'll keep it separate from the regular register that everyone sees. I started it with the amulet we found on the mummy from the tower. You'll find the entry on the first page."

When everything was photographed, inventoried, and securely locked away inside the safe, Ethan spun the dial and stepped back breathing a sigh of relief. "Come on. Let's quickly print the pictures of these artifacts"

"What are you going to do with the pictures?" Kate watched as he retrieved the camera and plugged it into the computer on the outer office desk.

Ethan sat down and pulled up the desired pictures of the golden artifacts as well as Anna's amulet.

"You do still have a safe deposit box, right?" His smile was shrewd. "Mind if we stash them there?"

Kate shrugged her good shoulder. "Not at all. And I just happen to have an amulet there that needs to be photographed, inventoried and put in this safe. How about tomorrow morning before we go down to the dig? The bank opens at eight. I'll get the bank to give you a second key."

"Sounds good. I was going to talk to you about getting the amulet from the box and moving it here. We definitely need to do that." He hit the print button and the photos began to print. He then deleted the pictures from the camera as soon as they finished printing, checking to ensure he had them all.

"As soon as we get the back room cleaned up we're going to eat. I can't wait any longer."

Kate snapped the rubber glove from her right hand and headed to the climate-controlled room to begin the cleanup. "I know. I know. Growing boys and their appetites. You just can't keep 'em fed."

~

"You cannot tell me that they aren't finding anything but mummies and bones in that archeological dig," the man's voice on the phone raised in a rage. "You will find out what they have discovered. They know that the first artifacts were stolen. They must be taking extra precautions."

"I will attempt to get the information from him. He will tell me. I'll force him to,"
the softened voice spoke with little confidence. *I must not show weakness. I must be confident and find the information he's looking for, or he will kill me.*

"He had better tell you, or you and he are dead." The phone clicked, ending the conversation.

It was hard to swallow as fear permeated every pour. *He'll kill me. I must get the information from Schmitz. He will tell me. One way or the other, he will tell me. I won't die because of him. I will find a way to get the information if I have to break every bone in his body.*

~

The next morning Ethan drove Kate to the bank where they placed the photos of the golden artifacts into the safe deposit box and removed the amulet. Then they climbed back into Ethan's pickup truck and took a circuitous route through the park to the archeologists' office, searching behind them all the way to ensure they weren't being followed. Once there, they quickly photographed the amulet, printed the photo and deleted it from the camera. When the amulet was secured in the safe with the rest of the artifacts, they hurried back to the bank to deposit the photo with the others. With that weight now off their shoulders, it was time to find out what was happening with Paul Schmitz. Ethan drove them over to the admin office to meet with Tasha.

After knocking softly and hearing Tasha's "come in," Kate entered her office followed by Ethan. "Hey, Tasha. I'm really worried about Paul. Any news?"

Tasha turned from her computer as they entered. "Hey there, you two. No, nothing. I called Mrs. Schmitz two days ago. The poor lady has cancer and isn't doing well. When I asked if Paul had been to visit, she told me that he hasn't been there in over a month. She suggested that maybe he'd gone to see a couple of college buddies where he attends at Illinois State University and gave me their names. I got hold of one of them, and he told me Paul hasn't been there. He told me the other guy is his roommate, and he hasn't seen him either."

Ethan sat on the corner of Tasha's desk while Kate dropped into the cushioned chair in front of her desk. "Well, that's not good. I was hoping his mom could give you some definite news on his whereabouts."

"Tasha, do you think he's walked away from the dig because he's involved?" Kate waved a hand helplessly. "I mean, two murders? The theft of the artifacts? With his disappearance it makes him look guilty."

"That it does, Kate, but we can't make assumptions." Tasha reached for a file folder on the side of her desk and pulled out a document. "Blake brought me a copy of Mike Pierce's coroner's report. Not a lot to go on, but one thing stood out. The caliber of the gun fired is the same as the one used to kill Prof. Rosenberg. A 9mm hollow point."

"So, we're definitely looking at the same killer." Ethan rested one elbow on a crossed arm over his chest and rubbed his chin with his fingers. "Anything else?"

"Seems someone observed their handiwork." Tasha flipped a photo around for them to see. "A longish, fine black hair was found on his shirt right in the middle of the blood stain. Someone most likely leaned over him after he was killed, and their hair fell on his shirt. That's DNA evidence."

Kate shook her head. "None of the suspects has longish, black hair. Anna's is long and blond. Carl's is brown and short. If Paul were here, his is longish and brown. This fits no one in the group."

"Could the hair have been somehow attached to Mike's shirt before he was killed?" Ethan asked.

Tasha shook her head. "Fortunately for evidence sake, no. There's blood on it, but not saturated like if it had been there when he was shot. It fell on top after he was shot.

"That means someone other than Anna, Carl or Paul killed the professor and Mike." Ethan stood, jamming his hands into his pockets. "We possibly have a professional killer on our hands."

"The operative word is possibly." Tasha slid the documents back into the folder and shoved it aside. "And we *possibly* have a professional killer after Kate."

A weight formed in Kate's chest as Tasha's words sank in. Tasha and Ethan both turned to her, concern in their eyes. The desire to flee the room and run as far and as fast as she could nearly overcame her, but Kate stayed rooted to her chair. The words that Molly Walker had once told her when she'd worked at the Great Smoky Mountains National Park filled her mind now when she needed them. That God doesn't give us "the spirit of fear but of power and of love and of a sound mind."

You brought that back to my mind didn't You, Lord? Thank you. I need Your power, Your love and certainly I need a sound mind. I need to be sharp right now to stay alive.

Chapter Twenty-One

"Are you sure it was a good idea coming without Ethan?" Kate climbed out of Tasha's car and shut the door. She'd grown so accustomed to having the tall, handsome man at her side as a bodyguard of sorts, she felt vulnerable. Placing her hand on her sidearm reassured her, but it's cold hard steel didn't replace the warmth and care that resided in Ethan's gaze every time she met his glance lately. The cold hard steel of her sidearm didn't affect the butterflies that she'd discovered resided in her middle region like the warmth of his gaze did. It was amazing how that worked. Now that she thought of it, even Craig had never gotten them to stir and flutter like Ethan did. *Why is that, Lord? Is that in Your plan somehow?*

"We'll meet him after a while." Tasha led the way along the sidewalk. "I just thought a change of scenery would do you good. The renovations out here at the Desert View Watchtower are going well, with a few hiccups of course, and will be done before long. I want to show you the paintings. They're simply beautiful."

Kate could see the Watchtower in the distance. It was a bit of a walk to get there from the parking lot. Tasha had told her all about the renovations and the difficulties she'd had with some of the contractors.

"Of all the places in the park, this is my absolute favorite," Tasha waved her arm encompassing the whole area, "and although Architect Mary Colter designed Hermit's Rest Gift Shop, I think she outdid herself with the Desert Watchtower. I just love how it rests right on the edge of the canyon and blends in with it. If you go down to the left along the canyon rim and look back to the

Watchtower, you'll see what I mean. And it looks ancient although she built it in 1932. It's how she designed it."

As they arrived at the Watchtower, Kate peered up at the cylindrical desert stone tower. "Wow, it's beautiful, Tasha."

"Well, you haven't seen anything yet, girlfriend. Wait till you see the inside. Then I'll take you around to the terrace."

Tasha reached to open the glass door just as a familiar voice called her and Kate's names.

"Tasha, Kate. What are you doing here?"

They turned to spot Cassie Rosenberg walking toward them from the parking lot where they'd just come.

"Cassie?" Kate eyed her spring costume. A short, white top trimmed with leopard over hot pink capris. Short leopard ankle boots encased her feet and a larger-than-life leopard purse hung from her shoulder. A pair of large sunglasses sat on top of her multi-layered white, hot-pink, black and neon-green hair.

"As you may remember, I work all over the park," Tasha pointed out. "And you? What are you doing at Desert View? You can tell from the posted signs and the yellow tape everywhere that it's closed for renovations. Everywhere except the terrace, that is. The public still has access to that."

"*Ja*, I know. I came down to get a few photographs from the terrace." Cassie held up an expensive digital camera then a subtle pout settled on her lips. "I am so bored with this continuing investigation, and I can't leave. I want so badly to go home to Frankfurt, but they won't let me. I noticed the two of you were on your way inside. I may never have the opportunity to visit inside the Watchtower unless you would allow me to accompany you. Will you take me with you?"

Boy was she laying it on thick. Kate watched as one of Tasha's eyebrows lowered slightly. Cassie was deliberately manipulating the situation and Tasha knew it too.

"Sure, you can come along," Tasha reached for the door handle, "but stay close to me, and don't touch anything. There are workmen inside. Don't get in their way."

A satisfied smile lit Cassie's face. "*Ja*. I will stay close to you, Tasha. Please, lead the way."

Tasha led them into a large, round low-ceilinged room with picture windows all around overlooking the Grand Canyon. This room, Tasha told them was called the kiva room. The ceiling was made of wood and the floor of huge smooth stones. A fireplace was built beneath one of the windows overlooking the canyon but in such a way so as not to detract from the view. Kate and Cassie followed Tasha up a small, narrow staircase to the second floor.

A walkway around the floor allowed visitors to closely examine the amazing Hopi Indian artwork that was painted by Indian artist Fred Kabotie. Tasha told them these paintings represented the spiritual and physical origins of Hopi life and was part of what was being restored as the original paintings had begun to deteriorate over time. Scaffolds were erected along the walls as a couple of artists worked to rejuvenate the original master's designs.

Looking to the left, Kate spotted a waist-high plastered wall barrier around a wide circular opening allowing her to see down to the kiva entrance below. Looking up, she spotted a similar opening to the third floor above, giving her a glimpse of more tribal paintings on that level.

Tasha led them to another narrow staircase to the third floor where the Indian paintings had been completed. On the fourth floor they found no paintings. Just observation windows and viewing scopes.

Returning to the kiva room, Tasha opened a side door and led them out to the terrace. "The Desert View Watchtower, in my opinion, captures the history, the time and the people of the Grand Canyon. We know of eight definite tribal nations that called the canyon home. Now, there's possibly more, right, Kate?"

Kate stopped in her tracks as her gaze met that of the bald German that had backed into her the day she and Ethan were at Bright Angel Trailhead. A smile of recognition lit his face, but it didn't reach his cold, dark eyes.

Goose flesh lifted the hair on the back of Kate's neck and ran down her spine. Why was he still here? Taking that long of a vacation at the Grand Canyon? Nodding, he tossed her a wave then turned back to the view before him, lifting his camera to snap pictures.

"What's the matter, Kate? Do you know that man?" Cassie tilted her head in his direction. "He's kind of cute, don't you think?"

"No, I don't know him." Cute? Not likely.

"Why did he wave at you then?" Tasha's eyebrow lifted in curiosity. "Looks like he knows you."

"He bumped into me the other day when Ethan and I were at Bright Angel. That's all." Heart beating faster than she could explain, Kate strolled out onto the point beyond the terrace where the view of the Watchtower and the surrounding canyon were spectacular. "Wow. Look at that view. It's amazing that you can go to different parts of the canyon and get such varying views."

Why did seeing Claus Von Richter again unsettle her so? He had the right to visit the park anywhere he wanted for as long as he wanted. It had just taken her by surprise, was all.

"Sure you're alright, Kate?" Tasha placed a hand on her arm.

Kate plastered a smile on her face, hoping it looked genuine. "Of course I am. I just can't get enough of that view. It overwhelms me every time I look at it."

"*Ja*, I know what you mean." Cassie snapped several pictures. "These colors would be beautiful in a fashion design. Not for me, mind you, but for someone, say, of your coloring. With more of the natural look, you know. I would love to design a wardrobe for you, Kate. It would be...let me think. More down to earth and practical, I think. With your natural auburn hair and peaches and cream complexion? Yes, these colors would go very well with you."

Kate eyed her skeptically. She was not the fashion designer type, and from what she'd seen of Cassie's designs, even if the colors were right, she'd be afraid of what the outcome of the garments themselves would be.

"Well, I don't know, Cassie. Thanks for thinking of me, but I'm not much for fashion."

"Oh, yes. I know this, Kate. It's very obvious." Cassie waved her hand in the air as if everyone knew this to be true. "But I could change all of that, and I would do it free of charge, darling."

Kate saw the humor in Tasha's gaze as she put a hand over the lower half of her face to stifle her grin.

"I appreciate your offer, Cassie. It's probably the most generous offer I've ever had, but I can't take you up on it. At least not right now. There's too much going on, and I just don't think now's a good time."

Cassie snapped another picture and lowered her camera.

Reaching into her purse, she retrieved a business card. "I understand, Kate. Just remember my offer. Here's my business card. Call me when life has settled down and you are ready. My only stipulation is, once the wardrobe is complete, you must model it for me on the runway. You'll be fabulous, darling. I can already picture it."

Kate couldn't. She was absolutely not runway material, and she had no plans to take Cassie up on her offer. No way.

"Well, we should be getting back." Tasha headed back along the point.

"Do you have to? Do you have a specific place to be or can I treat you both to lunch?" Cassie slid her sunglasses down on her nose. "It would be my pleasure."

They strolled back across the terrace and Kate noticed Claus was no longer there. She glanced around but didn't see him anywhere.

Tasha glanced at her watch and shrugged. "Not really. I suppose we could have lunch before we meet up with Ethan. Sure, why not?"

"Wonderful," Cassie clapped her hands together in glee. "Let's go. Just follow me, ladies. Fine dining awaits us."

~

Ethan settled Haley back inside the camper after their walk, gave her a treat which delighted her to no end and locked the door behind him. His four-footed companioned never judged him but was always glad when he made an appearance. He was glad Jill spent as much time taking care of Haley as she did, and she loved spending time with his furry girl. The teenager was definitely a godsend.

Rather than climb back into his pickup truck, he decided to walk over to Paul's trailer and knock on the door. If he was just hanging out and had lost track of time over the last several days, maybe a bang on the trailer door would rouse him.

The first thing he noticed was that Paul's old beater car was parked beside the deck. That was a good sign. Perhaps he was here after all. The trailer was a little shorter than Ethan's and a good bit older. It had been in its current location a while. The small wooden deck and the board steps that led up to it were gray with age and had spotty green moss in places. Dried brown pine needles lay scattered across it and protruded from the top of the stripped trailer awning. An old, ornate cast-iron patio chair sat beneath the awning beside a matching table, both with peeling moss-covered, white paint.

Ethan climbed the three steps to the deck and crossed to the door. Raising his hand, he knocked loudly several times hoping that if Paul was inside he'd hear, even if he had his earbuds in. Glancing at the windows for signs of life, he saw nothing. No curtains moving, no lights switched on. Nothing. Strange. Especially since his car was here. After knocking and waiting for a couple more minutes, Ethan tried the door handle and found it unlocked. Even stranger.

Ethan's gut twisted. Something definitely was off here. Tugging a rubber glove from his pocket, he slipped it on then pushed the door open a few inches. "Paul, are you here?"

No answer. A tingle on the back of Ethan's neck edged down his spine. Something didn't smell right, either. In fact, something smelled pretty bad.

With his gloved hand, he tugged the door closed and removed his cellphone from his pocket. It would be best to get Blake out here before he went any further. This was his jurisdiction, not Ethan's.

~

Blake and Ethan walked through the living room of Paul's trailer, as they began their search for what was causing the horrendous odor.

"This guy is one slob." Using the toe of his hiking boot, Blake shoved aside a pair of shoes from their path then edged forward. "How can anyone live like this?"

Furniture was piled with discarded clothes and stacks of archeology textbooks. The rickety coffee table was piled with dirty dishes and empty takeout containers. A wide screen TV and gaming system were positioned on a low cabinet on the opposite wall in front of the couch and coffee table.

"Priorities." Ethan held his nose pinched closed with his left ungloved hand and took a short breath through his mouth. "It's all in what's important to him. He's a brilliant young man with high grades. His gaming doesn't get in the way of his education, that's for sure."

In the kitchen they found the garbage can filled to capacity and a couple of filled garbage bags sitting beside it, a horrible smell emanating from them. The kitchen table was piled with a variety of books and more food containers.

Blake picked up a book and read the spine. He returned it to the pile. "I'd say his loves are reading, gaming and eating. Not necessarily in that order."

As they made their way to the one small bedroom in the back, they expected to find Paul, but he was nowhere to be found. The bed was unmade and dirty clothes were piled on the floor, emitting an odor. The tiny bathroom hadn't been cleaned in...well, hadn't been cleaned in a long time.

"Like I said, he's a slob." Blake waved an all-encompassing hand.

"And I'm going to hazard a guess that since we didn't find a body, the smell is from all the trash and rotting food." Ethan gasped in another quick breath through his mouth. "Can we get out of here?"

Blake glanced around the bedroom and nodded. "Let's take a gander as we pass back through to see if anything stands out that may give us an indication as to where he may have gone."

Ethan agreed and they headed back through the smelly trailer observing everything they could.

Once outside, Blake gasped for fresh air then asked, "Anything?"

"Yeah. There was a stain on the carpet in the living room." Ethan bent from the waist and breathed deeply as he wiped his watering eyes. He straightened and stared at Blake "It looked like dried blood to me."

"Blood?" Blake's eyebrows lifted before he nodded. "Okay, we'll process the scene and see what we find."

Ethan walked over to Paul's old beater car, Blake right behind him. It, like the trailer, was unlocked. Beneath the layer of takeout wrappers and discarded clothing, they didn't find much. Mostly archeology textbooks and notebooks with handwritten class notes.

Then Ethan noticed the keys were still in the ignition.

"Hey, take a look at this, Blake." He pointed at spattered red spots on the back of the driver's seat, the door, the steering wheel and a few faint spots on the windshield. "What do you make of that, other than that it looks like dried blood?"

"There's not enough to be the result of a gunshot wound." Blake took some rudimentary measurements then considered them again. "It's possible he was struck in the face or head then pulled from the car."

Ethan had been squatting to look at the marks, but when a thought struck him, he got up and walked back from the car to the trailer, examining the ground.

"Blake, there are drag marks from the car to the steps."

Blake followed the path Ethan indicated. "I see what you mean."

"But they aren't like the ones left by the professor. I'd say someone gripped Paul under the arms, dragging his heels in the dirt from his car to the steps, then up the steps. The dirt on his heels left marks on the steps and across the deck. I never noticed it before."

"Neither did I." Blake slapped Ethan on the shoulder. "Good eye, buddy."

"They must've taken him from his car inside, knocked him around to try and get information from him. That would explain the blood inside. Who knows if he cooperated or not or if he even knew anything. They probably took him away from here to further interrogate him for information concerning artifacts. It would be the only thing anyone would be interested in taking one of the archeologists for."

Blake shook his head in disgust. "Let's hope he's still alive. I'll get the team out here and see if we can't find some evidence that might help locate Paul."

"So, you're thinking the same thing I'm thinking. That someone's kidnapped him?" Ethan grimaced, running a hand through his hair. "And what if whoever killed the professor and Mike has Paul?"

"That would definitely complicate things." Blake released a heavy sigh.

Chapter Twenty-Two

W hat a wonderful meal that was." Cassie crumpled her napkin and dropped it beside her plate. "I love trying foods from all over the world. I've had the buffalo twice now since I've been here, and it's absolutely delicious. Too bad we do not have it in my home of Germany. Perhaps I shall have it flown in from time to time to remind me of the delightful time I shared with the wonderful rangers here at the Grand Canyon."

"I guess I always assumed that you lived in New York, Cassie." Tasha folded her napkin and dropped it by her plate as well.

"Oh, *nine*. I live in Frankfurt much of the time and travel back and forth to Paris. I have an apartment there."

"So you speak French as well?" Kate asked.

"*Oui*, but not fluently. I must say the French are *very* accommodating though." A smirk lifted a corner of her hot pink lips before she laughed suggestively.

Kate wanted to roll her eyes but gripped her ball cap in her lap and dropped her gaze instead. It was thoughtful of Cassie to take Tasha and her out to lunch, but she had spent most of the meal talking about herself and her career in fashion and modeling. If Kate could have gotten away with it she would've laid her head on the table and taken a nap. It had been that interesting to listen to.

"Well, I think Kate and I had better get back to work, Cassie." Tasha scooted her chair away from the table and stood.

Kate followed suit. Had she stood too quickly? Did she seem too eager? She hoped there would be a break in the investigation soon so Blake could wrap it up. Then Cassie could be on her way, and Kate could get back to the business of the archeological dig without looking over her shoulder every time she turned around. And whoever was left of the dig team could move on as well. Right now, life was too scary and too complicated.

Lord, please give us a break in the investigation. Please lead Blake to the culprit or culprits and help him to find the truth behind all this. Please put a hedge of protection around all of us who are innocent of evil.

"Oh, must you?" A pout formed on Cassie's lips as she slung her over-sized bag across her shoulder. "We were having such fun."

One of Tasha's eyebrows dipped in a half frown. "Sorry, but we have jobs you know. And we'd like to keep 'em. Right, Kate?"

Kate seated her ball cap on her head then nodded. "I'd like to."

"Will you allow Kate to go for just one afternoon? We girls will just...hang out, you know? Get to know each other better. Perhaps Kate can take me down the Bright Angel path. We'll take our time and not rush it, of course." The pout was joined by sweet, pleading eyes that may have worked on the majority of the men at the Grand Canyon, but Cassie hadn't counted on the fact that women didn't see that expression the same way.

Red flags went up in Kate's mind at the thought of going somewhere with Cassie alone without either Ethan or Tasha along. Yes, she still had her weapon with her, which was definitely reassuring, but she was not prepared to go anywhere with Cassie. She attempted to catch Tasha's eye, but her friend had her gaze squarely fixed on Cassie.

"I'm sorry, Cassie, but I need Kate this afternoon." Tasha settled her "Smokey-Bear" hat onto her curly head then smiled. "Thank you for a wonderful lunch. It was so thoughtful of you to bring us. You take care of yourself. Come on, Kate. We have things to do."

With an inward sigh of relief Kate smiled. "Thanks for lunch, Cassie. See you later."

"Yes, I will see you later. Perhaps we'll do something soon. I'll call you."

Kate cringed as Cassie's voice followed them out the restaurant door. *Please Lord, help Blake to find the killer soon.*

~

"Thanks for not agreeing to me going along with Cassie." Kate settled in beside Tasha in her park SUV. "Red flags were flying at the thought of not having you or Ethan around. I know I have my sidearm, but I've grown accustomed to having a bodyguard. And I'm not so sure that's a good thing. I've become dependent on others, and I don't like that feeling."

"It won't always be this way and life will get back to normal, girlfriend. Right now, it's far more important to keep you safe. When Cassie suggested that you go off with her while I go back to work? Uh uh, no way. Ethan would have my head, and rightly so."

Kate chuckled. "Did you see the look of pleading she turned on you?"

"Yeah, and if that's what she's been using to get her way around here, I can see why the men are giving in, but it doesn't work on me." Tasha snapped her fingers then returned her hand to the steering wheel.

Her phone buzzed and she reached into her shirt pocket and handed it to Kate. "Here, check it out for me since I'm driving. See who it is. I'm always worried it's the daycare about Ariel."

Kate tapped the phone screen and answered the call. "Hi, Blake. It's Kate. Tasha's driving so she handed me the phone. What's up? Okay. I'll tell her. We're on our way."

"What was that all about?" Curiosity lifted Tasha's finely-shaped eyebrows.

"Blake and Ethan have been to Paul Schmitz's trailer."

"Okay."

"Yeah. Blake asked us to meet them at his office. They have some compelling evidence."

Tasha nodded. "Well, okay then.

She pulled the SUV to the side of the road, made sure no cars were coming and flipped a U-turn. "Anything else?"

"Yeah, they found blood that's nearly a week old, and they believe that Paul's been kidnapped."

~

"Kidnapped?" Tasha leaned against the windowsill. "To what purpose? The killer has done just that previously. He or she has killed."

Ethan stopped pacing the floor and looked in her direction.

175

Ever since he'd found the blood in Paul's trailer and car, his mind had been racing to figure out how to find Paul. Where could the kidnapper have taken him? Was he still in the Grand Canyon area? And Tasha had asked the most important question of all, why had he or she taken him? He jammed his hands into his jean pockets.

"That question keeps circling around and around in my mind as well, Tasha, and the only thing I can come up with is this: the professor likely knew whoever stole the artifacts and possibly even caught them red-handed. They probably killed him to shut him up. Perhaps Mike overheard the conversation. Perhaps he overheard them talking about killing the professor and it caught up with him. They killed him. Paul helped the professor process that first mummy and well," he paused and his gaze settled on Kate. "I think it's time to tell them, Kate."

Blake moved forward in his chair, his expression curious as his eyes ping-ponged between Kate and Ethan. "Tell us what?"

Tasha straightened from the windowsill and she stepped in front of Ethan then her gaze swung to Kate. "What haven't you told us?"

Kate dragged in a deep breath and nodded. "Go ahead."

Ethan looked from Blake to Tasha and crossed his arms over his chest. "Blake's sitting down. Perhaps you should, too, Tasha."

"Just talk." Her tone was on the testy side and Ethan half grinned.

"Okay, here goes. When Prof. Rosenberg and Kate found that first mummy, not only did they find the mummy, but they found a priceless golden amulet around its neck. The professor had Kate snapping photos as he uncovered the mummy, and she took some of the amulet as well. After the other artifacts had been stolen the night before, the professor became agitated and forced Kate to take the amulet with her and hide it rather than share it with the team. The professor had the new safe installed that same day but forgot about it in all the excitement in finding the mummy and the amulet. He called her that night and asked her to bring it early the next morning to put it in the new safe. However, that's when she found him dead. She secured the amulet in a safe deposit box at the bank in Grand Canyon Village for safe keeping."

Ethan stopped his account and noticed the look of astonishment on Tasha's face. Backing up, she dropped into the chair next to Kate.

With a raised eyebrow, Blake turned a questioning eye on Kate, but Ethan held up a hand. "Oh, that's not all. Kate and I found a second mummy in the tower with a similar golden amulet around its neck. We believe each of these mummies to be former tribal chiefs possibly between two and five hundred years apart. Anna found a third body, a skeleton, possibly a female chieftain also wearing a golden amulet. The age of that one hasn't been determined yet."

"Please tell me all of the amulets have been secured either in the safe or in Kate's safe deposit box." Tasha waved her hand in front of her face like a fan.

"Oh, they're all secured in the safe," Ethan nodded.

"Hang onto your hat, Tasha. You haven't heard it all yet," Kate chuckled.

Ethan grinned. "Oh, it gets better. Kate discovered a treasure trove in the root cellar of the stone tower where she fell. From what I can figure out, someone long ago stole Incan treasure and brought it here. There was a sack full of various golden objects buried beneath the most beautiful, intact Anasazi clay pots. I estimate the age of the pots to be about eleven hundred years old. We know that the Anasazi were nomads and they roamed down along the edge of Mexico. At that time there was no delineation between Mexico and the US. The Incas were in power and someone stole their treasure. When the Anasazi moved on, the treasure came with them. At least that's what I surmise. How else would ancient Incan gold get this far north?"

"Wow, that's pretty amazing." Blake shook his head. "And what's more amazing is how you and Kate have gone to such lengths to protect the artifacts that are coming out of that dig. Are you sure that safe can't be broken into?"

Ethan grimaced. "I'm counting on the guarantee from the safe company. And so far," he knocked on the wooden desk, "either it's holding or no one's tried. I just pray it truly can't be cracked."

"So, it goes back to the night that Paul helped the professor process the first mummy," Kate said. "Do you think the killer thought they were hiding something and that Paul knows about it?"

"Yeah, possibly." Ethan turned his gaze directly on her, his heart beating like a trip hammer. She had no idea how concerned he was for her. "If they put two and two together and know that you were with the professor when you both discovered that mummy, and most likely they have, then they'll no longer be sending warnings. Paul doesn't know anything to tell them no matter what they do to him, so I'm afraid they'll be coming for you."

Chapter Twenty-Three

There are artifacts," the excited voice spoke into the phone. "They listed them off. They've found golden amulets as well as ancient Incan gold. They'll bring millions on the black market."

"How did you find this out when you couldn't before?" the querulous voice on the other end of the line snapped.

"We bugged her daypack. Kate Fleming has no idea that she's transmitting information to us. As they say, desperate times call for desperate measures."

"Get the artifacts. I don't care how you do it, and I don't care if you must kill someone. Get them!" the man yelled into the phone before clicking off.

At least he hadn't threatened to kill her this time. There was still time to redeem herself in his eyes by stealing the artifacts and turning them over to him. Her accomplice would help. Paul had said he wasn't aware of all those artifacts but was he holding out on the combination to the safe? After all, he helped Prof. Rosenberg process the first mummy when it was found. What exactly *had* they found? And surely, he'd been present when the professor had secured it in the safe. Further strong-arm tactics might persuade him to talk although he hadn't given anything away so far. Kate Fleming also knew what had been found, but one thing at a time. They already had Paul.

Then an idea formed in her mind, and she picked up her cellphone. A conversation she'd overheard from the bug in Kate's daypack.

"Hello, Mrs. Schmitz? Yes, I'm calling from the Emergency Department at the Grand Canyon Hospital. Your son, Paul's been in an accident...." She hoped Paul's mother would be too distraught to look up the fact that there wasn't a hospital at the Grand Canyon.

~

Paul had no idea how long he'd been in this tiny room but he'd give a guess that it'd been at least a week or a week and a half. It looked to be an old storage closet that he figured was in an unused building because in all the time he'd been here he hadn't heard anyone enter except his captors, whoever they were.

With no chair to sit on, Paul was forced to sit on the hard cement floor and lean against the wall. The floor wasn't wide enough for him to lay down flat to sleep, so he had to curl up in the small space, and he used an old ratty seat cushion he'd found behind a box for his pillow. Apparently, his captors hadn't known it was there, so he hid it during the day lest they take it from him. A bare light bulb that must have had a whole fifteen watts barely lit the space, but knowing the alternative was total darkness, he'd take it. His captors had fed him a few times, but nothing substantial. Rice cakes or bread and water, and certainly not three times a day. What he wouldn't give for a hot double cheeseburger and a side of fries right about now. A pepperoni pizza with extra cheese? Oh, yeah. But that kind of thinking was only self-torture, so what was the use?

In all that time, they'd kept him in the closet except when they wanted to question him, then they threw in a black hood which they demanded he place over his head. He was taken to another room that he couldn't see, questioned by someone who spoke to him, or rather screamed at him in an accented voice through a speaker, and then he was beaten by one of the captors. His left eye was swollen shut and his lips were cut open and still oozed occasionally when he forgot while he was chewing his stale rice cake. He figured his bruises had bruises, and he wondered when it would stop. He couldn't tell them what he didn't know. Would they kill him when they figured that out? The whole idiotic scenario reminded him of an espionage novel, but this was the Grand Canyon, for goodness sake, not Afghanistan or Iraq.

They questioned him about gold artifacts. Paul hadn't seen any so how could he tell them about something he hadn't seen? Leaning his head in his hands, he recalled the night that he and

Prof. Rosenberg processed the mummy after the professor and Kate Fleming found it. There hadn't been anything remarkable about the body other than it had been a really old Anasazi mummy. The professor had been excited about the find and had rambled on about it while they worked. He liked Prof. Rosenberg and had been sad when he'd been murdered, but Ethan was a good leader for the team, and he was fair.

As for the rest of the team, he didn't trust any of them, especially after the conversation with Anna and Carl concerning black market sales of artifacts. And snoopy Mike Pierce? He sure didn't trust him. Always sticking his nose where it didn't belong. What if one or more of them were in on his kidnapping? Anything was possible.

Heavy footsteps rang down the corridor outside the closet door, and Paul's stomach twisted with dread. With no windows to indicate what time of day it was, he had no idea if they were bringing him food or coming to beat him again to try and force information out of him. It was a mind game, wasn't it? The in-between waiting, not having any idea what was coming next. He hadn't had anything to eat in a while. Maybe they would give him something. Or maybe they wouldn't. It was a toss-up.

A key grated in the door lock just before it swung open and a black hood was thrown in. Heart sinking to his empty stomach, he reached for it, knowing that if he did so slowly, he'd pay for it.

Slipping it over his head, he didn't have long to wait before he was yanked to his feet by beefy hands that hauled him out of the closet and pushed him down the hallway to another room where he was shoved hard into a chair. So hard that the chair tipped over backward, smacking the back of his head against the floor.

Hands hauled Paul and the chair back into an upright position. Paul's head snapped forward, and he fought to control the dizziness and nausea that threatened to overcome him.

"We know there are gold artifacts in the safe at the archeologists' office, Mr. Schmitz," the loudspeaker voice yelled at him. "Tell us what the combination is and we will let you go."

"I've told you, I don't know anything. I'm only a second-year student. They never shared it wi...oohhff," Paul's words broke off as a fist uppercut into his jaw yanking his head up and sideways. Sharp pain reverberated through his jaw and skull. Would this never end?

"Mr. Schmitz," the voice raised in volume, "we've invited someone very special to you to visit with us. Perhaps she will help persuade you to give us the information we want. How long has it been since you've seen your mother?"

"My mother?" Paul whispered through cracked and bleeding lips. Why was she coming here? No, she shouldn't do that. She should stay home. These people would hurt her like they were hurting him. Was his brain addled from being hit so many times? They would do more to hurt her. They would kill her to get the information from him, and he had nothing to give.

Tears welled in his eyes and he felt them spill over and trail down his cheeks. Thank goodness the black hood hid them or his captors would probably torment him for that reason alone.

Pain seared through his face as a fist hit him again, only this time, everything went black.

~

"I got a call from a really distraught Mrs. Schmitz about ten minutes ago." Tasha dropped her briefcase on the kitchen counter and turned to Kate who had come in right behind her along with Ethan. "You're not going to believe this. After I finally got her calmed down enough to where I could understand her, she told me she got a phone call a little while ago from a woman here at the Grand Canyon Hospital saying her Paul was in an accident and that she should come immediately. They told her he was near death."

Kate dropped onto the bar stool by the counter. "That poor woman. No wonder she's distraught. But there's no hospital here at the Grand Canyon."

"Exactly." Tasha turned to put the coffee pot on.

Ethan propped a hip against the counter and linked his arms across his chest. "Sounds like our kidnappers are trying to lure Mrs. Schmitz here to use her for leverage to get Paul to talk. Not good but it suggests he's still alive."

"That's true. But when she doesn't show up, how long will they keep him alive? I urged her not to go anywhere, and I reassured her that Paul had not been in an accident. I called the local law enforcement in her area to take her into protective custody in case someone tries to kidnap her as well."

"You didn't tell her Paul had been kidnapped, did you?" Kate tugged at the sling, adjusting it on her neck.

"Not a chance. The poor woman has been through so much with her cancer, I didn't think that would be wise right now. Who knows what's going to happen, but for now, we'll wait. I told her someone had a poor sense of humor and had pulled a sick joke. It settled her down pretty quickly, probably because she'd talked with me before. I hope for that poor woman's sake we find Paul soon and alive."

"Yeah, that makes three of us." Ethan reached over and flicked Kate's braid over her shoulder. When her startled gaze flew to his, he gave her a long, slow wink. His eyebrow rose followed by a corner of his lips in a teasing grin. Tasha's back was still toward them while she prepared the coffee pot so there was no one to witness. Or so he thought.

"It's awfully quiet over there. What are you two up to?"

The eyebrow instantly dropped and the grin disappeared releasing a giggle from Kate.

"Absolutely nothing, Mother. What makes you think anything's going on?" Ethan's voice conveyed innocence as he rolled his eyes, eliciting another giggle from Kate.

Covering her mouth with her good hand, she knew her attempt was in vein as Tasha turned around and came back to the counter.

Both Ethan and Kate feigned innocent expressions as they gazed at Tasha. Her own gaze swept from one to the other, searching for a crack in their masks. Kate's fingers drummed softly on the counter and Tasha's gaze zeroed in on them. The fingers stilled instantly, Kate's expression never wavering.

Tasha's eyes moved back to their faces and she grinned. "Why don't you two just get married and be done with it?"

Ethan felt heat roll in a wave from the lower regions of his body--by his feet maybe? --toward the top of his head as his heart rate went into overdrive. His breathing seized up altogether. Next to him Kate was sputtering and turning all shades of red. Her gaze locked in the forward position and wouldn't move in his direction.

"Oh, you two are funny." Tasha reached for mugs and the coffee pot. "Maybe coffee will help settle you down. The fact that you're freaking out over my question says a lot, you know. If you didn't feel something for each other, you'd be laughing it off. I'm just saying."

Ethan swallowed the lump in his throat and realized that her words were true. He already knew he was in love with Kate. He just hadn't gotten around to thinking about marriage. But he'd thought about how wonderful it would be to wake up next to this woman, and the thought of waking up next to her every single day till death do us part? Yeah, that sounded pretty amazing too. Now to convince her of that.

~

Kate finished brushing her teeth and rinsed out the toothbrush. Dropping it into the cup, she stared at her reflection in the mirror but didn't really see it. Once again Tasha's words filled her mind. *"Why don't you two just get married and be done with it?"* As a matter of fact, they'd been ringing in her head over and over almost since she'd spoken them.

Remembering what had prompted the words was Ethan's actions as he flipped her braid, his long, slow wink, his flirty grin. They'd caused her heart to beat faster, her breathing to stall, her palms to grow sweaty. You know, the usual affects he had on her.

Kate flipped off the bathroom light and strode to the bed, climbing in and flipping off the bedside lamp. Settling a pillow beneath her broken shoulder for support, she fluffed the pillow beneath her head and burrowed into the bed. One good thing about coming to Tasha's to live, they'd given her a wonderful cloud-like bed to sleep in.

Once Kate had come to the realization that Craig would've wanted her to move on and be happy in another relationship, Ethan had never been far from her thoughts. And she may as well admit she was falling in love with him. She'd actually given him permission, in a round-about way, to court her if he chose. He'd seemed to be interested in her. His actions this evening would seem to indicate he still was. Would he follow through?

Lord, it's me again. I'm still sort of new at this so please bear with me. There's an awful lot going on here. We still need guidance in finding the killer. Please give us a break and lead us to them. And help us find Paul. Please keep him alive until we find him. And...is Ethan...is Ethan the one, Lord? Have You brought him into my life because You want us together? If so, then we need You to work things out. I love him, Lord. Please, in Christ's name, Thy will be done.

~

"She was not on the plane that I arranged for her to fly into Flagstaff on," she spoke in a soft voice. "My accomplice was to meet her and escort her here to the Grand Canyon."

"Then I will arrange for one of my henchmen to go to her home and bring her here," the man spoke in his raised voice. "She will be brought here one way or the other, and she will persuade her son to tell us what we wish to know."

"But of course, sir. As you wish." Her head ached from his loud voice. When this transaction was over she was moving on to other deals and would not work with this man again. His loud tones and at times yelling alone was enough to drive a person insane.

"You will await further orders until we have her in hand. Understood?"

"Absolutely, sir." She anticipated the slamming down of the phone and wasn't disappointed.

Chapter Twenty-Four

A re you alright, Anna? You don't look so good?" Kate set her daypack on the outer office desk as she and Ethan came into work Friday morning. "What's the matter?"

The other girl was sitting at the desk with her head buried in her hands but she glanced up enough for them to see her eyes which were dark-rimmed and bloodshot.

"I have a horrible headache and the thought of going down into that cavern this morning and doing any kind of work makes me nauseous. Even the skeleton princess in all her glory doesn't appeal today." She buried her face again.

Ethan stepped closer. "Is it just a headache or do you feel like you're coming down with something?"

"It's just a blasted horrible headache."

"Have you taken anything for it?" Kate zipped her daypack open. "I have something you can take if you haven't."

"I didn't have anything to take at my trailer." Anna lifted her head and held out her hand. "Yes, please. About ten of them will do."

Kate chuckled and removed a small bottle. "Let's start with two. Maybe in a few hours you can try a couple more."

As she reached back into her daypack something strange caught her eye. Something that hadn't been there before, and something that she certainly hadn't put there. Her heart froze in her chest as she feared what it might be. Elbowing Ethan to get his attention, she caught his eye and pointed at where it was attached near the bottom edge of the inside of the zipper.

Glancing at Anna to make sure her attention was elsewhere,

Ethan looked closer, a grimace settling on his features as his gaze swung back to Kate's. Placing a finger over his lips, he shook his head, indicating that she say nothing for now, then his lips formed the silent word "bug."

Kate's frozen heart dropped into the region of her stomach. A bug? Who had put it there? When had they put it there? And more importantly, what had they heard? Surely everything about the artifacts.

"Anna, perhaps you'd best return to your trailer and get some rest until your headache improves," Ethan suggested. "You're not going to get much accomplished down at the dig site in your condition."

Slowly raising her head and looking between strands of her hair, she nodded in slow motion. "You're probably right. About now all I want to do is go back to bed."

"Can you drive yourself home or do you need help?" Ethan asked.

"I have dark glasses." Anna slowly stood, picked up her purse, and slipped it onto her shoulder. "I'll make it. Thanks for the headache meds, Kate."

"I'll check on you this afternoon when we get back from the site, Anna." Kate patted her arm. "Get some rest. I hope you feel better quickly."

"Thanks."

They watched as Anna dragged herself out the door and to her car. She started it and drove away.

"Think she'll be alright?" Kate pointed at her daypack then shrugged as if to say "now what?"

Ethan stepped over to a cabinet along one wall of the office where they stored a supply of water bottles and grabbed one. "Yeah, I'm sure she'll be fine. Nothing some rest and a good sleep won't take care of."

Returning to the desk, Ethan twisted the cap off the bottle then reached inside the daypack and, grasping the bug between his fingers, dislodged it from beneath the zipper and took it out. Dropping the tiny listening device into the bottle of water, he replaced the lid and held it up for Kate to see.

"Is it safe to talk?" she whispered.

"Perfectly." Ethan jammed the bottle none too gently onto the surface of the desk. "Now that angers me. No telling how long that thing's been in your daypack nor how much information they've gleaned from conversations in Blake's office or at Tasha's. They're bound to know about the artifacts *and* the fact that we thwarted their efforts to bring Mrs. Schmitz out here."

Kate paced the floor back and forth a few times as she thought back to the conversation at Tasha's two nights before. What had she done with her daypack when she and Ethan had come in? Sometimes she dropped it on the couch, sometimes she took it to her room and sometimes she it left by the....

She spun around and pointed at the bottle of water. "Ethan, if I left my daypack by the hall tree at Tasha's, would that thing be sensitive enough to pick up our conversation in the kitchen?"

He shook his head as he considered her question, seeing where she was going with it. "Probably not, which means maybe they don't know we thwarted their plan. Yet."

"Ethan, they probably won't keep Paul alive long if they can't find his mom and bring her here to persuade him to tell them whatever it is they think he knows."

"Since they probably know about the artifacts, thanks to that thing," he pointed at the tiny device that looked a little bigger than it really was due to the distorted image caused by the water and the plastic bottle, "they most likely think Paul has the combination."

"If that's the case, then we can rule out Anna and Carl." Kate twisted her braid between her fingers as she tried to think. "They know Paul doesn't have the combination, and if they were the killers, once they discovered there were artifacts they would've gone straight for you, not Paul."

"That's a good point," Ethan agreed.

"Yes, that's a very good point, my dear Kate," a familiar voice spoke from the doorway and they both turned to find Cassie Rosenberg standing there in another fashionable spring hot pink and zebra striped dress with white sandals, her colorful hair arranged in an updo. Behind Cassie stood the German man Kate had seen twice before, Claus Von Richter. His gaze met Kate's and although a sardonic smile twisted his lips, his eyes remained dark and cold, sending a chill down Kate's back.

"It took you long enough to figure it all out. But of course, we cheated to discover the information we needed." Cassie strolled over and picked up the water bottle. "Ahhh. I see you found our little friend. Not soon enough, however. Too bad."

Cassie meandered over to Ethan's side and ran fingers down his cheek. He twisted his head away. "What's the matter, darling? We could have been such good…friends. Ahh. But I had a job to do. You were a mere distraction. A handsome distraction, but a distraction none-the-less."

She continued strolling around the room running her hand lightly over various objects then casually made her way to the safe. Cassie ran her fingers slowly over the smooth metal surface as if she were caressing it, then ran her hand down to the dial and spun it. Then laughing, she leaned her body back against the cool metal surface.

"Now that I know that you are the one with the combination, I'm sure we can…persuade you to open the safe for us, darling Ethan," Cassie crooned in a seductive voice. "I'm sure you'd be happy to do it for me, wouldn't you, darling Ethan?"

"Not on your life."

Kate noticed Ethan stood stock still. Was he carrying a weapon of any kind beneath the untucked button-down shirt he wore over his t-shirt? Or maybe on his ankle? Her .380 was in the holster on her utility belt and it was out of sight of Claus. Had Cassie spotted it? Could she draw it before he could pull whatever he was carrying?

"Then perhaps you'd open the safe for your precious Kate's life? Hmmm?" Cassie nodded at Claus.

The next several seconds flashed in a blur as Kate drew her handgun and fired at the same time Claus drew his and fired. She winged him in the upper arm, sending him backward. Ethan also drew and fired, but his shot missed because Claus had moved. Claus fired at Ethan who went down.

Kate's heart stopped in her chest then it felt like words were ripped from deep inside her. "Ethan! Nooo!"

She had no idea where he'd been hit, but after assessing the situation, she knew she had to get out of there. Was Ethan dead or alive? She had no way of knowing, but if she didn't run and get away, she would be dead in a matter of seconds too. She had to get to Blake or Tasha and get help.

Grabbing her daypack, she sprinted out the door, only to

remember that Ethan had the keys to the car. No need to head in that direction.

Cassie's words sounded behind her. "Get up, you fool. You must go after her. She will go to the gift shop and find help or catch the shuttle bus. Go. Stop her and bring her back."

With a glance over her shoulder at the office door, Kate ensured Claus hadn't come out yet. She knew heading toward the gift shop wasn't a good idea, so she took off down the steep trail toward the dig site. Hiding at the site was a bad idea because when he didn't find her at the gift shop, he'd eventually return and search for her there. Kate remembered the walkie-talkie in her daypack. Would Tasha have hers turned on? Would she be listening? It was a regular work day. Surely, she would be.

Mentally she crossed her fingers and prayed as she headed down the steep trail, afraid any minute that Claus would choose to follow the trail rather than head to the gift shop. Carl would be at the dig site already but if she went there, she would put his life at risk. If she didn't go there, maybe Claus wouldn't torture him. *Lord, please don't let him hurt Carl because of me.*

Oh, how she wished it were nighttime instead of morning. It was way too easy for Claus to see on the switchbacks below. Kate had to find someplace to hide, and unfortunately, she'd never been past the entrance to the dig site. She had no idea where she was going. Pulling out the walkie-talkie, Kate attempted to call Tasha and even tried her cell phone before she got too far into the canyon, hoping upon hope that a miracle might occur and the call would go through. Nothing.

Sobs clogged her throat and tears trailed down her cheeks as the scene in the office played over and over in her mind. Was Ethan dead? She'd lost one love. Had she lost another before it had even begun? *Let them have the artifacts but please don't let Ethan die. Please protect him, Lord.*

As Kate passed the entrance to the tunnel into the Anasazi city, she again prayed for safety for Carl but hoped that Claus would at least look for her there and give her a little more time to make her way further into the canyon. She tried the walkie-talkie again to no avail, but of course didn't bother with the cellphone. She was too far into the canyon at this point.

As she stuffed the walkie-talkie back into her daypack, she

spotted a trail map that Tasha had given her when she'd first started work at the Grand Canyon. Having simply glanced at it that day, she'd never really gotten familiar with it. Now she yanked it out and opened the tri-fold colored paper and studied it briefly while glancing back up the trail. With a little better idea where the trail led on paper, she folded it and slipped it into her shirt pocket beneath her daypack strap and began the steep descent once again. It would be a long journey around to connect with another trail leading back out of the canyon, but what choice did she have?

This is going to be all You, Lord, because I don't see a way through. I remember somewhere in the past I read in the Bible the story of how You led the children of Israel through the desert to the promised land. I'm pretty sure I'm not headed to the promised land now. It's looking pretty bleak. They were Your children and I'm Your child. Help me, Lord.

~

The walkie-talkie laying on Tasha's desk crackled to life but no words came through. Glancing curiously at it, she picked it up and depressed the call button.

"Come in, Kate. Say again. I couldn't hear you. Say again."

Tasha waited a few seconds and the crackling occurred again, but no distinguishable words. Odd. "Kate can you hear me?"

Nothing.

Reaching into a lower drawer of her desk, she withdrew some fresh batteries and, taking out the old ones from the walkie-talkie, replaced them with the new ones.

Tasha depressed the call button and tried again. "Kate, can you hear me? Come in, Kate."

Nothing. They'd have to change out Kate's batteries when she brought in her walkie-talkie later that day. It had been a while since they had.

Tasha laid the device on the desk and picked up her pen, returning to her paperwork. The Desert View Watchtower was nearly complete, but the Tusayan Ruins still had a way to go before that would be done, and there were several headaches to deal with on that project. As she buried herself in the paperwork, she forgot about the walkie-talkie until about twenty minutes later it crackled again, several times.

Grabbing it, she depressed the call button, concern growing.

"Kate is that you? Come in, Kate."

Crackle-crackle. Crackle-crackle.

"Kate, come in." Tasha reached for her daypack and car keys, continuing to call as she hurried to Blake Hunter's office at park police HQ.

Chapter Twenty-Five

E than lay on the floor of the archeologists' office, pain radiating through his side. He knew he wasn't severely wounded, but he kept his eyes closed and his ears opened.

Yes, Kate had shot Claus, but apparently not bad enough to stop him from chasing after her.

"Get up, you fool. You must go after her. She will go to the gift shop and find help or catch the shuttle bus. Go. Stop her and bring her back."

Ethan could hear the other man as he dragged himself up off the floor and as he grunted when Cassie shouted her orders at him. *Oh, Lord, don't let Kate go to the gift shop. He'll catch her there. Please keep her safe.* But if she didn't go to the gift shop or get on a shuttle, where would she go? The only alternative was into the canyon, and his heart sank at that prospect. Kate had only ever been to the dig site. She had no idea what the trail beyond was like.

Ethan waited until he heard Claus stomp out the office door, then he cracked his eyelids enough to see what was happening. Cassie stood at the door with her back to him. Silently he stood and made his way on rubber soles to her, putting his hand over her mouth to prevent her from calling out, and yanked her arms behind her back. With his foot, he pushed the door closed and moved Cassie toward a chair.

She struggled and tried to scream, her movements sending searing pain through his side. Ethan clamped his teeth together and shoved her onto the desk chair.

"Now, now, darling," he attempted to imitate her version of the word, "please don't struggle. It'll go a whole lot easier for you

193

if you don't."

Ethan reached into the desk and pulled out a roll of duct tape, securing her hands, then pulled his bandana from his pocket and tied it securely around her mouth before securing her feet with more duct tape.

Yanking his cellphone from his pocket, Ethan called Blake, giving him a quick rundown of what had just happened and where Kate most likely had gone.

"Tasha got a signal from Kate's walkie-talkie, Ethan, but no voice message," Blake explained. "It came through several times and she got worried. She only gets messages from the walkie-talkie when Kate's in the canyon. We're on our way out there now."

"Good. Send for backup. I've got someone that needs her Miranda rights read and held until she can be questioned. Cassie is one of our perpetrators, Blake. Claus Von Richter's the other, and unfortunately, he's out there looking for Kate."

~

As Kate moved further into the canyon and the sun climbed higher, it grew warmer. She hadn't brought a jacket with her and she certainly didn't need it now, but what would happen when the sun went down? May evenings were still cool and exposed to the elements, she would probably wish she had her jacket. For now, she'd just soak in the warmth and keep moving. As many times as she'd glanced up the trail and around switchbacks, she had seen no sign of Claus.

There was one advantage she had over him. She was wearing her short sleeved uniform shirt and uniform jeans and hiking boots. Claus wore his black leather pants and jacket and black turtleneck shirt. Black leather boots with slick leather soles encased his feet and wouldn't prevent him from slipping on this treacherous trail. Hopefully that would slow him down.

As she followed the trail down into the canyon, Kate pulled a bottle of water from her daypack. She always carried two, fortunately, knowing she'd be at the dig site and would need them. She could make these last. Mr. Von Richter, however, probably had none. Kate also had a supply of granola bars and nut packs. Except for the lack of a jacket she'd be fine for a while.

As the day wore on, Kate began to hope and pray that perhaps Von Richter had turned around and gone back or that he hadn't followed her down at all. She stopped to survey her surroundings and search back up the trail to see if she could spot him.

Glancing down at the laces of her boots she realized that one had come loose and she knelt to retie it. As she stood and wavered on whether to sit and take a break, a shot rang out, a bullet hitting mere inches from her shoulder and striking a boulder on the side of the trail.

Well, that answered that question. Having searched the trail, Kate hadn't been able to spot Von Richter, but he'd obviously spotted her. Putting her feet in motion, she took off down the trail, running where she could and shuffling her feet as fast as possible where she couldn't run. Keeping as low a profile as possible, she kept moving, not daring to stop again. *Lord, help me!* her heart continually cried out over and over.

~

Ethan watched as two park police officers led Cassie to a vehicle and put her inside. His gut churned knowing that woman had put Kate in danger and she was out there somewhere now being chased by a killer. He needed to get out there and find her.

"Ethan, please come over here and sit down." Tasha placed a gentle hand on his arm and scolded him, a grin lifting the corners of her full lips to soften her words. "Would you please let this EMT take a look at your side?"

"Tasha, I need to get out on that trail and find Kate. That madman is following her and she has no idea where she's going. She's never been further than the dig site tunnel entrance." Did his voice sound as agonized to Tasha as it did to him? His heart was a stone in his chest. Helplessness churned in his gut. Every second he stayed here was a second longer that madman had to find Kate. Ethan had to get to her.

"Ethan, listen to me, sweetie, if you don't let this man treat you before you go, you're going to have some major issues out on that trail. Just let him patch you up. Nobody faults you for wanting to go and nobody's going to stop you. Matter of fact, Blake's gearing up to go with you. But let this man check out your side first."

Ethan grunted and huffed out a heavy breath of air, then allowed her to lead him to the desk where, a short while earlier, he'd tied Cassie up to subdue her till Blake had arrived with reinforcements. "Fine but make it fast."

"Now, now, don't be rude." Tasha pointed a finger at him. "Let the man do his job and do it right."

Ethan eyed the EMT with a raised eyebrow. "Fine. Make it fast. *Please*."

The EMT chuckled. "This lady must be something special."

"Yeah. Yeah, she is." Ethan grimaced and grunted as the EMT prodded and probed.

"Then I'll be as quick as I can. I know she's got a killer after her." The EMT pulled out a hypodermic needle. "I don't see evidence of a bullet lodged in there. Looks like it went clean through, and it's just in the muscle. Missed the organs by a mile. I'm going to give you an antibiotic and wrap you up, but when you get back, you need to go to urgent care. Got that?"

"Got it."

"I'm pretty sure these will help too." He handed Ethan a few low dosage pain killers. "At least until urgent care can do better. Take them with you. The pounding of hiking on the trail will be noticeable if you don't."

Ethan barely waited for him to finish wrapping his side before he grabbed supplies and ensured his handgun was loaded and holstered and extra magazines were in place.

Blake had exchanged his uniform shoes for hiking boots and had grabbed a daypack from his patrol car.

"Ready to go?" Ethan headed toward the door. "If not, catch up with me."

"I'm right behind you," Blake chuckled.

"Be careful, fellas," Tasha called. "And bring our girl back."

"Count on it," Ethan called as he rushed down the steps. "There's *no* other option."

~

Gritting his teeth as he pounded down the trail, Ethan felt pain shooting through his side, just as the EMT had suggested it would. Without stopping, he pulled a bottle of water from his pack and took one of the pills he'd been given.

"Hurting pretty bad, huh?" Blake spoke from just behind him.

"Unfortunately."

"You must love her a lot."

"Who?"

"Really? You're going to play coy?" Blake chuckled. "You know I'm talking about Kate. This is me, Ethan. You can talk to me you know."

"What makes you think I'm in love with her?" Ethan doubted his attempt to keep his voice even had fooled Blake.

Blake laughed outright. "Well, let me see. You mean like how you couldn't wait to get out of the office fast enough to get down this trail to her? Even to the point of bleeding to death yourself? Not very smart, my friend. Then there's how you look at her *every* time you look at her. You know, like you can't look at her enough. Like how you can't keep your eyes off of her? Believe me, I get it. She's gorgeous. When I first met her, I was attracted to her, too, then I saw how you were attracted to her, and I backed off. I figured you were with her all the time, you know? I didn't stand a chance. And it's ok, because I really think she's attracted to you, too. No, I think it's more than just attraction. I think you two are in love, and I'm happy for you both."

Ethan stopped and turned to Blake. "Thanks. I appreciate that, man. There'll be someone special out there for you one day. God will bring her into your life when He's ready. Now, shut up and let's go find Kate."

~

The steepness of the trail never varied and at times Kate found she had to climb over boulders to continue on. It was a treacherous descent to say the least, and the fact that Claus was pursuing her prodded her on. What gave her a certain amount of pleasure was knowing that he was dealing with the same difficulties she was. Perhaps more. She'd seen the shoes he wore and they weren't adapted to this terrain. He must be experiencing problems with sliding on the steep, sand and pebble trail where her hiking boots gripped and supported her ankles. Thank the Lord for that. No matter how many times she'd glanced back trying to spot him, she hadn't been able to. But he had the advantage of being higher and looking down into the canyon. She just had to keep moving.

Beneath the long, wide rim of a huge layer of red rocks, the trail passed right in front of an old open-faced shack, it's shake roof covering rock walls that nearly blended with the canyon walls that spread in either direction. A water trough stood beside the building, a sign above it read Santa Maria's Spring. According to the map, it was a natural spring that ran year round.

Inside the tiny rock building, a chair beckoned her to sit and rest a while. As much as she longed to do just that, she pulled her bottle of water from the side of her daypack, took a few sips and moved past the tempting little shack and its welcoming chair.

Kate surveyed the canyon scenery before her. Even from this lower perspective below the rim, there was still a spectacular view. To sit in the little building in the chair in the shade and soak in this panoramic scene would be balm for her soul. But unfortunately, she couldn't afford to do that. Moving forward, she headed on down the trail, leaving the idyllic spot behind.

Doubtless Claus, too, would pass it up. With any luck he'd stop for a drink of water since he probably didn't bring any along. Cassie had sent him on the chase unprepared. Not smart. He was probably getting pretty thirsty by now. Perhaps some tiny parasites like giardia would slow him down. They lived in water like that, hence the need to treat it. Kate knew better than to drink water from natural sources without treating it first, but would Claus know that?

Glancing at the map and back toward the rim of the canyon, Kate realized she'd dropped nearly two-thousand feet in the two and half miles since she'd begun her descent, and her feet and calves were feeling every bit of it.

Ethan had once told her this trail had been *the* tourist attraction in the early twentieth century. Named after a man who lived alone but who was really quite social in the south rim community, the trail was actually hand paved with stones to accommodate guests to the luxury Hermit's Camp near Hermit's Creek that was built in 1911. A tramway was built from the canyon rim to Hermit's Camp, and an automobile was available to run around the camp. A Fred Harvey chef of the Santa Fe Railroad provided superb meals for the guests. Ethan explained that the camp operated for two decades before it closed and the canyon reclaimed it.

Kate had spotted sections of the paved trail, but for the most part it had fallen into disrepair and broken apart, its stones separated and moved with time. When man moved out, nature had taken over, erasing the evidence that he'd been here.

A shot rang out and Kate heard the echo through the canyon just before searing pain hit her in the side of her thigh.

~

"That's the second shot we've heard, Blake." Ethan scrambled over a boulder and slid down the trail on the other side.

"Then at least you know he didn't get her on the first shot." Blake followed him over the boulder.

"Yeah, well what about this one? That's not reassuring reasoning, buddy."

"Ethan, I can't say that I've ever really thought much about God. I wasn't raised in church like you once told me you were. But, man, I know you have faith. Where is it now? Aren't you supposed to be trusting the God you believe in?"

The emotions that fought for control in Ethan were like a wave that threatened to wash over and drown him. *Lord, help me. Blake's right. Where is my faith right now? I'm filled with anger, worry, doubt, fear. All the things that You tell us to give over to You. Help me to focus on You and remember that Kate's Your child. You know exactly where she is right now. Please keep her safe from that madman.*

"You are so right, Blake." Ethan attempted to control his breathing as he painfully scrambled over another boulder and attempted to move faster down the treacherous trail. "I'm sorry."

"Hey, I get it," Blake gasped for air. "You're in love with her. I know you're worried. Kate's a believer, too, isn't she?"

"Yeah, she is. She's been through a lot, but her faith is growing."

"I've seen a change in her since I first met her. She's right for you, man." Blake slipped on the trail then righted himself.

"You okay?" Ethan turned to check on him.

Blake waved him on. "I'm good. Don't stop. Maybe when all this is over we can sit down, and you can tell me more about this whole God thing. Not saying I'll do anything about it, but I'd at least be open to hearing about it."

Ethan grinned, his heart leaping with joy. *Lord, please prepare his heart and open his eyes to Your love and what Christ did for him on the cross. And help me to be the testimony he needs.*

"You got it, man. As soon as all this is settled."

"Think we're gaining on him?" Blake huffed.

"From your mouth to God's ears, as they say." Ethan took advantage of a straight ten-foot slide and rode it down rather than stepping carefully. Whatever risks he had to take to get to Kate, he would gladly take. He tamped down the emotions that threatened to resurface and again handed them over to the Lord. Kate was in better hands than his and he needed to leave her there.

~

As pain seared through her thigh, Kate stumbled and fell down the steep incline to the next switchback. Was Claus right behind her? Jamming her feet against a boulder at the edge of the trail to stop her momentum, she groaned at the pain throbbing in her thigh, picked herself up then stumbled on. She bit off the cry that threatened to escape from her lips. She couldn't afford to slow down even if she was injured. As she hobbled down the trail, she examined the wound as best she could. She was bleeding a lot but she couldn't stop now. She'd have to assess the damage later and hope she didn't bleed out in the meantime.

Glancing over her shoulder up the trail, she still couldn't spot Von Richter. As steep and unrelenting as the trail was, she couldn't afford to slow down. The switchbacks seemed endless through this section. According to the trail map this was the Cathedral Stairs. Something less pious and more sadistic would have been a better name. The Trail to Hades, perhaps? Kate couldn't imagine what this would be like in August. Of course, had a killer not been chasing her and she wasn't running for her life, perhaps things would be different. Under normal circumstances she would've stopped and taken advantage of the tiny rest house and enjoyed the scenery and the various animals she'd glimpsed since this trek had begun.

Several times she glanced up the trail trying to catch a glimpse of Claus but never could. Where was he? He'd fired on her twice. She'd seen his gun back at the office. It was a 9mm automatic which meant he had a magazine with the capacity of up to ten bullets. And who knew how many more mags he had in his pockets. He could shoot at her all day long until he picked her off. Yeah, she had an automatic, too, with two extra mags, but if she couldn't see him, they did her no good.

A 9mm? Was he the one that had killed Prof. Rosenberg and Mike Pierce? Great. And he was taking pot shots at her and had hit her. Glancing down at her thigh, she spotted the blood seeping down her pant leg. She wouldn't be able to keep this up for long without binding it up first. She had to stop soon.

Keeping an eye on the movement of the sun, Kate continued to pray that Ethan hadn't been seriously hurt and had been able to get help. But what if he had been seriously hurt? Or worse? What if he'd been killed? What if Claus had killed him? That thought had stuck in her mind. She hadn't been able to get out on the walkie-talkie, and she was headed deeper and deeper into the canyon with no one knowing where she was.

Kate shook her head. Trust in the Lord and lean not on your own understanding. Wasn't that the Proverb she'd read just that morning? Amazing how God had known she'd need those verses today. A heavy sigh escaped her as she kept plodding one exhausted foot in front of the other. She wanted nothing more than to be back safe and sound at Tasha's, but the dry and dusty trail spread forward beneath her feet. *Lord, help me.*

The throbbing in Kate's thigh increased, forcing her to stop. She had only a precious few minutes to treat the wound. Spotting an overhanging rock on the side of the trail fifty feet below, she stumbled on. It afforded a little shade and she dropped to her knees beneath it, facing back up the trail so she could keep a watch for Von Richter. Pulling her sidearm from its holster, she laid it on a rock within easy reach then yanked out her first aid kit. Pulling a pair of sharp scissors from the kit, she cut her pant leg. Thank goodness the scissors were in the kit. With her left arm still in the sling, it would've been impossible to tear the fabric one handed.

Gritting her teeth, she cleaned the wound as best she could then applied antibiotic ointment and covered it with a compression bandage, the bullet still inside. Nothing she could do about that now. Tossing the supplies back into the daypack and grabbing her gun, she awkwardly climbed to her feet and ran down the trail to make up for lost time. Pain flashed through her leg like a lightning bolt, but she couldn't stop.

The sun no longer hung overhead but had shifted toward the western rim of the canyon. Kate could spend the night in the canyon with no problem except for one concern. She had no jacket. Not even one of those little silver space blankets for emergency use. She'd planned to get one for her daypack, but just hadn't gotten around to it yet. There was an emergency fire starter in there, but she certainly couldn't use that. A fire would lead Claus right to her.

It would be a long, cold night, but Kate had to make it. She had to. There was no alternative. She wouldn't give up, either to Claus or to the cold. Somehow, she had to find a place to allow Claus to get past her so she could head back up the trail and find out if Ethan was still alive. Cassie had to be stopped and Claus had to be caught. And Paul? He had to be found. Was he even still alive?

As she continued to descend further into the canyon, she searched for a hiding place. Somewhere Claus wouldn't discover. Somewhere he would pass by and she could head back up the trail.

Kate's heart sank as nothing presented itself. Oh, for another hidden tunnel like the dig site. *Lord, it's just You and me, remember? I need some help here. A place to hide. Something. Please!*

~

As Ethan and Blake trekked further into the canyon at a breakneck speed that would have worried their mothers had they known, they said very little. Ethan spent much of his time in prayer as he raced down the trail. The knowledge that they hadn't met Claus Von Richter on his way back out of the canyon reassured Ethan that Kate was still alive. The second shot that was fired hadn't taken her out. The less reassuring thing was that Claus was still chasing her.

Never in his life would Ethan have thought he could've descended this trail at such a breakneck speed, but he attributed that to God's protection. Ethan had to reach Kate and he'd risk everything to do it. She had to be moving at a pretty good clip herself although she'd gotten a good jump on Claus. He and Blake weren't too far behind the German.

The sun had moved toward the western rim of the canyon. He looked at his wristwatch. Six-thirty. Ethan sucked in a heavy gasp of air making his side ache. They might be spending the night on this search. Would Kate hole up somewhere or would she try to keep moving? It would be nearly impossible without a light, and a light would give away her position. She'd know that, and Kate would never give away her position. If at all possible, she'd find a place to hole up for the night. But that was the question. Would she find a place before Claus Von Richter found her?

~

Tugging out her bottle of tepid water, Kate took a swig. But not too much. Just enough to quench her parched mouth and throat. Between the gunshot wound and her collar bone her whole being hurt. Praise God her ribs were down to a dull ache. It didn't hurt to breath as much anymore. If it had, this whole journey into the canyon would've been much worse.

Her head ached and she blinked. Did the scenery look a bit blurry? She blinked again. Uh, yeah, it did. Not good. Kate glanced at the position of the sun. It had disappeared behind the canyon rim and the temperature had already dropped several degrees.

As she kept moving, Kate tugged the trail map from her pocket to see what the next landmark or feature was. It wouldn't be long till the landscape changed and rather than the trail dropping into the canyon, it would begin to traverse across a plain of sorts, dropping occasionally into cracks and crevices as it headed toward Hermit's Creek and then on to the Colorado River several miles away. Kate would become a sitting duck out on that plain, and she certainly couldn't cross it after dark with a flashlight. She had to find a place to hide and soon.

Lord, I read recently in Your Word where You protected the three Hebrew men when they were thrown into the fiery furnace. You even went into the fire to protect them. Can You please provide a spot for me like that? To get me through the night?

~

"Kate's going to have to hole up soon, Ethan," Blake gasped, pointing at the fading light. "And so are we. It's going to be too dangerous to keep moving on this trail."

"I'm not stopping, Blake. Not till I stop Von Richter and know that Kate's safe." Ethan's heart beat like a jackhammer in his chest, half from exertion from treading as fast as he possibly could down the dangerous trail, but also from the knowledge that a madman was out to kill the woman he loved.

Blake's heavy sigh sounded behind him. "Buddy, you're either going to get us both killed or not, but I can't let you go it alone. I'd hate to find you over a cliff tomorrow morning. At least if I stick with you, I can report back exactly what happened."

"Thanks." Ethan's tone was dry.

"All kidding aside, there's going to come a point where Kate's going to become a sitting duck, you know."

"What do you mean?" Ethan's breathing hitched at the words.

"As long as she stays amongst the switchbacks and descending trail, Kate's the safest. Once she reaches the place where the trail crosses the plain toward the Hermit's Creek, she'll be more out in the open. Von Richter will be able to pick her off without a problem."

Ethan sucked in a breath of air and surged forward, determined to get to her. Glancing skyward, he knew the odds were against him. But His God was a mighty God, and the odds were in His favor. Always.

Chapter Twenty-Six

W as the cavern with the Anasazi city the only cavern in these maze-like canyons? After taking two Tylenol earlier, Kate's head still pounded and her vision had grown blurrier. Was that a side effect of the headache? It had to be. Her shoulder and gunshot wound were almost unbearable. Plopping one foot in front of the other, she somehow kept moving forward. *God are You still there? Can You hear me? Please help me!*

Kate stumbled and nearly fell, but she reached out a hand and caught herself on a boulder along the side of the trail causing her daypack to slip down her good arm. The unexpected motion jarred her, sending a jolt through her shoulders. A cry slipped from her before she bit her lip to silence the noise. Gasping through the pain, she clamped her teeth together. Kate couldn't afford for any sound to reach Von Richter and help him pinpoint her location.

The sun had long disappeared behind the western canyon rim and light was fading fast. Kate caught a glimpse of a group of large boulders several feel off the trail a hundred yards or so ahead. Was it possible there was an opening to crawl into? Would there be snakes inside? Kate cringed at the thought. She'd have to use her flashlight to check it out. It had a red lens that would prevent it from being seen at a distance. She didn't have a choice. Better that than bed down with a diamondback rattlesnake or worse yet, a family of them.

Stumbling onward, Kate reached the boulders and tugged her flashlight from her daypack. When she pulled it out, the clip on the side caught on something. A roll of brown paracord? Wow, she'd forgot she had that in there. An idea popped into her head. What if she set a trap for Von Richter? She could put an end to this now. But how would she get him out of here? She would worry about that later. Trap him and run.

Glancing back up the trail, she searched for Von Richter but it was difficult to spot any movement in the growing darkness. Everything blended together. Her blurry vision from the pounding headache simply made matters worse.

Kate remembered that she'd passed a group of large rocks and boulders that covered half the trail about twenty feet back up the way she'd come. Several Utah juniper saplings grew along the trail on either side throughout this area. As quickly as she could, she made her way back up the path. She had no choice but to slip her left arm from the sling. She needed both hands to tie the end of the paracord to one of the saplings about five inches above the ground, but her hands were shaking from…what? Pain, exhaustion, fear that Von Richter would come down the trail any minute and find her here?

Kate stopped, flexed her fingers, and forced herself to slow down and tie the cord into a strong double knot around the sapling. If only her head weren't pounding so, causing her vision to blur. She had to do most of it by feel because the darkness was closing in. That actually worked to her advantage in hiding her from Von Richter but made it hard for her to see what she was doing.

When one end of the paracord was secure, she unwound more and stretched it taught across the trail behind the boulder and rocks to another sapling where she struggled to tie it securely. Von Richter would have to go around the boulder that hid the cord, and when he did, he'd trip on it and fall. When the cord was secured to the second sapling, Kate cut the extra cord and stuck it in her pocket. She had handcuffs for his wrists but would need the rest of the cord to tie Von Richter's feet.

Hurrying back to the boulder formation she'd scoped out as her hiding place, Kate stepped carefully off the trail and maneuvered around to the side where a depression of sorts was large enough for her to sit and lean back. She would be well hidden here, and she would be able to hear when Claus hopefully tripped on the cord. Kate would have to move quickly to get a jump on him, but she would keep Ethan's face before her. Claus Von

Richter had shot Ethan, and whether or not he was dead or alive, Kate was going to stop this evil man.

An exhausted sigh escaped from Kate. She was so ready for this to be over. Goose flesh raised on her arms as the temps continued to drop. Flipping the red lens into place on the flashlight, she positioned the hood around the light before turning it on to prevent it from being seen at a distance. Flicking on the switch, she held the red light on the depressed rock area beside the boulders only long enough to search for unwanted residents then turned it off. With it on the opposite side from Von Richter's position, he wouldn't have been able to see the faint red light.

Breathing a sigh of relief that she wouldn't have to evict any rattlesnakes, Kate removed her daypack and sat down on the flat rock away from the trail and leaned back. She stretched out her injured leg, slipped her gun from its holster, and held it in her hand, prepared to fire then listened for Von Richter's approach.

Lord, I have no idea what to do next. I don't know how I'm going to get up quick enough with this injured leg to take him down. I need Your intervention. Please, help me. And help that tripwire to take him down.

~

A tingle ran down Kate's spine moments later at a sound somewhere up the trail. Pebbles skittered against rocks. Was that an animal? Or Von Richter? Kate listened as the sound changed and grew louder, coming closer. The sandy ground scraping beneath hard, smooth-soled shoes froze her heartbeat. Her stomach clenched as the hair raised on the back of her neck. She dared not breathe lest Claus Von Richter should hear her. She knew it was him. Who else would it be? *Lord, help me!* Every nerve ending in her body was instantly alert even as she remained still, afraid to move.

His steps advanced steadily down the trail, kicking pebbles as he approached. Claus slipped, his smooth soles grinding against the ground and eliciting what Kate assumed was a curse in German, before he grunted, caught himself and stopped.

His footsteps started down the trail again. He had to be getting close to the paracord trip wire. *Please, Lord. Stun him or disable him or something long enough for me to get to him, cuff and tie him up.*

As Kate waited, her lungs began to pant like a freight train, and she forced herself to breathe in deeply, slowly. She had to take this guy down. It was him or her. And at this point, she had the upper hand, so *he* was going down.

Kate heard a yell followed by rocks sliding and a thud, then silence. Pushing to her feet as quickly as she could, and with her gun in one hand and the flashlight, minus the red lens, gripped just beneath it in the other, Kate lit up the trail and hurried to where she'd laid the trap for Von Richter. There he lay, face down on the sandy trail, his hands out to his sides. His gun lay a couple feet from his right hand, and Kate made a beeline for it, kicking it where she could find it later but where he couldn't reach it when he came to. She observed him from a short distance. That is if he were truly out.

Claus faced away from Kate, and even though he lay still, she wasn't convinced he was knocked out. She had a pair of handcuffs on her utility belt and if she approached him to cuff him, he might overpower her. It would be easy to do since she was injured and in a sling.

Kate approached his feet and kicked one. "Von Richter, get up. I know you're awake. Get up now."

Von Richter didn't move.

Kate remembered she'd shot him in the shoulder earlier that morning, so she moved to his side and nudged his injured shoulder with her foot.

Von Richter roared in pain and, flipping over, grabbed Kate's leg, dragging her to the ground. Kate's gun slipped from her fingers just as she fired off a round. Where did it go? The flashlight dropped a few feet away, lighting up Von Richter's face and highlighting the angular plains marred by bloody cuts and scrapes from his fall and by rage.

Kate banged her head on the ground, sending jarring pain through her skull. It only added to the headache she already possessed, but the flashing lights before her vision were new.

Von Richter's hands clamped around Kate's throat, his thumbs slowly pressing against her windpipe. It quickly became hard to breathe no matter how much she tried to suck in air. The evil smirk on his face began to waver before her eyes in the faint light from the flashlight. The pounding in her head increased by the second.

The gun had been in her hands just seconds ago. Where was it? There was no point in pulling at his arms. He was too strong for her. If she couldn't find the gun, then.... no, don't...give...up...yet.

The pressure on her throat put pressure on her fractured shoulder causing great pain. She wanted to scream, but she couldn't. There was no air to breathe, much less scream.

With her right hand, Kate searched along the ground. Von Richter seemed too intent on strangling her to notice or else he couldn't see her hand in the darkness. She reached as far and wide as she could until... was that it? Her fingers touch something. There. Yes, she had...something...something with...angles?

Kate's vision clouded and swam before her as the pressure on her throat increased. She couldn't breathe. Mere seconds was all she had as blackness threatened to draw her in. Grabbing the rock and yanking it up with every bit of energy left in her being, she smashed it into the side of Von Richter's head and the evil smirk on his face changed to confusion. Yanking it up a second time, she smashed it again, then a third time before he slumped forward on top of her.

His fingers eased from her throat opening her airway so that she gasped for air, but his weight on her chest was nearly as bad. Taking short, panting breaths, Kate was able to draw in breath as she attempted to shove Von Richter's body off of her. It took a monumental effort with her right arm to push him across her fractured shoulder.

Kate lay there staring at the myriad of stars gleaming in the ink-blue sky overhead as she breathed deeply the cool night air.

"Thank you, Lord. I'm alive," she rasped loudly, limp with relief, pain and exhaustion. "I'm alive."

~

Ethan and Blake heard a gunshot on the trail not too far ahead and within minutes spotted a white light. The scene they found was truly remarkable. Kate lay on the cold desert floor, her eyes closed, sending Ethan's heart into a panic. *Please, dear God, don't let her be dead.* Laying right beside her, face down on the ground, his legs across Kate's, lay Claus Von Richter, dead and bleeding from a head wound, never to harm another person.

Ethan hurried to Kate's side, touching her face and arms. He looked at the blood covering the front of her uniform. "Kate, sweetheart. Kate, can you hear me?"

Kate's eyes fluttered opened "I can hear you."

Her faint voice was rough as sandpaper.

"Darling, what happened here? Are you shot?"

Kate tried to swallow then shook her head before whispering. "No, but I need water."

Ethan pulled a bottle of water from his daypack then, after shoving Von Richter from Kate's lower body, he lifted her into his arms, resting her back against his chest and shoulder. "Here you go. Drink this."

Kate drank slowly, pain etching her face.

Blake rolled Von Richter over and examined the body. "Well, I don't think he's going to be bothering anyone anymore."

Kate shook her head.

"What happened, Kate. Can you tell us?" Ethan gently swiped the hair from her face, tucking it behind her ear.

Kate nodded. "I'll whisper. I set a tripwire trap. When he fell, he pretended to be knocked out. I kicked his gun into the underbrush, then I kicked his shoulder where I shot him this morning and he got mad. I was trying to get him up to cuff him. Not smart on my part."

Kate coughed then continued. "He dragged me to the ground and started to strangle me. Slowly, torturing me. I guess he was enjoying it and wasn't paying attention to my right hand. I was feeling around for my gun but I only had seconds before I passed out and grabbed the first thing my hand touched. A good-sized rock."

Ethan wrapped her tenderly in his arms. "Thank God you did."

"Blake, shine your light this way." When Blake accommodated him, Ethan tipped up Kate's chin, taking in the already bruising skin around her neck. Anger filled him at what Von Richter had put this precious woman through. Glancing down at her thigh, he noticed the compression bandage that was covered with blood. "Kate, what happened to your leg?"

"Von Richter shot me." Kate leaned her head sideways against his chest. "The bullet's still in there. I barely had time to bandage it. I had to keep moving. When he shot me, it was a while before I could stop. When I did, it was a quick patch job then I had to run."

Anger welled within Ethan. Von Richter had shot Kate after all. She'd have to be medevac'd out by helicopter and taken to the hospital in Flagstaff where the bullet would be removed. There was no way she could walk out of the canyon.

Using a much stronger powered radio than Kate had, Blake arranged for a rescue helicopter. After the transmission was completed, he clipped the device back onto his belt and squatted beside Ethan and Kate. "They're on the way. There's no place to set down anywhere near here, so they'll have to hover over this area and extract us from above."

Ethan nodded. "Understood."

Kate's head lolled against his chest and he looked down to see she'd dozed off. Grinning, he hugged her closer to him. He'd let her catch a few z's until the chopper arrived. She was exhausted. His side ached from where Von Richter had shot him that morning, and he was glad Kate wasn't leaning on that side. But even if she were, he'd grin and bear it for her sake.

Ethan dropped a kiss on the top of her hair.

"Mmmm," Kate murmured as she stirred slightly. "Ethan?"

"I'm here, sweetheart."

"I'm glad." Her voice was barely more than a whisper then she dropped off again.

In the darkness, Ethan was thankful God allowed Kate to be safely in his arms. *Thank you, Lord. I'm beyond grateful that You protected her for me. I love her, Lord, and I love you.*

Chapter Twenty-Seven

Blake had given their coordinates to the dispatcher and when the whirring sound of helicopter rotors grew near, he turned on his LED flashlight, sending its bright beam into the night sky. Within minutes, the chopper with its flashing lights, hovered just above their position. A basket with an accompanying rescue ranger was lowered to the ground.

"Kate, sweetheart. Wake up. We have company." Ethan gently squeezed Kate's good shoulder and placed a kiss on her temple.

"No, I'll just stay here." Kate rested her head against his chest and burrowed in. "I like it here."

Ethan's lips curved into a silly grin that reached right down to his heart. It took two swallows to clear the lump from his throat. Sweet. He'd do something about that for her later, but right now he had to get her to the hospital.

"Hello, gentlemen." Ethan made introductions. "The patient has a gunshot wound to her right thigh as well as a broken collar bone from a previous injury. It was mending, but with her day, I wouldn't be surprised that it's been reinjured."

"Alright," the rescue ranger nodded. "Let's get her in the basket and back to the chopper. We'll begin treatment in the air on the way to the hospital."

"Here, hold her up while I stand." Ethan stood then lifted Kate into his arms and lay her into the aluminum basket. Blankets were wrapped around her as she began to shiver.

"Ethan," Kate began.

"Shhh." He placed a gentle finger over her lips. "I'll meet you up top in just a few. These guys want to get you up there and start treating you. Be a good patient and do what they tell you, okay?"

Kate nodded.

Ethan bent and dropped a quick kiss onto her soft lips. Then the rescue ranger gave the signal for the basket to be lifted.

Ethan watched as Kate rode up with the rescue ranger and was deposited into the belly of the flying machine. The rescue ranger returned with the empty basket.

"I suppose you want to take him back." He tossed his head in Von Richter's direction.

Ethan would've been happy to leave the villain for the coyotes and buzzards, but he knew they had to take the body back.

"Yep," Blake nodded. "Let's pack him up. Got some sheets we can wrap him in? I'd rather Kate didn't see him again."

"We can arrange that."

Within minutes Von Richter was wrapped and lifted to the helicopter where he was placed in the back out of view. A body harness was lowered first for Ethan and then Blake to make their ride to the top and then everyone was belted in and Kate's gurney was secured.

"Ok, gentlemen, the pilot's ready to fly." Another rescue ranger clapped both Ethan and Blake on the shoulder. "If you'll take your seats and belt yourselves in, we'll head out."

Ethan snapped his seatbelt and linked his fingers across his lap. Exhaustion caused his muscles to relax against the soft leather and fabric seats. It would be at least a forty-five-minute flight to Flagstaff. He could close his eyes for a few minutes. Glancing over at Kate as the rangers worked on her, he saw that they'd put an oxygen mask on her face, installed an IV drip and were treating her gunshot wound. Most likely she'd be in surgery soon after she arrived. Her eyes were closed. Was she asleep? He sure hoped so. She'd had one heck of a day. He closed his eyes and nodded off.

~

"Kate, can you hear me, sweetheart?" Hadn't she heard those words recently. Only this didn't feel like her rocky little seat where she'd hidden from Claus Von Richter. No, definitely not. Was she floating? She was reclining for sure, and the surface was…well it was so much softer than the little rocky seat. Was that Ethan calling her? His voice was so far away. As much as she tried, she couldn't open her eyes. Her eyelids were so heavy.

Someone was shaking her arm. No, no. Go away. All she wanted was to fade away and sleep. Just sleep.

Blackness descended and that was all she knew.

It must have been sometime later Kate became aware that someone was gently stroking her arm.

"Kate, sweetheart. Wake up." Ethan's voice pleaded again. It sounded so much closer now than before. Her attempt at opening her eyes was met with success and the handsome, if worried, face of Ethan appeared before her.

"Thank you, Lord." He breathed a relieved sigh then drew her hand to his lips. He rested it there several moments as his gaze searched hers.

"Ethan? How long have I been asleep?" Was that her voice? It sounded like raspy sandpaper against a rock.

Keeping her hand in his, he grinned then winked. "Far longer than any decent person should sleep in a day, but we'll excuse you given the circumstances. You slept a solid eight hours, then when we tried to wake you, you refused and slept another four. All that was after your surgery to remove the bullet. Needless to say, you had a little something to help you sleep."

"That must be why I feel like I've been hit by a Mack truck."

"Most likely," Ethan nodded, chuckling. "I'd have let you sleep longer but you know these doctors and nurses. Too much of a good thing is bad for you. We can't let you sleep too much, now can we. They wanted to make sure you were coming out of the anesthesia. You were pretty exhausted and you weren't coming out of it. We tried to get them to leave you alone and just let you sleep. After the ordeal you went through yesterday and especially last night, you just needed rest."

Kate glanced down at the huge bandage encasing her thigh then returned her gaze to Ethan. Tugging her fingers from his, she raised her hand to his face and gently cupped his scruffy cheek. Of course, there had been no opportunity for him to clean up or shave since yesterday morning, but somehow his rough appearance was just as appealing as when he was clean shaven.

"Ethan, it was sheer agony when I thought you were dead. I didn't want to leave you behind, but I knew I had to get out of there or they'd kill me too. Sometime you'll have to tell me the whole story of how you survived when Claus shot you and how you found me, but until then thank you for coming after me and rescuing me."

The blaze that flamed in Ethan's gaze at Kate's words sent heat throughout her body. Swallowing hard, she started to withdraw her hand, but he captured it within his fingers and lifting it, placed a kiss on her palm.

"Sweetheart, you do what you have to in order to rescue the one you love, and I couldn't get to you fast enough."

"Ain't *that* the truth," a familiar voice spoke from the doorway before Blake appeared around the cloth curtain that divided the semi-private hospital room.

"Blake?" Kate cast a curious eye in his direction as he produced a colorful bouquet of a variety of flowers in a glass vase.

"For you, my lady. Fresh from the hospital gift shop."

Kate smiled but didn't dare shake her head. It was still a little fuzzy and achy. She didn't want to chance setting it off on that horrible headache again.

"Thank you, Blake. They're beautiful. Please set them on the tray table where I can see and enjoy them."

"My pleasure."

"Did anyone ever tell you that you have terrible timing?" Ethan glared at him as he linked his arms across his chest.

Blake nodded as he pursed his lips and lowered his brows in thought. "Yeah, occasionally."

"Add me to the list," Ethan growled.

"Well there you are, girlfriend." Tasha breezed into the room, her presence bringing sunshine with her. She placed a purple and pink polka dotted gift bag on the tray table next to Blake's flowers. "I brought some goodies you might like. A few of your personal items, like your Bible, as well as some fun things I picked up for you."

"That was thoughtful, Tasha. Thanks." Kate tried to readjust her position on the bed but gasped as pain ricocheted through her shoulder and leg.

"Let me help you." Ethan lifted her and settled her more comfortably. His gray gaze locked with hers, mere inches away bringing a wave of heat to her cheeks and sending her pulse stampeding at his proximity. As the heart monitor began to beep loudly, Ethan straightened and glanced at it, a grin on his lips. His gaze once again slid to hers, this time with a raised brow. A nurse rushed into the room to check on Kate, then reassured, reset the monitor and left. Of course, his proximity had made her heart race, but had it set off the heart monitor alarm? Kate swallowed hard then started coughing.

Avoiding Ethan's gaze, Kate tried to concentrate on what Tasha was saying.

"Blake told me how Von Richter nearly strangled you, girlfriend. I brought you some throat lozenges. They're in the bag." Tasha pointed at the gift bag. "You should probably whisper until your throat heals. It sounds like broken glass scraping over cement. Painful. Mmmm mmmm."

"Thanks, Tasha. I will," Kate whispered.

Tasha continued, changing the subject. "An intense search has begun for Paul Schmitz in every building, shed, shack and outbuilding within the park. Cassie Rosenberg has been interrogated and so far, has been less than co-operative. She refuses to give up his location."

"Yeah, I just wanted to stop in and see how you're doing, Kate." Blake propped his hands on his hips. "I'm heading back with Tasha in a few minutes. I'll also interrogate Cassie in the morning to see if I can find out anything new."

"Thanks for checking on me, Blake. I'm sure I'll be fine once I get this thing off my leg." Kate pointed at the heavy bandage. "I'll be praying Paul's found quickly."

Reaching over, Ethan twined his fingers with hers. Kate felt heat rush into her cheeks but she certainly didn't pull her hand away. A satisfied smile settled on Tasha's full lips and a grin on Blake's

"*We'll* be praying he's found quickly." Ethan gave a gentle squeeze of her fingers. "And please keep us posted."

"It seems you have a strong case against Cassie." Tasha turned to Blake. "I just don't understand why she would kill her father."

"Maybe we can find that out." Blake turned with a salute as he and Tasha said their goodbyes and headed out the door.

~

Moving around to Kate's right side, Ethan brought a chair as close to the edge of the bed as he could and lowered the bedrail, then took a seat in the chair and leaned toward her. The whole time

Kate watched him with a mixture of caution and curiosity. His heart rate kicked into high gear at the nearness of this woman. He was about to lay his heart out for her to pick up and cherish or to stomp on and walk away. Which would she do? It hadn't been too long since she'd pretty much given him permission to court her. Would she hold to that, or would she change her mind? He loved Kate with everything in him, and he was ready for a till death-do-you-part relationship. Was she?

"Now, where were we before we were interrupted?" Ethan picked up Kate's hand and twined his fingers with hers. "Ah, yes, I remember. You were thanking me for rescuing you, and I, in turn, was in the middle of telling you that you do what you have to in order to rescue the one you love. Wasn't that about where we left off?"

Ethan watched as Kate swallowed hard then licked her dry lips. How could such a simple action be so tantalizing? *Keep your mind on the task, man.*

Kate nodded, her voice barely above a whisper. "I…I think that's where we were."

Ethan felt the corners of his lips tugging upward. "Then let me assure you, sweetheart, that's exactly the case. I love you more than life itself. As I said earlier, I couldn't get to you fast enough. I risked life and limb coming down into the canyon to find you, and I prayed all the way that God would protect you. I'm not even sure how I got down there without killing myself, except that God placed my feet where they needed to go."

Kate's gaze was locked on his as he spoke and now a smile lit her face. "I'd say the Lord has a plan for us, darling Ethan. If there's one thing I've learned by falling in love with you, is that the heart has the capacity to love so much and more than once. I was very much in love with Craig, and I'll always love him. But, Ethan, I love you with all my heart. There's no competition between you. You don't have to worry about that. I'm all yours."

Ethan swallowed twice before the lump in his throat dislodged. Lifting a hand, he cupped Kate's cheek and caressed it with the pad of his thumb. When she responded by snuggling into his palm, Ethan could hold back no longer and leaned forward claiming her sweet, soft lips, sealing the love they shared.

Deepening the kiss, a heady sensation filled him that nearly made him forget where he was. All he wanted was to continue holding this woman who nearly drove him to distraction.

"Aahhhmmm," a voice cleared from a few feet away. "Aahhhmmm."

Had someone just cleared their throat? Twice?

With regret Ethan pulled back slightly to see that Kate, too, was completely immersed in their kiss. Then the sound of beeping met his ears, and he turned to find the disapproving glower of the shift nurse as she stood with arms locked across her chest, toe tapping on the linoleum floor.

"So, you're the culprit." She stomped over to the heart monitor and turned off the alarm. "I really do have better things to do than to come running every time you get my patient's heart twittering."

"Sorry." Ethan grinned, not really contrite.

The nurse looked at him sideways as she headed out the door. "Sure you are."

Ethan turned to find a grinning Kate watching him. "I'm not complaining."

Chapter Twenty-Eight

H ey, girlfriend. How are you doing?" Tasha strolled into Kate's hospital room the next morning. "I'm here to spring you. Doc said you can go home today, and you and Ethan need a ride. It's a long walk from Flagstaff back to the Grand Canyon, don't ya know? And I don't think you're up to the walk."

"Good morning, Tasha. Yay! I can go home." Kate struggled to sit up a bit and nodded. The pain was still there but apparently the meds they were giving her in her IV had dulled it somewhat. "Yeah, I remember the drive out from when I first arrived. I'd rather not walk home."

Ethan stood from the recliner in the corner where he'd slept all night. His hair stood on end and he yawned, stretching his arms and back to release the kinks that a night in the less-than-comfortable recliner had given him.

"My, my, that must've been a comfortable sleep, sweetie." Tasha gave him a hug.

"Don't knock it till you try it, then knock it all you want." Ethan moved to Kate's side and helped her adjust the bed and her pillows to sit up more, then he placed a tender kiss on her lips.

Tasha gaped at the gesture. Her finger did a circle in the air between them. "So, did something happen here after I left yesterday?"

Ethan feigned a confused expression. "What do you mean?"

Tasha's gazed bounced between them as did her pointing finger. "I mean *that*. You know. The kiss."

Ethan leaned down and gave Kate a slightly longer kiss this time then straightened. "You mean like that?"

Tasha glowered at him. "Yeah, like that."

219

Kate's cheeks warmed as she chuckled. Reaching across, she poked Ethan in the leg. "Yeah, I guess you could say something happened."

"Really? Like you two finally realized you're in love?" Tasha squealed and did a happy dance. She yanked the curtain back dividing Kate's bed from the next one to see if anyone was there. Fortunately, the next bed was empty. "Oh, that's so awesome! I knew it! I just knew it. It was only a matter of time before you two figured it out. I was praying for you, you know. Praise the Lord! Answered prayer."

"Don't we know it." Ethan grinned and dropped an arm around Tasha's shoulders. "Thanks for that, by the way."

"Hey, God knows what He's doing." Tasha wrapped her arm around Ethan's waist and gave him a squeeze. "But on to other good news. I wanted to tell you they found Paul last night."

A gasp slipped from Kate. "Alive?"

Tasha released Ethan and slipped onto the chair by the bed. She nodded, a huge smile lighting her face. "Yes, alive."

"Praise God." Kate's voice rasped softly as she breathed a sigh of relief. Ethan stepped over and grasped her hand. "Where and how?"

"Well, a park-wide search led to an old unused office building where he was being kept in a storage closet. The building sat unused for about three years and is waiting to be torn down. The park service is going to build something else there in the near future. In the meantime, Paul was being tortured and beaten for information on the artifacts. Cassie and Claus Von Richter attempted to get his mom out here to further get information from him. Information he didn't even have. And Kate, Claus never intended to kill you. He wanted to stop you and bring you back. But don't think things would've been any easier for you. They would've tortured you for the information as well. And in your case, you have the information."

Tasha let those words sink in and a chill ran through Kate when she considered what they would've done to her to extract that information.

"Thank God it didn't come to that." Ethan's words echoed in her own mind. "But in a sense, that's what they've done to her since the beginning. A long, slow torture. What with all the warnings. They just hadn't gotten to extracting information yet."

"Very true," Tasha agreed.

"Have you found out why they were torturing Paul?" Kate asked. "It's obvious they wanted the artifacts, but were they going to sell them on the black market?"

A wide grin split Tasha's lips. "That's where the most amazing information comes in. Blake's been in touch with both the FBI and Interpol."

"What?" Kate and Ethan asked in unison.

"Yep. Seems Cassie isn't willing to go down alone. She finally broke and sang like a bird when Blake interrogated her. A black marketeer named Abdul Ruhamni not only threatened her life to get those artifacts but he buys and sells in the millions on the black market. Interpol has located him in the middle east and is on their way now to take him down."

Kate stared at Tasha, her jaw slack. Was her mouth hanging open? She clamped her lips together.

"You've got to be kidding." Ethan sat down on the recliner in the corner. "Who knew this was an international black-market scandal. And where did Von Richter come into this?"

"Cassie was the one who contacted Ruhamni about selling artifacts to him," Tasha explained. "She just knew that her father would find them here at the dig. She'd been after her father for money for a while, but he refused to give her any. Said he had none to give her. She didn't believe him."

"Archeology isn't a profitable profession," Ethan ran his hand through his tousled hair, "at lcast not to the extent that Cassie expected."

Tasha shook her head. "No, and she wanted a lot of money. So, she contracted with Ruhamni for valuable artifacts. He sent Claus Von Richter to assist Cassie in getting the artifacts and to ensure she kept her end of the contract. They opened the safe and stole the first artifacts. They weren't of great value, but unfortunately those artifacts are likely gone for good."

"All we have left of them are photographs," Ethan said. "We were able to inventory and photograph them before they were stolen."

"The information has been passed on to Interpol so if they should ever show up in a sale somewhere, they may be recovered,"

Tasha continued.

Ethan stood and paced along the side of Kate's bed. He stopped and faced Tasha again. "How is Paul now?"

"He's in serious condition. They flew him here. He has several broken bones, a serious concussion, facial lacerations, and internal bleeding. He was taken into emergency surgery when he arrived. He's resting now. Perhaps by the time they're ready to discharge you we can stop in and say hi to him if he's awake."

"Poor Paul." Kate rested her head against the pillow. "All that and he didn't know a thing."

"I've sent Gage to accompany his mom here. I know she's not in the best of health, but I think she needs to be here for him, and I think it'll be good for her to be needed."

"That's great," Ethan agreed, "but don't put her up at his place. That would be a terrible idea."

"So I've heard." Tasha wrinkled her nose.

~

When Kate was finally discharged a few hours later, Ethan wheeled her down to the third floor to visit with Paul before they headed out to Tasha's car.

"Wait here while I make sure he's awake and ready for company." Ethan parked Kate along the side of the hallway and Tasha waited with her while he entered the open doorway. The double-occupant room was only occupied by Paul, and Ethan went right to his bedside.

Paul lay with his head swathed in gauze bandages, his face covered with smaller bandages and his right arm in a sling. He was covered by blankets so further injuries were difficult to discern.

"Hey Paul, are you awake?" Ethan spoke in low tones so as not to awaken him if he was sleeping.

"Hi, Dr. Wagner." Paul's one uncovered eye slowly slid open. "I'm awake. Just resting. I came out of the anesthesia but just can't get up the energy to read or watch TV or anything yet."

Ethan patted his shoulder. "There's no rush, you know."

"I know. I don't think I'm going anywhere right away."

"Probably not right away," Ethan agreed. "Feel up to some company? We won't stay long. Don't want to tire you. We just wanted to say hi and see how you're doing."

"Sure."

Ethan stepped back to the doorway and wheeled Kate in, followed by Tasha.

"Hi, Paul." Kate took his hand and patted it. "I'm so sorry this happened to you."

"Thanks, Kate. I appreciate that." Paul turned his head to look at her with his good eye. "Looks like you had some trouble too. What happened to you?"

Ethan met Kate's gaze and realized her hesitance, so he told Paul what had happened to her.

"You've got to be kidding." A smile lifted as much of Paul's lips as possible considering the bandages and damage to his face. "There really were gold artifacts coming out of the dig? That's awesome, Dr. Wagner. I was beginning to think it was just a great find with the Anasazi city and all, but to actually find some artifacts? That's great. Do Anna, Mike and Carl know about the artifacts?"

Ethan exchanged glances with Kate and Tasha. "Paul, you wouldn't have known, but Mike was murdered a couple days after you were kidnapped. He was shot."

"What?" A shocked whisper was ripped from Paul.

Kate reached over and squeezed his hand as tears slipped from his eye. He lay for a while not saying anything then he uttered softly, "I guess I'm the lucky one after all, huh? I'm still alive."

Paul turned his head toward the window. "I guess Anna and Carl are okay then?"

"Yeah, they're fine."

He turned his face back toward them and tried to smile. "Do they know about the artifacts?"

Ethan met first Kate's then Tasha's gazes and grinned. "Well, Anna knows of some. Carl, not so much. But that'll all be changing now that the real thieves have been caught. You know you're going to have to hurry and get well so you can get back to the dig. There's still a lot of work to be done."

"Really?" Relief filled Paul's voice. "I thought I'd be sent back to school after I heal and you'd fill my position or something."

Ethan chuckled and turned to Tasha. "What do you think? Can we find work for him to do around here, even if it has to do with paperwork and simple jobs while he mends, then he can return to the dig?"

"I don't see why not." Tasha smiled as Paul's one good eye bounced between her and Ethan. "It would be a shame for him to lose his place and have to reapply for another position at another dig. They're pretty hard to come by, from what I hear."

"They certainly can be," Ethan agreed, linking his arms across his chest.

Kate chuckled then whispered. "You two are terrible. Would you stop putting Paul through this agony and just tell him he can stay?"

Ethan patted Paul's shoulder and held up a finger. "Okay, you can stay. With one condition."

"Sure, what's that."

"You don't overdo."

"I promise."

"Good. Now we're going to get out of here so you can get some rest. We'll see you soon. Take it easy, Paul"

"You got it."

~

At park police headquarters the next morning, Kate and Ethan met Blake Hunter in the hallway outside the interrogation room.

"Good morning, Blake," Kate's voice was less like broken glass this morning. "Tasha said you wanted us to meet you here. What's up?"

"Morning, guys. Yes, I did. Come with me."

Blake opened a door and led them inside a darkened room where a technician sat before a digital panel. He nodded as they entered but without a word, turned back to his buttons, lights and switches. To their left a one-way glass picture window covered the better part of the wall and there on the other side sat Cassie Rosenberg in all her fashion glory: zebra stripes mixed with leopard, neon-green and purple. Her rainbow, white and black hair was spiked. Was this to distract the interrogator? If that was Blake, her plan was doomed to failure.

Cassie sat at a table, one leg crossed over the other in a leisurely manner, her arms linked across her midriff. Gum smacked in her mouth, and Kate doubted Blake would tolerate that for long. Cassie glanced around the room as if inspecting a public toilet.

"I thought you two would want to see this. You have a vested interest, after all." Blake pointed a thumb toward the picture window.

"Here, Kate, have a seat." Blake pulled a chair forward. "I don't think you'll be able to stand long on that bum leg of yours."

"Thanks, Blake." She dropped into the chair and stretched her leg out in front of her.

The door opened and Tasha stepped in, closing it quietly behind her. "You haven't started yet I see. Good. I wouldn't miss this for the world."

"Nope. Come on in." Blake waved a hand. "Alright. You three wait here. I'm going to begin. Then wait till I return."

He stepped out of the room and they saw the door of the room where Cassie sat open and Blake stepped in. Closing it behind him, he took the seat across from Cassie, his back to the one-way glass window. She blew a bubble with her bubble gum then popped it. Without a word, Blake reached for the small trash can in the corner, and he forced her to spit her gum into the can. A pout marred her usually pretty face.

Blake began his questioning. Most of the information concerned things that Kate, Ethan and Tasha already knew. What they were most concerned about was why she'd killed her father.

Eventually Blake worked the questioning around to the murders of Mike Pierce and Professor Dietrich Rosenberg.

Blake reached into the file folder that he'd brought into the room with him and pulled out two photographs, laying them on the table in front of Cassie. They were the pictures of Professor Rosenberg and Mike Pierce, taken after they were murdered. Casting a quick glance at them, she shoved them away in distaste. Blake pushed them back.

"Look at them, Miss Rosenberg. Look at them closely. Did you murder your father and Mike Pierce?"

Cassie refused to look at the graphic pictures again but shrugged her shoulder and rolled her eyes. "Why would I kill them, Officer Hunter?"

Blake stood and leaned against the table as his voice grew harsher and louder. "I'm the one asking questions here, Miss Rosenberg. Not you. Now answer my question. Did you murder your father and Mike Pierce? And remember, you have been read your rights and you are sworn to tell the truth."

Cassie remained silent but looked shaken.

Blake reached into the file folder and retrieved another photo. "Perhaps this will jog your memory. This is a photo of hair strands taken from Mike Pierce's body after he was shot. A black hair that not only looks like the hair in the small section of black that you have, it matches in length too. However, Miss Rosenberg, the evidence doesn't stop there. It matches your DNA as well. Imagine that."

In the darkened room behind the one-way glass, Kate watched Cassie's features and it seemed, with the pictures that Blake displayed and the evidence that he produced, Cassie began to wilt a little at a time. Would she fold completely? Or would she somehow rebound and cover up, trying to lie her way out of this? But DNA? You can't cover that up.

"That's impossible." Cassie's words were no longer filled with assurance as she attempted to wave away his words with a slightly shaky hand. "I...I was not there."

"Really? The evidence would prove otherwise." Blake reached down to the floor and lifted a small cardboard box to the tabletop. Opening it, he retrieved a clear, plastic evidence bag with a 9mm automatic handgun encased inside. "You wouldn't happen to recognize this, would you?"

Cassie's lips clamped tightly together, her chin lifted in defiance. Eyes narrowed as she watched Blake in silence.

"No? Well, I am surprised," Blake continued. "We found it in your room at the El Tovar Hotel when we searched it late last night."

Fire ignited in Cassie's gaze as she glared at Blake, but she remained silent. Kate could tell Cassie was unsure how to handle the situation. She just hoped she didn't clam up and call for a lawyer before Blake got more information out of her.

"It's Claus's gun," Cassie blurted out. "He must have left it in my room. What an imbecile. It was he that killed my father and Michael Pierce."

With the evidence bag in hand, Blake casually strolled around the table, stopping just behind and to the left of Cassie. "Hmmm. That's odd. Claus's fingerprints were nowhere to be found on this gun, but yours are all over it. Funny, that. I'd say that proves the gun belonged to you. Not Claus. Oh, don't worry. Claus had one too. He was definitely an accomplice to murder, but this one's yours, Cassie. You see, we even ran a check on it. It's registered to you. Not even stolen. You bought it and registered it. It seems you're an honest criminal. Claus? Not so much. His was bought on the black market. Filed off serial number. No way to trace where it came from. But this one is definitely yours."

Blake completed the circuit around the table and stopped in front of Cassie, laying the gun on the smooth surface. "This gun fired the bullets that killed both Professor Rosenberg and Mike Pierce, and you killed them. Now why don't you tell me *why* you killed them."

Kate watched as Cassie completely wilted before Blake's stare. He'd provided the evidence linking Cassie with the deaths of Professor Rosenberg and Mike Pierce and she knew it. Kate had mixed feelings over this knowledge. Cassie had become like the relative no one wanted to have around yet grew on you over time, but that didn't come close in comparison to the relief that the horrible nightmare of the last few weeks had come to an end. The killer had been caught and there would be no more looking over her shoulder. No more fear of being chased, harmed or killed. They could get back to the business of the archeological dig and move on with life. Move on with.... She glanced at Ethan standing beside her.

His gaze was on her, a grin lifting the corners of his lips. Had he read her mind? He reached for her hand and twined his warm fingers with hers. Whether he had or not, his heart was attuned with hers and that was all that mattered.

Blake's raised voice snagged Kate's attention back to the interrogation room. "Miss Rosenberg, tell me why you killed your father. Did you hate him so much that you had to kill him?"

"Yes! Yes! Yes!" Cassie screamed. "I hated him so much. I hated him more than the likes of you will ever understand."

Silence filled the room for a few moments as Cassie's face twisted into a mask of hatred and bitterness. Tears streamed down her face. mixing mascara into the wetness. Her hands with their hot pink nails clenched together on the tabletop. A sob racked her body before she settled down sniffing it back and breathing deeply.

Blake retook his seat and spoke softly, encouraging her to

confide in him. "Why did you hate your father, Cassie? Had he done something to you?"

Cassie closed her eyes for a moment, and when she opened them, she was more in control. Her gaze was distant, as if she were thinking of a long-ago time. "I hated him, but I had not planned to kill him. He always wanted me to study archeology, and I didn't want to. I hated the thought of getting my hands dirty. When I was young he would force me to go with him to his digs, but I would scream and cry the whole time I was there. If he would make me miserable, I would make him miserable. My mother was in fashion and that's what I wanted to study. When she died five years ago, he refused to give me money to support my studies. We argued horribly. I asked him many times for money but he wouldn't give me anything. Said he had nothing to give me, that archeologists make very little. I did not believe him. With all the artifacts they find, I just don't believe it. So, when this dig came up, I decided to get in touch with a black marketeer who would pay me big money for the artifacts my father would find. I contracted with him."

Her voice grew softer. "I never intended to kill him. Just to threaten and scare him into giving them to me to sell on the black market."

"Tell me what happened that night, Cassie." Blake edged closer, his voice becoming mellow. "Why did you go to the archeologists' office?"

Cassie wiped her face with the back of her hand, smearing the mascara across her cheeks. "I intended to demand more money, but my father once again said he had none to give me. He said he was tired of telling me the same thing and to stop asking. I was furious. So I went outside and grabbed a tree limb from the edge of the tree line by the office. I suppose he thought I left, but I came back inside and while he was looking at some papers, I swung the limb and bashed him in the head. Claus was waiting in the car, so I went out to get him to come move Father's body out back of the office. Father was still alive when Claus dragged him out back so I shot him. We left him beneath the trees thinking the coyotes or some other animals would dispose of him quickly. And they would have if Kate Fleming had not found him in the middle of their meal."

"And Claus? Where did he come in?"

"Abdul Ruhamni, the black marketeer, sent him to help me

with the artifacts and to put pressure on my father. Other than the killing, he did the dirty work."

"And Mike Pierce? Why did you kill him?"

Cassie sighed heavily. When she spoke, her voice was nearly monotone. "Claus and I came to try to open the safe again one night and Mike was there. He asked why we had come. I grew nervous because I had no good answer so I shot him. I knew the archeology team members were under investigation and they would be the first ones questioned and assumed guilty. I told Claus to lay low and pretend to be a tourist. I just played my own role. The daughter of the murdered Professor Rosenberg. No one would connect me with Mike Pierce."

"You had it all wrapped up nicely, didn't you, Cassie?"

She remained silent, her gaze on the tabletop.

Blake stood and turned toward the one-way glass and nodded once. Kate watched as the park police officer in the darkened room picked up the phone on the wall and mumbled into the receiver then hung up.

"Cassandra Rosenberg," Blake tugged his handcuffs from his utility belt as he walked around the table behind Cassie and helped her to stand, "you're under arrest for the murder of Professor Dietrich Rosenberg and Michael Pierce."

He snapped the handcuffs on Cassie's wrists as she stood still, the life seeming to have left her. All the fight and spirit that she had exhibited before now no longer in evidence. She was a broken woman.

The door to the room opened and two park police officers led Cassie from the room and toward a holding cell.

Kate dragged in a deep breath, her head down.

Ethan's finger slipped beneath her chin, lifting her gaze to meet his.

"You okay, sweetheart?" His concern was evident as his eyes swept over her face.

"I'm fine. It's just that I've lived with fear and dread almost since I arrived at the Grand Canyon. It's going to take some time getting used to not looking over my shoulder every time I do anything or go anywhere. It's such a new feeling, I can't really grasp it yet."

Ethan chuckled and knelt beside the chair, wrapping her in his arms. "We'll work on that together, okay?"

The door of the observation room opened and Blake stepped in.

"Well done, Blake." Tasha patted his shoulder. "You pulled that confession out of Cassie like the pro that you are."

"Thanks." Blake shook his head, sighing heavily. "She wasn't going to make it easy, though."

"No, she wasn't. I'd say you earned your bread and butter today, buddy." Ethan stood up and reaching over, clapped him on the back.

"And we'll all sleep easier tonight," Tasha nodded.

"And I can go home to my own bed," Kate smiled. "I think I've slept in it a total of three nights."

Epilogue

It's a real pleasure to meet you, Mrs. Schmitz," Kate shook the older woman's hand. "Paul has told us all about you. I know he's thrilled that you're here."

"Why thank you so much, Kate. It's nice to meet you too." Paul's mother might be sick with cancer, but there was nothing wrong with her handshake. Her grip was killer. "It was so nice of Tasha to invite me to this cookout. I was just sorry that Gage had to rent a car and drive me cross-country rather than fly me here as originally planned. My doctor doesn't want me to fly, you understand. He's funny about some things."

"Yes, that's understandable." Kate agreed.

"I would've loved to be able to help with the preparations for the cookout if I could've arrived sooner."

Kate waved her hand to dismiss her words. "You needn't worry on that account. We had plenty of help."

Mrs. Schmitz reached over and patted her son's leg. "It's just so wonderful to be here with Paul. I hate that he went through such a terrible time, but I'm thankful they found the culprits and have put them away. Once Gage explained what had happened, I began praying for him. I pray the Lord will work in his life and have been for many years."

The bandages covering Paul's face couldn't hide the pensiveness that her words elicited. Was he considering a change in his spiritual life? Sometimes a tragic episode in one's life makes them realize their mortality and helps them see that they need Christ. Kate would also pray for Paul that he would make that step of faith.

"If you'll excuse me, Mrs. Schmitz, I'll let you and Paul visit.

I'll talk with you later."

"Why certainly, Kate. Have a lovely time."

Kate slipped away and slowly meandered through the guests standing around Tasha and Lance's backyard talking. The end of May was here and the long-awaited warm weather had decided to stick around for the season. The couple had invited their friends over for a Memorial Day weekend cookout and the day was perfect for it. Kate had dressed in a plaid, collared, sleeveless, button-down shirt and baggy linen capris to cover the not-as-bulky bandage over her healing leg wound. Her hair was in a braid.

Lance stood in front of a huge BBQ grill, a "Grill Sergeant" apron covering a t-shirt and shorts, a pair of BBQ tongs in one hand and a hamburger flipper in the other. Hamburgers and hotdogs were lined up on the grill in symmetrical order. You'd think he was a drill sergeant rather than a park police officer.

"Kate," Tasha called from the kitchen. "Gotta a sec?"

"Sure." Kate slowly managed the four wooden steps to the deck then strolled into the kitchen. "What do you need?"

"I know you can't use that left wing yet, but can you carry this bucket of ice out to the table for me? It's got a handle so it'll be easy."

"No problem."

"It won't be long before you get that sling off."

"Tell me about it. When they x-rayed it two days ago, they said it's healing fine. I may even get it off early. Wouldn't that be great? Then I could start physical therapy and begin building up my strength. I'm going to have to do the same thing with my leg eventually."

"That's awesome, girlfriend. And don't you worry about the leg. It'll be fine too. At least nothing was broken." Tasha came around the counter and gave Kate a hug. "Things are working out, aren't they? The good Lord said they would for those who love Him."

Kate hugged her back. "Yes, they are. And I thank Him for giving you to me for a friend. What a blessing you are, Tasha Johnson. And don't you forget it."

She cleared the lump from her throat and the mist from her eyes. "I better get this ice outside."

Kate paused at the top of the steps and viewed the crowd as

they chatted with one another. What remained of the archeology team was here. Besides Paul, there was Anna and Carl. They both had warmed to not only her, but Paul and Ethan. They would finally work as a team now. Gage was here as was Blake. There were a few others that she had recently met as well, but her heart soared when she turned to descend the steps and Ethan waited for her at the bottom.

Reaching for the bucket of ice with one hand, he clasped her hand with the other. Without a word he led her to the table, deposited the bucket then led her around the house where a bench stood beneath a tree in the front yard.

Kate laughed as he tugged her onto the seat and wrapped her in his arms. "You don't think they'll miss us?"

"They're going to have to do without us for a few minutes. I haven't been alone with you all day, and I need my Kate fix. That's right, I'm hopelessly addicted. For life."

Turning slightly, Kate draped her right arm over his shoulder, running her fingers into the hair at the base of his neck. "You know, that's okay by me."

Ethan took Kate's face between his palms and planted a firm but gentle kiss on her lips. Her heart bumped in her chest then kicked into overdrive. He always had that effect on her. While she was still trying to catch her breath, he lifted his face and turned her facing away from him, tugging her back against his chest. Then he wrapped her securely in his arms.

"I'm not squeezing you too tight, am I?" Ethan flicked her braid aside and whispered in her ear.

She opened her eyes. Was this all a dream and she'd wake up in her bed after all? Reaching down, she pinched her arm. Ouch. Nope. Not a dream.

"No, you're not squeezing me too tight, Ethan," Kate whispered, her mouth dry.

"Good. I don't want to hurt your shoulder or your newly healing leg wound." Ethan laid his lips on Kate's temple.

"No, I'm good." Did her voice squeak?"

"Awesome." His lips trailed down to her cheek. "I love you, Kate. Will you marry me?"

Those silly butterflies took that moment to take flight in her stomach. Were they as thrilled with his question as she was? Kate turned her face as far as she could to meet Ethan's gaze.

"I love you, Ethan, with everything that's in me. Yes, I'll marry you."

Ethan tugged a little black velvet box from his pocket and opened it in front of her. Taking the diamond engagement ring from its bedding, he took her left hand as it stuck out of the sling and slipped it on her finger.

"Oohhh," Kate breathed. "It's gorgeous, Ethan. Simply gorgeous."

"Just like you, sweetheart. Will you marry me soon?" Yearning filled his gaze as it swept her features. He shook his head doubtfully. "I don't know how long I can wait. You're enough to try a man's patience, you know that?"

Kate sent him a sideways glance. "You'll have to take that up with my mother, darling. She's going to want to have a part in it. I suppose you were born and not hatched, right? You've never said much about your mother. Want to spill?"

Ethan dropped his head to her good shoulder. "Do I have to?"

"Yes."

"No, I wasn't hatched and, yes, I have a mother. Yes, she's going to want to have a part in the wedding." He lifted his head, a bright-idea smile on his face. "I have a better idea. Let's just elope."

Kate grinned at him. "And deny our mothers the opportunity to help plan our wedding?"

At his glum expression, Kate turned and draped her legs across his, wrapping her good arm around his middle and giving him a hug. "I'm teasing you, Ethan. Let's get married here at the Grand Canyon. South rim at Hermit's Trail. Just before sunset. We'll invite our families, but we'll plan the wedding ourselves. Hands off, mothers. How about that?"

Ethan drew her close, placing a kiss just below her ear. "It sounds like a plan. How about tomorrow?"

Kate chuckled. "I don't think we can get family here that fast, sweetheart."

"No? Shucks. Day after tomorrow?"

"Well, here you two are," Tasha's voice called from the corner of the house as she strode toward them. "What are you doing? Oh. Never mind. I don't want to know."

Kate lifted her left hand to display the engagement ring. "I bet you do too."

Tasha raised her hands to the sky and did a happy dance. "Thank you, Lord. That's answered prayer. Hallelujah, I praise Your holy name, Lord. You answered *my* prayers. Ethan and Kate are getting married. Praise God! Hallelujah!"

She danced her way toward the back of the house to spread the good news, then turned to call back to Kate and Ethan.

"By the way, the hamburgers and hotdogs are ready."

The End

Author Bio

A native North Carolinian, J. Carol Nemeth has always loved reading and enjoyed making up stories ever since junior high school, most based in the places she has lived or traveled to. She worked in the National Park Service as a Park Aid and served in the US Army where she was stationed in Italy, traveling to over thirteen countries while there. She met the love of her life, Mark Nemeth, also an Army veteran, while stationed in Italy. After they married, they lived in various locations, including North Yorkshire, England. They now live in West Virginia, where, in her spare time, Carol and her husband enjoy RVing and sightseeing. Carol and Mark are active in their church and enjoy their two grown children, son-in-law, and three grandchildren.

Sign up for my newsletter at www.jcarolnemeth.com/ and receive a free short story.

Thank you for purchasing this book. If you enjoyed reading it, please consider leaving a review at the purchase page at www.amazon.com/

Mountain of Peril, Faith in the Parks Book 1 - Buy Link goo.gl/XMM32A

Yorkshire Lass- Buy Link goo.gl/uodShD

Dedication to Love - Buy Link goo.gl/WU9L22

Wilderness Weddings National Park Historical Collection - Buy Link goo.gl/3SC8XZ

A Beacon of Love – Buy Link goo.gl/vqTR7Q

A Soldier's Heart – Buy Link goo.gl/ZRD9Yf

A Soldier's Hope – Buy Link https: goo.gl/QvzkmG

Amazon Author Central – goo.gl/SHnk5H

www.JCarolNemeth.com

www.facebook.com/J.CarolNemeth

https://twitter.com/nemeth_jcarol

https://www.goodreads.com/author/dashboard

Made in the USA
Columbia, SC
06 January 2021